The full moon shone brightly as it crowned the sky in a large, round sphere of luminescence. Mattie pulled her robe tightly around her as a cool breeze brought goose bumps to her arms.

"Well, Mr. Moon?" she asked whimsically. "Any ideas? Where do you think I can find a Lord Ashton?"

She tried again. "How about it, big boy? You can see everything from where you are. Is there any man like that out there for me? Asking you the same question? Do they even make men like that anymore?"

Mattie leaned her arms against the railing and ignored the lights of the condominiums across the sidewalk—so close she often wondered if she could throw a coin onto the balcony opposite. She was pretty sure, however, that she didn't want to throw a coin onto the balcony opposite to test the theory. Coins were pretty dear at the moment, especially since Tom had moved out. He'd helped with a few of the living expenses—groceries, anyway.

"Hey, up there!" she called out. "Are you listening to me? How about a sign? Some hint that this isn't the rest of my life!"

A dog barked in the distance and a door slammed somewhere. Mattie waited, half expecting the moon to actually drop the man of her dreams onto her balcony.

The dog barked once again. Then it was silent. Mattie held her breath and listened. Nothing. No sign. No riding-booted footsteps. No tall figure in yellow silk pantaloons and a blue cutaway coat magically appeared on her balcony. No raven-haired man arrived to pull her into his arms.

She shivered in the cool night breeze and hugged herself. Living in such a vivid fantasy world wasn't good for her—she realized that. She was fully aware she had to stop her obsession at some point in the near future, and return the book to the library. Take up knitting, watch TV, study calligraphy.

Mattie's mind raced with a number of activities she could and should pursue—activities that would be much more productive than fantasizing about a character in a book who could never exist outside of the imagination of the author...and readers.

With a last pleading look at the unresponsive moon, she sighed and turned back toward the door. Her knees buckled, and she felt herself falling.

MOONLIGHT WISHES IN TIME

BESS MCBRIDE

MOONLIGHT WISHES IN TIME

Copyright © 2013 Bess McBride

Contact information: bessmcbride@gmail.com

Cover Art by *Tamra Westberry*

Formatted by IRONHORSE Formatting

Published in the United States of America

ISBN: 1491086424
ISBN-13: 978-1491086421

DEDICATION

For all my time-travel romance reader fans. Here's something new for you. I sincerely hope you enjoy it!

For Diana Coyle, who has helped me in immeasurable ways, including beta reading this book for me!

For Tamra Westberry, who always does such wonderful covers for me. As I always tell her when she delivers a masterpiece, "You get me, you really get me!" This cover is no exception.

Dear Reader,

Thank you for purchasing *Moonlight Wishes in Time*. *Moonlight Wishes in Time* is Book One of the *Moonlight Wishes in Time* series, a series of Georgian-era time-travel romances featuring time travel by moonlight.

Like many of you, I grew up reading Regency romance novels, especially Georgette Heyer. While I cannot pretend to do justice to Georgette Heyer's work, here is my humble attempt at a Georgian-era romance. *Moonlight Wishes in Time* is set in England in 1825 following the Regency era.

Although I am American, I am an Anglophile in that I love all things British and Irish. I love the lyrical language of Georgette Heyer's and Jane Austen's dialogue, and I enjoyed trying to incorporate some of the dialogue into my own story while keeping the book a little more "readable" for modern-day romance enthusiasts. My advance apologies to my British and Canadian reader friends who will note that the majority of the story is written and spelled in "American English" though the majority of the characters are English.

I know that I, like many of my fellow time-travel romance readers, have wondered: What if I traveled back in time somehow and fell in love with someone from the past? What would I do if he asked me to stay with him...in his time? Could I really give up all the things I've grown up with—the comfortable amenities, modern medicine, clean water, sanitation? Matilda Crockwell from *Moonlight Wishes in Time* wonders that very same thing.

The other thing I've always wondered is what would it be like to be as successful and prolific as Georgette Heyer! But that's another story...

Thank you for your support over the years, friends and readers. Because of your favorable comments, I continue to strive to write the best stories I can. More romances are on the way!

You know I always enjoy hearing from you, so please feel free to contact me at bessmcbride@gmail.com, through my website at http://www.bessmcbride.com, or my blog Will Travel for Romance.

Thanks for reading!

Bess

PROLOGUE

William Sinclair stood in the garden of Ashton House with his hands clasped behind his back, staring at the moon and wishing for he knew not what. A vague, ill-defined sense of yearning, of longing, plagued him, but he could not put a name to his desire. He was not happy. The course of his life was not as he might have wished. He felt…empty. Without joy, without hope. Incessant dinner parties and country balls, dreary evenings of cards and drink, and the attentions of vapid young women who fawned over his fortune no longer held any interest for him. He grimaced and shook his head. No, that was untrue. They had *never* held any interest for him.

Perhaps it was time for him to take a wife as his mother wished. Perchance a wife would help fill the void. But which one of the insipid young ladies in his circle could possibly interest him for a lifetime—or even for one month? It seemed as if each one been educated by the same governess in the arts of fanning, blushing and pouting. None of the young women his mother invited to her parties appeared to have even the slightest notion that a gentleman might want a companion of intelligence and conversation, perhaps even a bit of wit.

Other than his sister, and occasionally his mother, he had yet to meet a woman who made him want to smile or laugh. As was expected, most of the young ladies in their circles were encouraged to make advantageous marriages. Too often, he had seen the desire for wealth and luxury in their eyes.

He did not fault them for desiring to better their lives, but he had hoped for so much more from a marriage. His parents' marriage had been tolerable—perhaps they had even grown fond of each other over the years—but they had not loved each other. As a young girl, his mother

1

had been urged to marry his father for position and comfort, and she had acceded to the dictates of her parents.

He supposed it was possible the yearning to be loved for all that he was—in the absence of riches—was the thing he desired most in the world. How else would he know whether the lady loved him, or loved his fortune? He was not, however, of a mind to dispense with his estate to prove the thing, nor could he as his family depended upon him.

"When will you grant me that which I desire most?" he murmured to the moon. Knowing from long practice no response would come, he turned away with a restless sigh to return to the house, at present gaily lit for one of his mother's dinner parties. A dinner party in which his mother hoped he would meet his future wife.

He tripped over something soft and pliable on the ground and cursed as he sought to avoid injury to the creature by leaping over it. Losing his balance, he fell, rolled over onto his knees and came up sputtering. One of the dogs? Injured?

"What in the infernal blazes—" He jumped to his feet and peered at the pale, fluffy creature rolled up into a ball. The lights from the house cast a faint glow on the animal. No, not an animal. Long hair flowed away from a white face. A woman? Surely not!

CHAPTER ONE

Fresh and squeaky clean from her shower, Mattie Crockwell shook out her still-damp hair, climbed into her favorite overstuffed easy chair and settled in to spend another evening with the man of her dreams. She tucked her beloved tattered pink thermal blanket around her legs and eyed the novel on the small table beside her chair with anticipation.

As she had every night for the past several months, she opened the well-worn library book and leafed through the pages until she found her bookmark.

"The moon shines for us because it has given me my heart's desire."

Mattie mouthed the hero's words as she read them for at least the twentieth time. She was sure she knew almost every word of dialogue by heart. Hokey, her practical side said. Purple prose, she'd heard it called. But she didn't care. In the privacy of her own bedroom, no one needed to know about her secret fantasy life in the Georgian era. That was just for her.

Luckily, the library computer had not balked at her fifth consecutive three-week renewal. The out-of-print book wasn't available for her to have as her own, *to possess*, and she occasionally toyed with the idea of just not returning it.

But that was the wrong thing to do, and Mattie tried very, very hard not to do the wrong thing. Thanks in large part, she suspected, to her parents' Midwestern values.

As she had so many times before, she turned to the cover to study the colorful depiction of the hero—a tall, raven-haired man whose distinctive cheekbones, chiseled jaw and broad shoulders screamed confidence and assurance. The heroine—a voluptuous redhead with masses of flowing curls, impossibly long dark eyelashes, and a graceful swan neck—

luxuriated in the capable embrace of Lord Ashton of Sinclair House as he lowered his face to hers.

Mattie sighed and resisted the temptation—yet again—to plant a kiss on the hero's face. Had she given in to her whimsical urges, it was likely the cover of the book could have rapidly approached the conditions of the Blarney Stone in Ireland—not that she had ever seen that icon in person. She read on.

"And mine! Now kiss me, William," the heroine breathed.

Mattie rolled her eyes, as she always did. Okay, so the dialogue could improve, she thought. She remembered her mother giggling when she read passages of her favorite romance novels to then sixteen-year-old Mattie. Mattie had dutifully groaned with the scorn of youth, but read every single one of her mother's books as soon as she stuck the finished novels in a bookshelf.

Mattie's chest ached in that way it always did when she remembered her mother—gone over a year ago from ovarian cancer. She pressed her lips together, took several deep breaths, and allowed the pain to ebb—a skill she'd developed when her father had died only a year before her mother.

She returned her attention to the cover and ran a loving finger across her hero's face. Lord Ashton's story had not been in her mother's collection of paperback novels, and Mattie had happened on it in the library one day—probably a donation from a little old lady cleaning out her house. The book was older, originally published in the 1850s, with numerous reprints over the years. However, Mattie had checked at the library, and discovered it was, sadly, out of print. No biography was included in the book, and the author had used initials, making it hard to determine whether the writer was a man or a woman. She suspected a woman. *I. C. Moon.* Isolde Claire Moon? Isis Catherine Moon? Worse yet…Ichabod Crane Moon?

Mattie smiled to herself, shook her head, and for the next two hours, she reveled in the passionate embrace of Lord Ashton until she reached the end of the book with a sigh of regret, tempered only by the certain knowledge that she would begin at page one again the following night.

A shake of her shoulder-length hair revealed it had dried, and she laid the book down with care and rose from her chair to prepare for bed. Six a.m. would come early, and all too soon she would awaken to discover she had only dreamt of being in the arms of the handsome Lord Ashton. The only excitement in store for her tomorrow evening was the thought that after her bath, she would settle back into her chair once again with her novel—and Lord Ashton.

A quick check of her closet satisfied her that her clothes were ready for work the following day. A light blue blouse and dark blue slacks with matching sweater were free of wrinkles and ready to slip on, despite early-morning bleary eyes unable to differentiate between black and blue slacks.

Mattie stepped into the bathroom, grabbed her toothbrush and loaded it with organic mango-orange tartar control toothpaste. As she brushed her teeth, she wondered about dental hygiene in the Georgian era. Did they have something like toothpaste? Toothbrushes? Surely they did, she thought. Oh, surely they did!

She rinsed her mouth and surveyed the bathroom—a nondescript standard apartment configuration of bathtub/shower combination, sink and toilet. Her book didn't quite address hygienic matters, and she wondered if she could manage to live in the Georgian era without her favorite organic toothpaste, soft toilet paper, body lotion, makeup remover or hot running water. Not a chance, she thought! Not a chance!

The tinkling sound of her cell phone set her on a run toward the nightstand next to her bed. She dived onto the luxurious pillow-top mattress and caught the phone on the fourth ring—just before the call went to voice mail. A check of caller identification revealed it was her friend, Renee.

"Hello. What's up?" Mattie said, as she rolled over onto her back and stared at the white and brass ceiling fan whirring silently overhead.

"What's up is I'm sick and I'm not going to work tomorrow," Renee said on a ragged voice, which deteriorated into a deep cough.

"You sound awful," Mattie said with a wince. "Did you just come down with this? You sounded fine at the bank on Friday."

"I was fine on Friday," Renee wheezed. "Some customer must have given me the cold. I keep swearing I'm going to use antibacterial hand wipes after every transaction, but I never do."

Mattie chuckled. "I already do. I told you to start using something before. And now look at you."

"Yeah, look at me. Thanks for the sympathy."

"I *am* sympathetic, pal. Really. Lots of sympathy. Do you need anything? Medicine, anything from the store?"

"No, thanks. Mike went to get me some cold medicine earlier. I took a big dose and now I'm going to pass out. I just wanted you to know that you're on your own driving into work tomorrow."

"Okay, kiddo," Mattie said. "Take care of yourself. I'll call you tomorrow night and see how you're doing."

"I'll probably be dead."

Mattie laughed. "Okay, well, let me know the date for the funeral."

A chuckle followed, which deteriorated into another choking cough before Renee managed to squeak out a good night.

Mattie set her phone back on the nightstand and climbed off her bed to wriggle out of her robe. She laid it on the foot of the bed, turned out the bedside lamp and slipped under the comforter.

Once her eyes adjusted to the darkness, she noticed the room seemed abnormally bright. Moonlight streamed in through the open-curtained window, and she debated climbing back out of bed to close the curtains or pull down the blinds.

She turned away from the window and squeezed her eyes shut, eagerly anticipating the arrival of her nightly dreams with Lord Ashton. But the bright moonlight hit the white wall opposite the window, reflecting off it and into her eyes. Restlessly, she turned over onto her back and draped an arm over her face to block the light.

Lord Ashton... Where are you? Lord Ashton... You can come any time. She waited and willed, fervently hoping she wasn't doomed to return to the long, lonely nights of tossing and turning she had known over the past year.

Blissful sleep continued to elude her.

Frustrated, Mattie jumped out of bed, pulled the blinds down with a yank, let the curtains drop, threw herself back under the covers and slammed her eyes shut. Her heart raced with all the activity, and she took several deep breaths to calm down. She waited again, holding her breath, willing Lord Ashton to come. Pent-up air escaped her after a moment, and she settled for some more deep breathing.

Five minutes passed...or an hour, she wasn't sure which. Had her luck finally run out? Would this be the first night in months she wouldn't dream of her beloved Lord Ashton?

Mattie gave up and pushed herself into a sitting position, irritation with herself and angst for her dream lover wreaking havoc with any ideas of serenity. She contemplated getting out of bed to start the book all over again—even at the late hour—just to get back into the warm mood she'd had earlier. She threw a longing glance at the empty spot in the bed next to her. What did Lord Ashton look like without his double-breasted jacket, pantaloons and Hessians, she wondered? Her toes curled delightfully at the thought. What did he wear under those things, anyway?

No matter what he wore, Lord Ashton would certainly be better than the last man to inhabit that side of the bed—her ex-boyfriend, Tom. Although Tom bore certain similarities to Lord Ashton—tall with dark hair—he lacked the strong, assertive jaw, flashing gray eyes and English accent of her hero. And he cheated—or so she'd found out a year ago—just after her mother's death. Lord Ashton would never cheat on his beloved. Never. He was too honorable, too chivalrous, too…gentlemanly.

"You've got to snap out of this depression, Mattie. Your mother wouldn't want this," Tom had said a week after the funeral.

"I'm trying," she'd whispered, helplessly looking for a clean pair of jeans to wear, as Tom wanted to take her out to dinner to cheer her up. It seemed like she hadn't done laundry in a month—the month her mother had been in the hospital fighting to stay alive.

"Are you?" he'd said as he stood in the doorway of the bedroom waiting for her. "I have to tell you, I think you're wallowing a bit. You knew this would happen. You've known for months—ever since she was diagnosed."

"I thought it would be easier," Mattie said as she shoved her feet into a pair of sandals. "Knowing. Planning. But it isn't." She searched for some sort of shirt to wear, uncaring.

"Yeah," Tom said. "Doesn't look like it." He looked at his watch. "Are you about ready?"

Mattie nodded, though she wanted nothing more than to burrow into a corner of her walk-in closet and cry.

Several hours later, they left the restaurant, Tom in good spirits, and Mattie even more despondent than when they'd entered the seafood joint.

She'd suspected for some time that Tom had been unfaithful to her, but she hadn't known for certain until that evening. The waitress, who always waited on them, seemed unable to avoid touching him at every opportunity—from allowing her hand to rub his when she handed him the menu to covering his hand as she took Mattie's credit card from him. The gestures had seemed inordinately intimate, and Tom had beamed at the waitress throughout.

"Tom," she'd begun heavily, almost too depressed to even care, "are you seeing that waitress?"

"What waitress?" Tom had said after a moment, keeping his eyes on the road.

"Please," Mattie had said dryly. Oddly, she had no desire to cry over Tom—not like for her mom. Though they had lived together for about a year, she didn't feel the sense of loss that she thought she should.

Tom's heavy sigh gave her the answer before he spoke.

"What do you want me to say, Mattie?"

"Yes or no, that's all," she replied wearily.

"You've been gone a lot. You know, staying at your mother's place, then at the hospital when she couldn't stay home any longer."

"Yes, I've been gone," she agreed with a pang of guilt. "You don't have much staying power, do you?" she said more than asked. She turned exhausted eyes on his profile. Dark haired, maybe not as handsome as she'd once thought, his face fuller than when they met, his chin sort of weak looking rather than strong and chiseled.

"No, I guess not," he said with a feeble half-smile as he glanced at her. "I'm sorry."

Mattie turned away to look out the car window. The moon rode high in the sky, bright, round and full. What she wouldn't have given to be up there.

"What are your plans?" she asked as she contemplated perching on the moon and watching the world go by.

"Plans?" he'd asked.

"You have to leave. You can't live with me anymore," Mattie said, too tired to even care about the long nights of loneliness looming ahead.

Although Tom had argued weakly, he'd packed his bags that night and left. They'd exchanged a few phone calls, but he had quickly moved in with the waitress, and Mattie heard from him that the younger woman was pregnant, and they were planning to marry. Mattie hadn't dated since Tom had left, preferring to bury her head into her mother's old romance novels. And then Lord Ashton had come along: charming, dashing, principled and honorable—everything she longed for in a man.

Wide awake, Mattie slipped out of bed, grabbed her robe, stuck her feet into her slippers and made her way down the carpeted hallway to the kitchen. The incessantly bright moonlight had found its way into the kitchen as well. Just how big was this moon, anyway? *ET* size? She slid open the glass doors and stepped out onto the small balcony of her second-floor condominium.

The full moon shone brightly as it crowned the sky in a large, round sphere of luminescence. Mattie pulled her robe tightly around her as a cool breeze brought goose bumps to her arms.

"Well, Mr. Moon," she asked whimsically. "Any ideas? Where do you think I can find a Lord Ashton?"

She tried again. "How about it, big boy? You can see everything from where you are. Is there any man like that out there for me? Asking you the same question? Do they even make men like that anymore?"

Mattie leaned her arms against the railing and ignored the lights of the condominiums across the sidewalk—so close she often wondered if she could throw a coin onto the balcony opposite. She was pretty sure, however, that she didn't want to throw a coin onto the balcony opposite to test the theory. Coins were pretty dear at the moment, especially since Tom had moved out. He'd helped with a few of the living expenses—groceries, anyway.

"Hey, up there!" she called out. "Are you listening to me? How about a sign? Some hint that this isn't the rest of my life!"

A dog barked in the distance and a door slammed somewhere. Mattie waited, half expecting the moon to actually drop the man of her dreams onto her balcony.

The dog barked once again. Then it was silent. Mattie held her breath and listened. Nothing. No sign. No riding-booted footsteps. No tall figure in yellow silk pantaloons and a blue cutaway coat magically appeared on her balcony. No raven-haired man arrived to pull her into his arms.

She shivered in the cool night breeze and hugged herself. Living in such a vivid fantasy world wasn't good for her—she realized that. She was fully aware she had to stop her obsession at some point in the near future, and return the book to the library. Take up knitting, watch TV, study calligraphy.

Mattie's mind raced with a number of activities she could and should pursue—activities that would be much more productive than fantasizing about a character in a book who could never exist outside of the imagination of the author...and readers.

With a last pleading look at the unresponsive moon, she sighed and turned back toward the door. Her knees buckled, and she felt herself falling.

CHAPTER TWO

"Good heavens! Madam! Madam? Can you hear me?" William said as he turned the woman over and checked the pulse at her exposed throat. She lived, but seemed to be unconscious.

He dropped to one knee and scooped her up into his arms. She was light as a feather, and as fluffy as a newborn pup to boot. Her head dangled over his arm and he peered at her face, trying to make out her features, but the light from the moon was insufficient to illuminate her face or to ascertain whom she was. From the appearance of her clothing, though, she was certainly not one of the servants.

He looked toward the house. What was he to do with the woman? A warm yellow glow at the side of the house caught his eye. The kitchen! Mrs. White would know what to do with her. Perhaps Mrs. White might even know who she was.

He carried her across the lawn and around the side of the house toward the kitchen. With his hands full, he gave the door several good kicks. A scullery maid pulled open the heavy oak door and gaped at him with rounded eyes.

"Let me in, girl!" William pushed past her with his burden, who grew mercilessly heavier by the minute.

"Susie, get yourself off to bed now, there's a good girl." Mrs. White, a plump gray-haired woman who had been with the family ever since William could remember, shooed the young gawking girl out of the kitchen before turning to pull a rocking chair toward the fire.

"Here, Master William, set her here."

William lowered the woman into the rocking chair by the cheery fire and straightened, reaching an unconscious hand to his aching back.

"Master William," Mrs. White remonstrated. "You shouldn't ought to have carried the young lass. You're not as young as you used to be."

William gave the cook a withering look that did not seem to bother the short woman in the least. He continued to rub his back and returned his gaze to the young woman.

"What do we have here, master? Wherever did you find her…and what is that garment she is wearing? Is she one of your guests? Did she…em…imbibe overly much?"

"Mrs. White! Do you actually think I would bring an inebriated guest down here to the kitchen? And a woman at that? What do you take me for?"

"Well, Master William, you have pulled some pranks in your time," she said dryly.

They both regarded the unconscious woman draped in the chair, her head lolling to the side. Reddish-brown hair the color of cinnamon spilled over her shoulders and onto the pink confection she wore.

"Are those slippers, Master William?" Mrs. White wiped her hands on her apron and bent to peer closely at the fuzzy shoes on the young woman's feet. "My goodness, they are indeed!" She turned to William with a faint accusing look, bright red spots coloring her full cheeks.

"Master William, the young lady is in her sleeping garments. You never took her from her bedchamber, did you? Is she a local girl?"

He thrust out his hands in defense. Mrs. White could be a formidable woman when she thought an injustice had occurred.

"Now, just a moment, Mrs. White. I found the…ah…young woman on the lawn out there." He nodded in the direction of the garden. "Fainted, I presume. In point of fact, I fell over her. I have never seen her before in my life. I was hoping you would know who she was. Perhaps a new servant?"

"None to my knowledge, Master William. Is she a guest of Miss Sylvie? They look to be of an age." Mrs. White turned away to grab a clean white cloth and run a pitcher of water over it. She returned and pressed the cold compress onto the young lady's pale forehead.

"Well, Mrs. White, I will leave her in your hands. She is not a guest of Miss Sylvie. I am certain you can sort her out and return her to her proper abode."

William turned away, but felt his arm grasped in a vise grip.

"Oh, no, sir. She isn't one of your stray puppies you have always been so fond of leaving here in the kitchen for me to see to. And here's one of them now. Rufus!" The older woman acknowledged the red setter that trotted into the kitchen and came to a halt at William's feet, wagging his tail and staring up at him with adoring eyes.

William bent to scratch the dog behind the ears.

"But Mrs. White, I must return to our guests. I have been gone far too long as it is. Mother will have my head."

"Oh, I think you know your way around your mother, Master William."

He gave her a cheeky grin, pulled a fob watch from the pocket of his vest and stiffened.

"It is almost eleven o'clock. The guests will soon be leaving. Watch over her for me. I will return within the hour to discuss what is to be done with her."

Mrs. White sighed and pressed the cool cloth to the young woman's forehead once again.

"Don't bat your gray eyes at me, Master William. I've known you too long to be taken in by that. I'll see to her for the next hour, don't you worry, but I hope you aren't leaving me with a lunatic from some asylum."

He grinned, bent near to kiss the older woman's cheek and strode out the door with a sigh of relief, allowing himself the pretense of believing he would not return to the kitchen. He clasped his hands behind his back as he walked around the side of the house to the grand balcony and climbed the curved stone steps. Of course, he would return. He had promised.

William reached the balcony fronting the large French doors, which led into the ballroom. Before entering, he turned to survey the moon once again. He remembered wishing for his heart's desire just before he had stumbled over the woman. The strange apparition in his garden was not what he had envisioned.

He strode through the house to reach the drawing room where he had left his mother, sister and the guests playing cards and drinking coffee after dinner. He winced as he recalled his mother had yet another rout planned for the next evening, so insatiably was she bent on finding him a suitable wife. So far, he had managed to thwart her best efforts.

"Will! There you are!" His sister, a vision in a lilac silk gown, approached. "Where have you been? Several of the young ladies of our acquaintance asked after you. As did our mother." She turned her back on the room, gave him a wink of one of her bright blue eyes and grinned. "Were you hiding, brother?" she whispered as she tucked her gloved hand through his arm and turned back to the room with a polished smile for public eyes.

"Do you blame me?" he edged out through an even smile as he surveyed the large room. "I cannot abide these gatherings that mother must always host in her unrelenting pursuit of a daughter-in-law."

"Not a daughter-in-law, dear brother," Sylvie said softly. "An heir for the estate, as you well know."

Their mother spotted them and made her way across the room. A tall, elegant, golden-haired woman who had passed her beauty onto her daughter, Mrs. Sinclair tapped her closed fan against her left hand in a sign of irritation.

"There you are, William. You have been neglecting our guests, I think. I have not seen you this past half-hour."

"Forgive me, Mother. I stepped out to the garden for a bit of fresh air. I did not think to be away so long. Time simply flew by."

"Moon gazing again, were you?" She quirked a well-groomed eyebrow at her son, the gesture elegant and graceful on her.

"Oh, the Roberts are leaving," Sylvie said. "I shall bid them good night." She drifted away. William watched her easy escape with envy.

"It is a full moon tonight, Mother," he quipped. "Who knows what magical mysteries might happen on a full moon?" He nodded and bowed slightly to a matron in purple satin and matching feathers in her silver hair, accompanied by a young woman of nondescript coloring and expression.

His mother inclined her head. "Lady Spencer, Miss Spencer, it was so good of you to come tonight. I do hope we shall see you tomorrow evening?" The women responded with delight and moved away.

"I thought you had outgrown such fancifulness, my son," his mother continued. "Nothing will occur on a full moon that cannot occur on any other night. Specifically, a decision by you on one of these young ladies as your wife."

William gritted his teeth.

"I do not think so, Mother. I will decide when I am ready. Not before."

She raised her closed fan to her mouth and sighed for his benefit.

"There will be other opportunities. Perhaps the right young woman was not at our small gathering tonight but will attend the dance tomorrow night. If not, I shall widen the search."

William lifted a finger to his cravat. It seemed to be choking him at the moment.

"Please do not put yourself out, Mother. Were the right woman to come along tonight, I would not recognize her in any event, as I wear blinders in an effort to resist your scheming. I do not wish to be coerced in this matter."

"You are thirty now, my dear. And I am considerably older. How long shall I wait for grandchildren?"

William turned to eye his youthful-looking mother. No wrinkles lined the corners of her blue eyes, no strands of gray dulled her bright golden hair, no plumpness marred the elegant figure in dark blue silk.

"Mother...please. You have many years ahead of you. Perhaps you should consider remarriage yourself. It is no secret that Lord Hamilton has held a fondness for you these many years."

She snapped open her fan to hide the heightened color in her cheeks.

"Do not be silly, William. I am a merry widow. I have no intention of ever remarrying."

"I see." He bowed as a portly gentleman passed. "Well, then, why can you not extend the same courtesy to me? Perhaps I do not want to marry either...ever." He knew the inexorableness of his duty and berated himself for his childish retort.

Mrs. Sinclair turned to him, her public smile curving into a more intimate one of affection and empathy.

"I sympathize with you, my dear, I do. But do you honestly think that you have that choice, William? What will happen to the estate when you die? Will you pass it on to some as yet unborn niece or nephew bearing another man's name? You owe your father more than that. You owe your ancestors more than that. The land has been in your father's family for centuries."

She turned to incline her head to another departing guest—a short, rounded woman in a satin emerald green gown.

"So pleased to see you tonight, Mrs. Brookfield. Please stop by for tea soon."

"I would be delighted, Mrs. Sinclair. Perhaps Thursday?"

"Thursday would be lovely, Mrs. Brookfield. I look forward to seeing you then."

Mrs. Brookfield passed on.

William straightened from his bow to the older woman.

"I apologize for my boorish behavior, Mother. You are right, of course. I know you are, but I despair of finding a woman who holds my interest, a woman with whom I could envision a palatable future."

She closed her fan and tapped William's arm with it.

"You are too fastidious in your tastes, William. Simply choose a girl of good breeding and sound reputation. Affection and friendship will surely follow."

When his mother turned her attention to other departing guests, William pulled his watch from his pocket and glanced at it. She did not miss the gesture and turned a shrewd eye upon him.

"Are we keeping you, dear? Did you have other plans this evening?"

William smiled, well used to his mother's omniscient ways.

"Not at all, Mother. I was simply checking the time as a matter of curiosity. I feel somewhat tired this evening."

"Only several more guests remain to bid farewell, William. We shall soon see the end of them for another evening."

"Mother!" he reproached playfully. He pressed his lips together as Lady and Sir Wallingford, and their pale daughter, Emeline, made departing curtsies and bows.

"Yes, William? Are you saying you feel differently?" His mother smiled serenely when the Wallingfords had passed.

"Not at all. I agree with you wholeheartedly. If you despise these functions so, why must you put us through them?"

"Because your sister needs gaiety and you need a wife."

"Ah, yes," he murmured. "The wife."

The last of the guests departed within twenty minutes, and William was able to bid his mother and sister good night, stating he would take a glass of brandy in his study prior to retiring for the night. As the last rustle of silk skirts disappeared up the stairs, he hurried back through the dining room and clattered down the stone steps to the kitchen. He pushed open the heavy wooden door and came to an abrupt halt.

There, standing before the hearth holding her hands to the fire, stood the young woman—dark, reddish hair hanging about her shoulders in a most primitive fashion, the ridiculously fluffy garment draped about her person, and equally unsuitable shoes upon her feet.

She swung around upon hearing him enter.

Cheeks rosy from the fire burned suddenly brighter. Her eyes widened, he supposed in fear. She opened her mouth to speak but no words came.

Good gravy! Was it possible she did not speak English? Or perhaps could not speak at all?

William sighed with relief when out of the corner of his eye he saw Mrs. White bustling forward. He really did not feel equal to handling the strange creature who stood before him, hands now covering her mouth, cheeks suddenly pale, a decided unsteadiness to her stance.

He slid his eyes toward the cook.

"Mrs. White! Is she faint? She looks as if she is about to—"

He jumped forward to catch her just as she would have slid to the stone floor. She slumped into his arms, and he staggered for a moment.

"Oh, my goodness, Master William! Not again. The poor girl. Put her here, sir." Mrs. White pulled the rocking chair forward. "Gently now. Have a care."

William half dragged her into the chair once again. Her head lolled to the side.

"What ails her, Mrs. White?" William turned to the cook. "Did you have a chance to speak with her? Did you take some tea? A refreshment?

Shall I send someone to fetch the doctor?"

"No, Master William. I do not think you should call for the doctor at this time. She awakened some time after you left, and I was able to exchange a few words with her. I think you should talk to her before you send for anyone. She is just as likely to end up in Bedlam as anywhere else at the moment, and I hate to see the poor thing shipped off to such a place."

William straightened and eyed the older woman with a raised brow.

"What do you mean, Mrs. White? What has she said? Is she some sort of...em..."

Mrs. White shook her head, gray wisps of hair straying from her cap. She gazed at the unfortunate creature in the chair with a knit between her brows.

"I can't explain it, Master William. She seems somewhat...lost. When she awakened, she asked where she was." Mrs. White bent forward to lay a hand against the young woman's forehead. "I told her she was here at Ashton House. She didn't seem to understand. And she has a very strange way of speaking English. A foreign accent of some sort. Perhaps from the south of England? The coast?"

William bent to study the apparition in the rocking chair with misgiving. What was he going to do with her?

"How long do you think she will stay like this?" he asked.

As he spoke, dark lashes fluttered on pale cheeks.

"She awakens now, it seems." William clasped his hands behind his back and straightened.

"Yes, Master William, and I wish you the best of luck."

He threw Mrs. White a suspicious look before he turned back toward the young woman. Vivid hazel eyes stared at him, eyes the color of the forest in fall.

"Mr. Sinclair?" the young woman whispered. So, she did speak English. Excellent!

He executed a small bow.

"Yes, madam. William Sinclair, at your service. Mrs. White will have told you who I am."

As before, her eyes widened when she saw him, and she attempted to struggle to her feet.

He reached as if to stay her, but thought better of it and reclasped his hands behind his back.

"Stay seated, madam. You seem to have sustained some shock. I would not have you rise precipitously only to swoon in my arms once again."

"Swoon?" she repeated in a small voice. She gave up her efforts as

Mrs. White, having hurried over to moisten a cloth once again with cool water, pressed it against her forehead, thereby keeping her in the chair.

"There, there now, dear," Mrs. White murmured soothingly.

William stared in confused fascination while the young woman tried to peer at him from under the cloth. She twisted to the side to see him better, and Mrs. White struggled to keep the wet cloth to her forehead.

Mrs. White looked over her shoulder at William and then straightened with a sigh.

"Well, if the two of you must stare at one another, you might as well hand me that cup of tea, Master William." She nodded toward a long wooden table behind him.

William's face colored, and he straightened. He turned around and picked up the teacup and saucer and handed them to Mrs. White, who in turn offered them to the young woman. She shook her head.

"Well, madam"—William cleared his throat—"how may we be of assistance to you? Mrs. White tells me she thinks you are...lost." He cleared his throat. "Do you live nearby? In the village, perhaps?"

The young woman shook her head, and William threw an uncertain glance at Mrs. White.

"You are not a guest in this house, certainly? I would have met you before now. Not a friend of my sister's, surely?"

She continued to stare at him with wide eyes. Another slight shake of her head.

"Come, now, madam. Tell us who you are and how we may return you to your home. I found you outside on the lawn, fainted dead away, not two hours ago."

She opened her mouth to speak but pressed it shut again.

"Very well, Mrs. White." William turned towards the cook in frustration. "She seems disinclined to speak to me. Did she say anything else?"

Mrs. White shook her head with a sympathetic glance at the young lady, who sat rigid in the chair with her arms wrapped tightly around herself.

"Oh, dear. You would do well to tell the master where you come from, my dear," Mrs. White urged. "He cannot help you if he does not know."

William turned back to the small thing, wishing he could wash his hands of the affair, and knowing he could not walk away from her. Not that Mrs. White would allow him to leave her in any case.

"Your name, madam. Can you at least give us your name?"

Her lips moved, the lower lip charmingly fuller than the top. He heard a whisper and bent forward.

17

"I beg your pardon?"

"Mattie."

He furrowed his brow and straightened once again.

"Maddy? A very unusual name, to be sure."

She shook her head.

"No. Mattie," she repeated. "Short for Matilda."

"Ah, Matilda. I see now. A fine name. Matilda…?" he coaxed.

"Crockwell."

"Indeed. Miss Matilda Crockwell. Excellent! And where do you live, Miss Crockwell? How did you come to be in the garden…in…em…?" William left the words hanging. It was not seemly to speak of her clothing.

The unfortunate creature stared at him but seemed unwilling to say anything more. He was at a loss.

He decided on a different tactic, raising his voice just a bit and speaking slowly and clearly.

"Do…you…require…a…physician?"

A twitch at the corner of her mouth took him by surprise.

"No." She shook her head and raised a pale hand to cover her mouth. Was she laughing?

A sparkle of gold on her slender wrist caught his eye, and he squinted at it.

"Is that…? What is that you wear on your wrist, may I ask? Is that a timepiece of some sort?"

Miss Crockwell lowered her hand to look at the jewelry, then covered it with her other hand. She narrowed her eyes and nodded mutely.

"How very unusual! I should like to study it further at another time." He pulled his watch from a pocket in his waistcoat. "The hour grows late, madam, and I am afraid we are keeping Mrs. White from her sleep. Is there no information you can offer us to help you find your way home? Surely, you have only just risen from bed yourself? In that attire? You cannot live far?"

Miss Crockwell shook her head once again.

"I don't know." The words came out in a whisper.

"I beg your pardon?"

"I don't know where I live. I don't know where I am."

William looked at Mrs. White, who shrugged helplessly.

"But surely Mrs. White informed you that you are at my estate, Ashton House. You must be staying nearby, else how could you have ended up in the garden? Perhaps a midnight walk from the nearest inn? The Village Inn, perhaps? Do you have lodgings there?"

She shook her head, lovely auburn curls swaying against her face.

William cleared his throat and focused on the task at hand—discovering her identity.

"I don't think so."

He turned to Mrs. White, but she shrugged her shoulders helplessly. He returned his attention to Miss Crockwell.

"You do speak English with an accent. Are you a servant? Perhaps from one of the neighboring houses? Did something happen to you to make you run in the night?"

William suspected he might be on to something. Roland Satterfield was known for bothering the maids in his father's house. Though if this young woman had run from her employment, the gold bracelet timepiece on her wrist could only have been stolen. In his experience, maids did not possess such jewelry. Still, the poor thing seemed too frightened at the moment to be taxed with suggestions of thievery.

She shook her head once again.

"No, not a servant."

He sighed pointedly. She was sorely trying his patience.

"Well, madam, I must insist you tell me what is to be done with you. You hardly know your name. You do not know where you live, nor what your status may be. Is there anything you can tell us so that we may help you?"

Her next words took him by surprise.

"I think if you just let me go back to sleep, I'll get back to where I'm supposed to be."

"I beg your pardon?" He exchanged a troubled look with Mrs. White.

"Sleep. I think I'm probably dreaming, so if you could just let me get back to sleep, then I can get out of your hair."

William took a step back. What odd language she used.

"Out of your hair?" He peered at her. "When I found you on the lawn, you were…ah…sleeping. And you fell asleep—or fainted—just a few moments ago. Still, you are here. This is not a dream, madam."

She grasped the arms of the rocking chair. White knuckles showed her distress. It was then that William noticed something even more unusual about her.

"Good gravy! Is that…paint on your fingernails, Miss Crockwell?"

Mrs. White bent over and peered at Mattie's hands just before she thrust them into the pockets of her garment.

"Yes," Miss Crockwell answered.

William rubbed the back of his neck.

"How very odd you are, to be sure, madam. Are you from England?"

She shook her head.

"Pray tell then, where are you from?"

"The United States."

Mrs. White gasped.

"Of America?" William choked. "Then surely you are no servant. How did you come to be here?"

Miss Crockwell shook her head. "I'm in England, aren't I?" Her voice grew small, and William leaned forward to hear her.

"But of course you are, madam. Where else would you be?"

"Back home?"

The hopeful look on her face tugged at his heart. It seemed as if the young woman were truly lost. What were they to do?

"Have you had an accident recently? Perhaps you hit your head?"

Miss Crockwell's face brightened and she nodded. "I did. I fell...on my balcony."

"That's it then, Master William."

William nodded. "I agree, Mrs. White. It is likely she has had some sort of head injury and does not now understand where she is."

Miss Crockwell gave him a look from under veiled lashes that he did not quite comprehend.

"This is what I think we must do for tonight, Miss Crockwell. The hour is late, and everyone needs to sleep. Mrs. White will escort you to one of the guest bedrooms. In the morning, if you still have not recovered your memory and your address, we will call for the doctor. You do understand, of course, that we need to be...ah...discreet in this matter."

Miss Crockwell watched him carefully but said nothing.

"Master William. You know I don't go above stairs. How would I know what room to put her in? Mrs. Bailey will have my head. Perhaps you should ring for one of the maids."

William eyed her with a frown on his face.

"No, that will not do. We cannot have every servant in the house wondering about Miss Crockwell." He looked toward the kitchen door with a harried expression.

"Very well then, Mrs. White, *I* will take her above stairs myself."

"Master William. Begging your pardon, but don't you think you ought to wake your mother and ask her advice?"

"No, Mrs. White, I would rather not do that just yet. If Miss Crockwell regains her memory in the morning, I could whisk her away to her address with none the wiser except you and I. You have held my childhood secrets these many years—therefore, I have no fears in that quarter."

Mrs. White flashed a toothy smile.

"That is certain, Master William."

William held his hands out to Miss Crockwell to help her rise.

"Shall we, madam?" Her widened eyes gave him pause. "Mrs. White, I think you must accompany us at least for propriety's sake. She looks somewhat wary. I do not blame her."

Mrs. White nodded and wiped her hands on her apron.

"Yes, Master William. I can see that. Come now, dearie. Let me help you up, there's a good girl."

Mrs. White pulled Miss Crockwell from the chair, and William led the way to the door of the kitchen. He grabbed a candle from the sconce in the wall and pulled open the heavy wooden door. A slight creak of the door hinge stilled him, and he listened intently. Hearing no other sounds, he moved through the door and beckoned for the women to follow. Miss Crockwell seemed reluctant—appearing, in fact, as one heading to the guillotine—but Mrs. White had a plump arm firmly around the smaller woman's shoulders.

They climbed the stone steps in silence and reached the family dining room. William passed through the dining room and led the way to the main hallway. With a finger to his lips and a glance over his shoulder, he beckoned to them to follow him up the great staircase. Miss Crockwell's eyes grew wider still, as if she had never seen the inside of a house before. She did indeed look frightened, and he wondered if putting her into a room by herself was a wise thing for her, or for the safety of his mother and sister. What if she were an escapee from some institution?

He glanced over his shoulder once again. The idea seemed unlikely. Her clothing appeared clean, albeit somewhat strange, bringing to mind a large pink rabbit. However, if she were from America, that certainly might explain things.

They reached the landing to the second floor, and William paused once again to listen. No sound. His mother and sister seemed to be safely tucked in bed. He led the way to a door directly across from his own bedchamber, with every intention of leaving his own door open throughout the night in case the hapless young woman decided to stray. He should have had Mrs. White take her to her own room, but something told him that Miss Matilda Crockwell was not from the working class. He did not like to put her in the servant's quarters.

He opened the door and stood back while the women preceded him into the room. Miss Crockwell entered slowly on Mrs. White's arm and paused just inside the door as William shut it behind them. He lit a candle on the side table, illuminating the room. He set his own candle down beside it.

"My sister and mother sleep farther down the hall. My room is directly opposite this one. I shall sleep with my door open tonight should you require anything."

"Don't worry, Mr. Sinclair. I'm not dangerous, and I'll be quiet if that's what you're worried about," Miss Crockwell surprised him by saying. "I'm fairly sure I'll be gone in the morning, so you won't have to worry about me anyway."

William and Mrs. White both stared at the unexpectedly loquacious Miss Crockwell, who moved away to study the furnishings in the room.

"I never suggested…" William paused. "Might I ask? Where do you think you will be able to go in the morning—without clothing, without conveyance?"

She turned to face them. "Well, this can't be real, can it?" She smiled ruefully and held up empty palms. "I mean…who really gets their dreams?"

William exchanged a look of concern with Mrs. White once again.

"I am afraid I do not understand."

Miss Crockwell gave her head a quick shake, russet curls swaying on her shoulders.

"Never mind," she murmured. "I'm just mumbling. I feel so tired. I think I'll just lie down for a few minutes." She moved toward the bed, and Mrs. White stepped forward to pull back the coverlet.

"Goodness me, I think you should, miss. You'll feel much better in the morning after you've have some rest. I'll bring you a cup of tea myself…if I can manage to avoid Mrs. Bailey in the morning."

William stared at Miss Crockwell for a moment as she sat down on the edge of the bed. He was aware of a distinct feeling of dismay when she said she would be "gone by morning." In fact, he rather had the absurd notion that he wanted her to stay for an indefinite period.

"I will bring the tea, Mrs. White," he said. "It will not do to have Mrs. Bailey wondering who is staying in the Green Room until I have a chance to devise a story."

Mrs. White moved to the door.

"As you wish, Master William. Good night, miss. Sleep well."

"Good night, Miss Crockwell," William said, feeling as if he had a million questions for the strange young woman from America. He would have to bide his time. "I am just across the hall if you need anything."

"Good night," she said as she seemed to study his person intently. Unused to such steady regard from a woman, his cheeks bronzed. He gave her a tight bow, picked up the candle and held the door open for Mrs. White.

He turned back with a final glance to see Miss Crockwell raise a hand in farewell—a seemingly final gesture that gave him an uneasy feeling. He felt certain he would not sleep a wink that night.

CHAPTER THREE

Mattie pretended exhaustion as she waited for the door to close behind William Sinclair. Once the latch clicked, she jumped up and ran for the candle. Lifting it high with a trembling hand, she surveyed the room.

Even by the light of only one candle, she could see that the high-ceilinged room was decorated in varying shades of green. The coverlet was white but the walls were painted pale green, and dark green velvet drapes covered the windows. She hustled over to the window and pulled back one of the heavy curtains. The moon rode high in the sky, full, round and familiar in a world suddenly gone mad. She could see little of the grounds, but the lawn seemed extensive. She dropped the curtain and turned around.

A glance at her watch showed it was almost 1 a.m. her time, the date September 17th. Why then was she standing in the bedroom of a house very obviously several hundred years old? She sank down onto a dark green velvet and gilt love seat in front of a large hearth and set the candle down on a small marble occasional table to her left. The flames of her candle reflected on the large white carved mantle. The love seat, an antique collectors' treasure in her time, seemed new and was surprisingly comfortable. She had always wondered what one of the "settees" of her novels might feel like.

A glance over her shoulder at the massive four-poster bed draped with velvet hangings made her shiver. The thing looked forbidding in the dark. What she wouldn't do to flick on some bright lights and dispel the darkness in some of the corners of the large room. Mattie pulled her knees to her chest and wrapped her arms tightly around her legs while she contemplated her predicament.

What had happened? The last she knew, she was on her balcony babbling at the moon. Then she awakened in the massive kitchen of what appeared to be some sort of historical house...in England. The cook, Mrs. White, a sweet lady who looked and acted as if she were straight out of some Regency novel, had offered her tea and asked her to wait for the "master" to return. "Master" indeed, Mattie smirked.

Ashton House! Mattie twisted her neck and surveyed the shadowed room once again. When asked, Mrs. White had given her to understand that she was at a place called Ashton House. So odd that it should be named after the hero in her favorite book—the handsome and charismatic Lord William Ashton.

And then—as if things couldn't get any more surreal—the man of her dreams, the hero of her book, whose face was plastered across its cover, had walked into the kitchen. And she'd fainted dead away.

Was she caught in the midst of some strange dream? It seemed nothing like the dreams she'd been having for weeks—those delightful encounters where she, gowned in lovely silks, floated about beneath a brilliant chandelier in William's arms as they waltzed across the ballroom floor. The stark reality of this dream—the impotent light of the candle which only added more creepy shadows to the room, the dismay on William's face when he saw her and the feeling of complete and utter aloneness as she stared at the cold fireplace—were nothing like her dreams.

She slid down on the settee and rested her head against a tasseled roll pillow. Squeezing her eyes shut, she willed herself back to sleep, back to the sensuous dreams of life and love with William Ashton in England's Georgian era. That the waltz was still frowned upon as slightly "vulgar," and William could, in reality, have little to do with her since she was "in the trades" troubled her not one little bit. That was the beauty of dreams. One could adjust them as needed. She had apparently just made some odd adjustments in this one.

Her eyelids twitched, unwilling to remain closed, and she opened her eyes and sat up. She rose restlessly and crossed over to the window once again, pulling open the curtains to gaze at the moon.

"Hey, buddy, is this a dream?" Mattie asked aloud. She thought she could really see the face of the man in the moon. "Because this is not quite what I had in mind. The edges are a little rough. I'm supposed to be happy and in the arms of a man who loves me."

Mattie swallowed hard. The harder she stared at the moon, the less romantically mystical it appeared and the more it looked like a round sphere of cold rock made bright by the sun.

"This isn't a dream, is it?" she whispered as she clutched the velvet curtains in a death grip. "I'm really in someone's house somewhere in

England in I-don't-even-know-what-year-it-is, aren't I?"

The moon didn't so much as blink in response, and Mattie loosed her grip on the curtains and turned away, wiping perspiration from her upper lip though the room was cool. She felt slightly nauseous.

What was she going to do now, she wondered with rising panic. How long would this last? Could she get back if she wanted? How? Tap her heels three times? She looked down at her slippers. They would make no tapping noise. They weren't even red, she thought idiotically.

Mattie looked toward the door. She heard no sound in the hallway. Maybe she could slip out and at least explore the house while she was here. If she woke up the next morning in her own bed, she would regret losing the chance to look around. And if she had truly traveled back in time, there was no telling how long she would be here. She thought she'd better make good use of the time and reconnoiter the area.

She crossed the room and pressed her ear against the door. Only the noise of her rapid, shallow breathing broke the silence. She pushed on the door handle, hoping she hadn't been locked in. Mattie hadn't missed the looks of concern that had passed between William Sinclair and Mrs. White. They thought she was crazy and didn't quite know what to do with her. She considered herself lucky she hadn't been turned over to some sort of authorities by now, or at least chained below stairs in the dungeon.

Despite her anxiety, Mattie managed a weak grin at the vision.

She eased open the door, no small feat as it appeared to be made of thick, solid wood, nothing like the hollow metal doors in her apartment. She stuck her head into the dark hallway. No one stood guard at her door. No one patrolled the hallways, wondering if she were going to make good an escape or murder the family in their beds.

Mattie shook her head. These people were too trusting by far. There was no way she would ever let a stranger stay in her apartment. No way. They probably should have locked her up in a dungeon.

The hallway was dark, too dark to see anything, and Mattie dashed back to grab the candle. She returned to the door and stuck her head and the candle out into the hallway.

As William had promised, his door was open a crack. Surely enough time had passed that he must be asleep. She slid out from behind the door and stepped into the hallway, her trusty slippers quiet on the thick carpet.

Mattie hesitated. If William were going to come dashing out of the bedroom to tackle her, he would do it now. She would be ready.

Silence. Apparently, the handsome Mr. Sinclair was asleep. Mattie turned to the left toward the stairs and moved down the hallway, holding the candle high and wondering how she could avoid burning off her eyebrows with the silly thing.

She reached the top of the staircase and paused. Still quiet. No servants arising before dawn to light fires and scrub stone floors. Or was that Cinderella?

Mattie rested a hand on the smooth surface of the wooden railing and moved down the large staircase. The hall below seemed vast and dark, but little by little, the light from her candle broke through the shadows, revealing a large entryway with doors leading off in every direction. She reached the bottom step and contemplated her next move as her fingers absently roamed over the delicately carved wooden finial of the staircase in the shape of an acorn.

The flickering light of her candle reflected off the highly polished wood floor. She looked up to see a large chandelier hung over the entryway. When fully lit, it promised to be stunning, as the crystal teardrops would cast a radiant glow around the room.

"Miss Crockwell, do you require something? May I be of assistance?"

Mattie jumped and whirled around, barely hanging onto her candleholder. Close behind her on the staircase stood William Sinclair, still dressed in shirt, waistcoat, trousers and shoes, but with loosened cravat. He had shed his coat. He rested a hand on the banister while he watched her carefully.

"Oh, I'm sorry. I just wanted to see the house." She wasn't really sorry and didn't really attempt to hide it.

"Can you not sleep?" He stepped down onto the floor and took the candle from her, holding it aloft.

Mattie shoved her hands in her pockets and kept a wary eye on him. He really looked exactly like the artist's rendering of the hero on the cover of her book. The resemblance was uncanny. But she hadn't anticipated the sparkle in his eyes from the flickering candle.

"No, not really. I don't know if I should," she muttered.

He gave a short laugh.

"You do not know if you should? I am uncertain as to your meaning, Miss Crockwell."

He didn't wait for a response.

"Please allow me to escort you to the study. Since neither of us can sleep, we might have a small refreshment and discuss what is to be done with you." He gave her a short bow and nodded in the direction of a door at the end of the entryway.

Mattie shuffled toward it. William reached around her to open the door, and she stepped in. He followed her inside and shut the door quietly behind them. She moved to the middle of the room and turned around to watch him light the candles in several candelabras above the massive wooden mantle over the fireplace. The room sprang to life. Dark wood paneling gleamed with a high polish. Shelves filled with books covered three of the walls. Colorful landscape paintings adorned the open spaces between. Luxurious furniture dotted the room—a dark blue sofa and several gilt-edged chairs centered on the hearth flanked by gleaming wooden tables of mahogany. William led her toward the fireplace, settling her on the sofa before moving away to a sideboard.

"May I pour something for you? Some Madeira, perhaps?"

Mattie recognized the name of the drink from her books. She had no idea what it really was. Wine? Whiskey? She nodded, noting that he opened up another glass bottle and poured something different for himself.

"What are you having?" She craned her neck to see what he was doing, surprising herself that she could talk to him in any rational fashion at all. He was the embodiment of the man of her fantasies, right down to the clothing. She swore the cover of the book showed William Ashton in the same yellow silk pantaloons.

"I shall have port, but that would be too strong for you," William said.

He returned with two tulip-shaped glasses and handed her one with a generous portion of burgundy liquid before he settled himself in one of the chairs facing both her and the fireplace.

"Forgive my appearance," he said in a politely formal tone. "I heard your footsteps and thought it best to hurry after you before you found yourself in the cellar or some other such place." He took a sip of his drink and gave her a small smile, albeit a wary one. "This is a large house. I was not certain you would find your way easily, nor was I certain of your destination."

Mattie sighed inwardly at the curve of his lips. A dimple in his chin fascinated her, its boyish vulnerability belying his conservative tone. Could the man be any more handsome? Thick, dark hair curled around the sides of his ears, an errant lock falling across his forehead. Mattie bit her lips together to suppress an idiotic grin. Had she just thought "an errant lock"? She forcibly prevented herself from rolling her eyes as she found herself slipping into the language of her historical romance novels.

"I'm not sure where I was going. Just exploring." She took a tentative sip of the Madeira. Never having been much of a drinker, she sputtered at the strong alcoholic taste of the drink. It seemed to burn its way down her esophagus to her stomach.

William leaned forward, his brow knotted in concern.

"Miss Crockwell, are you all right? May I offer you something else?" He reached for her glass, but she pulled away.

"Oh, no. This is fine. I just don't drink very much. It's actually not too bad," she murmured as she took another, still smaller sip of the potent fruity wine. "Oh, yes, that's better," she said with an appreciative nod.

She looked up to see William staring at her with a bemused expression. The burning in her stomach had evolved into a warm sensation, and she pulled her legs up under her robe and relaxed against the back of the couch, suddenly feeling quite at one with the world. She swirled the rich liquid in her glass and sipped again. It was definitely getting better and better.

"Was it something I said?" she asked with a quirk of her eyebrow as he continued to stare.

He gave a start.

"I beg your pardon?"

"You're staring at me, Mr. Sinclair."

Mattie thought his cheeks bronzed, but who could tell in a room lit only by the romantic flicker of candles?

"Forgive me. I know it is rude, but I am not quite sure what to think about you, Miss Crockwell." He relaxed into his chair, but Mattie noticed an unsteadiness to his hand as he raised his glass to his mouth.

Her lips twitched. The poor man, she thought. He had no idea what to do with her, did he? She took pity on him.

"How can I help, Mr. Sinclair?" she asked.

"You could begin by telling me how you came to be here, Miss Crockwell," he said.

Mattie shrugged with a nonchalance she didn't feel.

"I really don't know. You'll think I'm crazy—which I know you do already—but one minute, I was on my balcony chatting with the moon...and the next thing I know, I woke up in your kitchen."

"Is it a habit where you come from to...em...*chat with the moon*?" His lips twitched despite the fact that he continued to regard her as a scientist might observe a specimen in a laboratory.

"Sometimes," she said with a self-conscious smile.

He dropped his eyes to his glass and studied it for a moment as he twirled the liquid.

"I must confess to doing exactly that when I found you, Miss Crockwell." His expression, when he looked at her, seemed uncertain.

"What's that?"

"Em...engaging in a conversation with the moon. Wishing on the moon, one could say," he said with a shrug of his shoulders and a faint smile.

"Really!" Mattie took a rather large swallow of her wine, enjoying the warmth in her throat. She felt quite cozy in the library at the moment, seated across from a gorgeous man who had the longest legs she'd ever seen, and who happened to also make wishes on the moon.

"And what were you wishing for, Mr. Sinclair, may I ask?" Mattie asked, surprising herself again with her newfound boldness. Good gravy! Was she flirting? Shy, quiet Mattie? Who was lost in some sort of time warp?

William rose abruptly.

"May I refill your glass?"

"Oh, yes, please. It's lovely. Very fruity." Mattie was faintly aware that her body had relaxed into a lounging position on the settee, one arm draped over the back, her legs extended down the length.

William returned with her glass and resumed his seat. He tossed back another swallow, and Mattie followed suit.

"And so, you were saying?" Mattie prompted, an imp egging her on.

"I beg your pardon?"

"About wishing on the moon? What could a handsome man like you, with obvious wealth"—she waved an airy hand about the room—"and comfort possibly need to wish for?"

A flicker of candlelight revealed a definite bronze tinge to his cheeks. He crossed and re-crossed his legs.

"Many things, Miss Crockwell," he prevaricated. "What was it that *you* wished for?"

"Oh, you know, the usual things." Mattie knew he'd given her the slip, but her brain wasn't working well enough to seize the moment.

"Yes? The usual things? Such as?"

Mattie took another swallow of the pungent wine.

"Life, love, a handsome man in a cravat and yellow silk trousers— that sort of thing."

He coughed, and Mattie thought he looked a bit startled. Had she said something she shouldn't have, she wondered? What had she said?

"I see," he murmured with a slight smile.

"Yes, I knew you would," she mumbled as she took another gulp and slipped a little farther down on the settee. She wasn't sure what he saw at the moment, but that was okay.

Through hazy eyes, she watched as William jumped up to retrieve the glass that dangled precariously from her limp fingers. She wouldn't have dropped it, she thought.

"Miss Crockwell, are you unwell?" He set her glass aside and bent to examine her with concern.

Mattie, feeling a complete lack of inhibition at the moment, reached for the ends of his cravat and pulled him towards her.

29

"I think I'm drunk, Mr. Sinclair. Kiss me now before I pass out."

Mattie felt him attempt to pull away, but she didn't seem to care at the moment.

"Madam! Miss Crockwell, please. This is most unseemly. I cannot take advantage."

"Resistance is futile, Mr. Sinclair." She grinned at the hackneyed line, but it seemed so appropriate for the moment.

Mattie wrapped her arms around his neck and pulled him down to her. To keep his balance, he went down on one knee at the edge of the settee. As his warm lips touched hers, Mattie sighed with the gloriousness of the kiss. Stars exploded, and she knew no more.

****

Mattie opened her eyes to a faint gray light peeping into the room from around the edges of the heavy velvet drapes. She gasped and bolted upright, pushing aside the heavy coverlet. She looked down at her pajamas—a white cotton camisole and her favorite pink baggy flannel bottoms with a pattern of red and purple hearts. Where was her robe? A glance down the length of the bed showed it was draped across the foot. She turned to look at the pillow next to hers. Her last memory had been of kissing William. Well, mauling him, really. The pillow next to hers was plump. There was no sign anyone had slept on it the night before…or so she dearly hoped.

A stab of pain assaulted her head, and she pressed her palms to the sides of her skull. She hadn't had a hangover since her college days, more than five years ago. What had possessed her to drink so much? On an empty stomach? She certainly didn't remember much after grabbing William's cravat and kissing him.

At the memory, Mattie slid back down onto the pillow, wishing she could ease the ache in her head, and even more desperate to erase the memory of forcing William to kiss her.

There seemed to be little doubt. She was not in a dream. The sun had every intention of rising, the night had passed, and with it every idea that she might still be asleep. She was still in the nineteenth century. Somehow, someway, she had wished herself into her romance novel, and she had no idea how to get back.

A nearby movement startled her, and she froze for a moment. *Oh, please, not rats*, she begged. Was something scurrying across the floor of the bedroom?

She turned slowly toward the source of the brief noise. One long, masculine leg draped over the arm of a gilt-edged chair near the bed, while the other stretched out along the floor in front of its owner.

William! He slept in a chair near the door, and very uncomfortably from the looks of it.

Mattie rose up on one elbow and tried to make out his face in the dim light. A shadow covered the lower half of his face, extending from the fascinating, thick sideburns that grew down below his ear lobe. The dark waves of his hair lay in casual disarray, completely different from the carefully coiffed curls of the night before. One arm stretched above his head, ruffles at the end of his sleeve, the other hand dangled over the arm of the chair.

He moved to adjust himself in the chair, once again making the slight noise Mattie had heard, and then he opened his eyes. His gaze seemed unfocused for a moment as he looked at her. He blinked several times, ran a hand across his eyes, and peered at her again.

Mattie offered him a tentative smile.

William's eyes widened, and he jumped to his feet.

"Madam...Miss Crockwell. Forgive me! I did not plan to fall asleep. I thought merely to rest here for a moment to see that all was well with you."

Mattie sat up in bed and watched with fascination as he ran a hand through his wavy hair and scanned the room with something like horror on his face.

"I sincerely beg your pardon. I shall leave at once, and no one the wiser. Forgive me for placing you in this untenable position."

Mattie opened her mouth to speak, but William swung around and strode to the door. Before he left, he turned around.

"Rest assured, Miss Crockwell, that nothing untoward occurred in this chamber last night. You have my word. I shall return shortly with a cup of tea for you, and then we must discuss what is to be done."

He slipped out the door quietly, leaving Mattie with her mouth hanging open, empty words of reassurance on her lips.

With a sigh, she slipped out of bed. A wave of dizziness hit her, and she grabbed the nearest bedpost to steady herself.

Hangover! How could she possibly have a hangover in her first few hours in the nineteenth century?

Mattie staggered over to the curtains to pull them wide. An early-morning mist covered the lawn in front of the house, and she could see little except that she appeared to be on the second floor of a rather massive house, judging from the leaded pane windows that began at her waist and ran up to the high ceilings. She turned away to study the room once again, aware of a nagging urge. Which way to the bathroom? Would it be down the hall? She fervently hoped not. William would not be happy if she were discovered by family and servants wandering around in her pajamas.

A door on the opposite side of the room caught her eye and she made her way around the bed, enjoying the luxurious, silky feel of the Oriental carpet beneath her toes. She eased the door open and peeked inside. Though the small room was dark, she could make out a metal tub of some sort, a dresser with a large basin and bowl, and another container on the floor. A chamber pot!

She slammed the door shut and gritted her teeth. No! She had absolutely no intention of going in a chamber pot. None! She swung away and tossed herself into the chair where William had slept, hoping her needs would simply pass.

Mattie crossed her legs and studied the room once again, keeping an alert ear out for William's return. Now that the curtains were open and gray light filled the room, she could see that the impression of green she'd received the night before was accurate. Everything in the room seemed to be green, from the patterned wallpaper of pale moss green down to the silk cushion of the chair on which she sat. Only the large white-painted mantle and the gleaming surfaces of various pieces of antique wooden and marble-topped furniture broke the atmosphere of green. Well, she thought with a shake of her head, antique only to her. The pieces were probably new to the owners.

Mattie noted an exquisite dressing table nestled against the wall near the fireplace, and was in the process of getting up to investigate it when a light tap sounded on her door, followed by the entrance of William, balancing a silver tea service.

Mattie jumped up to take the tray from him while he turned to close the door. She staggered under its weight and tottered over to the table beside the sofa. Setting it down with a clank, she turned to look at William, neatly dressed in boots, form-fitting beige slacks, a fresh neck cloth, a burgundy vest and another one of those wonderful coats with long, flowing tails, this one a dark blue that accented his broad shoulders and narrowed to his waist.

William paused for a moment with his head turned toward the door, as if listening intently for any sounds from the hallway. Apparently reassured, he turned and looked at her. His eyes widened, and he dropped his gaze to the floor as he made his way to the bed to grab her robe. He handed it to her and turned around.

"If you please, Miss Crockwell."

With a grin, Mattie slipped the robe over her arms and tied the sash in the front.

"Better, Mr. Sinclair?"

He turned and kept his eyes on her face.

"Yes, much better, Miss Crockwell." He inclined his head and indicated she should sit on the settee. "Will you take some tea? Mrs. White laid out some food."

"I'd love some tea. My head is killing me!" Mattie sank down onto the sofa and poured two cups from a lovely porcelain rose-patterned set, noting with pleasure several pieces of toasted bread and a small saucer of butter.

"Killing you?" William murmured. "So severe as that?" He took a seat on a nearby chair and regarded her gravely.

"No, that's just an expression," she sighed as she handed him a cup of tea. "It feels that bad. I'll never drink again, I swear."

"The fault is mine, Miss Crockwell. I apologize for offering you such a strong beverage last night. I should have seen you are not accustomed to drink." He drank some tea and studied her over the cup.

"Not really," she murmured with a smile. She picked up her own saucer of tea and took a sip from the delicate cup. The comforting, hot liquid slid down her throat with ease, and she relaxed. William sent several glances her way, and she thought she ought to say something...anything.

Mattie dropped her eyes and took a breath.

"Mr. Sinclair. I want to apologize for my behavior last night. I really can't believe that I...um..." She really didn't want to finish the sentence.

William held up a hand and shook his head quickly. He looked away toward the empty fireplace.

"Think no more about it. You were not yourself."

"Well, I would never have...uh...grabbed you when I was sober, but after a drink or two, there's no telling what I'm capable of." She played it off with a grin, but a quirk of one of William's dark eyebrows startled her.

"I'm kidding," she said hastily.

"Kidding? Do you mean to say you jest, Miss Crockwell?"

She nodded and hoped he didn't see her lips twitching. The man hardly seemed to have a funny bone in his body. Come to think of it, she didn't remember the hero in her book having a sense of humor either. It just never came up.

"Yes, Mr. Sinclair. Jest, joke."

"I see." He took another sip of tea.

Mattie, giving in to the rumblings in her stomach, set her cup down, snagged a piece of toast and bit into it. Still warm from the oven, the bread seemed to melt in her mouth, even without butter.

"This is delicious," she breathed.

"Mrs. White will be pleased to hear it," William murmured.

She munched on the toast and wondered if there was something else she should say. She knew he must want answers…explanations.

William set his cup down on the table and leaned back. He rested his elbows on the arms of his chair and steepled his fingers as he studied her with a frown between his eyes.

Uh oh, Mattie thought. Time for the talk. She swallowed the last piece of toast and waited.

"Miss Crockwell." He paused, as if unsure what to say.

"Yes, Mr. Sinclair."

"Can you… Can you tell me now how you came to be here?" He nodded toward the window. "On the lawn…in the middle of the night? Have you recollected anything more specific of the events which brought you here?"

Mattie clasped her hands in her lap and squeezed. What if he decided she was crazy? What would he do? Send for the authorities to take her away? Commit her to an institution? She was fairly certain people had few rights in the nineteenth century, and she doubted they would tolerate any notions of traveling through time—however much she doubted the event herself.

"Well, the thing is…" She hesitated and looked up to meet his eyes. "You're going to think I'm crazy."

He shook his head as if to dispute her, but she nodded firmly.

"No, Mr. Sinclair. You will. Just like I would think you were insane if this happened to you and you showed up at my door." Mattie jumped up restlessly, desperate to come up with something more plausible than the truth, but nothing came to mind.

William stood when she did and clasped his hands behind his back. She dropped back down on the settee, unsure her shaking legs would hold her while she talked, and William retook his seat.

"How may I make this easier for you, Miss Crockwell? You seem to be in a great deal of distress. I give you my promise I will not think you insane. Will that suffice?" A lift at the corner of his lips caught her eye. An almost imperceptible half-smile. Could she trust him?

"I'd rather you promise that you won't have someone take me away to an asylum. I would find it more reassuring if you promise to let me go, even if you think I'm insane."

William stared hard at her, and she pressed her lips together to signify she wouldn't talk without his assurances.

A slight shake of his head set her heart hammering.

"I do not think I can blindly assure you of the latter, Miss Crockwell, until we have discussed the matter. If you had a safe place to be, I believe you would already be there. If I let you go"—he frowned—"a ridiculous notion indeed, as I do not detain you in any way, where would you go?"

"So, you are saying I am free to go…if I need to."

"Come now, Miss Crockwell." He leaned forward, one elbow on his knee. "You are speaking in circles, and I am thoroughly confused. If there is some safe place to which I can convey you, let me know at once, and we can depart for it before the rest of the house awakens."

Mattie didn't feel in the least reassured.

"Did you ever have a favorite book? One you read over and over because you couldn't get enough of it?"

William's expression suggested he already thought she was insane.

"I beg your pardon?"

"Oh, never mind. That wasn't a good way to start. Let's see…"

"Miss Crockwell." William pulled his watch from his vest pocket and consulted it. "We do not have much time to sort this matter out. My mother and sister will soon rise, and there is nothing which occurs in this house that they do not soon ferret out. I wish to…ah…return you to your lodgings if you would but be so kind as to direct me."

Mattie threw a harried look toward the door, somehow expecting the Georgian ladies to pop in at any moment.

"Okay, okay, I'm trying. No, I don't have any lodgings nearby. I'm not from England. I'm from the United States. I don't exactly know how I got here. As I told you last night, the last thing I remember is stepping out on my balcony at home in Seattle and wishing on the moon. I wished for…" Mattie bit her lip and shook her head. "Well, it doesn't matter. But what I wished for seems to sort of have come true. That is, not quite, but a little bit. Though not quite what I thought."

She raised her eyes from her clenched white knuckles to steal a glance at his face.

William sat back in his chair and clenched his own hands together, staring at her with an expression of unease. The situation looked grim for her.

"I'm not crazy, Mr. Sinclair. I'm not. I don't know what happened. When I get up in the morning—if I'm not already awake—I'm supposed to go to work at the bank. It's Thursday morning, September 17th." When she told him the current year, she winced as his eyes widened and he jumped to his feet.

He stared down at her for a moment, and she tried to meet his eyes steadily.

"Surely, you jest once again, Miss Crockwell."

She shook her head.

He clasped his hands behind his back and swung away, to begin pacing in front of the hearth.

"So, you would have me believe that you have"—he paused and faced her for a moment with an incredulous look on his face—"come from the future?"

CHAPTER FOUR

Mattie winced. Did he have to make it sound so much like science fiction?

"Yes," she whispered.

William stared at her again for a long moment before he resumed his pacing once again.

"And how do you believe you came to be in this time?" he asked in a carefully measured voice.

Mattie shrugged. "I don't know. I have this favorite book, and I was reading it, and then I couldn't sleep, and so I went outside. The moon…" She gestured skyward.

He stilled and turned to look at her once again, a crease between his brows.

"Yes, the moon. You mentioned that before. And what time was that exactly?"

"Around ten thirty at night my time. I don't know what time that would be here." She shook her head with the ghost of a smile on her face. "Or even what year this is, frankly."

A corner of William's lips tilted.

"The year is 1825, Miss Crockwell."

Mattie nodded, unsurprised. She had suspected from the cut of his clothing that she'd landed somewhere in the Georgian or the Regency era. In fact, she was in the exact year in which her book was set.

"I imagined as much, Mr. Sinclair."

William turned toward the fireplace, bracing one arm against the mantle and the other behind his back as he stared down into the hearth. Mattie watched his stiff back as if she could divine his thoughts from the rigidity of his spine. He certainly didn't appear relaxed in any way.

She pulled her knees up and wrapped her arms around her legs, beginning a gentle rocking of which she was barely aware. The heretofore romantic idea of traveling through time to meet the man of her dreams seemed suddenly a very foolish idea—one fraught with dire implications. Visions of ending her days in a cold stone building chained to the wall while she ranted that she worked in a bank and really didn't belong there after all presented themselves as frightening possibilities.

She watched William's shoulders rise as if he took a deep breath. His back seemed to visibly relax, and he dropped his head. He turned to face her, keeping both hands behind him. While his eyes traveled over her childish posture, he made no mention of it.

"I believe something untoward has occurred here, Miss Crockwell, though I do not know what. I must allow that I too wished on the moon, at exactly the same time as you—though, as with you, my desires were not met in quite the way that I had envisioned. But it is this fact that leads me to believe that between us, you and I have brought about some strange phenomenon which I cannot begin to comprehend." He regarded her gravely. "The question is…what is to be done now, and how can we return you to your time?"

Mattie breathed a sigh of relief, images of a dark, foreboding insane asylum drifting away.

"I don't have the faintest idea."

William echoed her sigh as he took his seat once again, gazing at the hearth in an unfocused fashion.

"I think the answer may lie in the full moon upon which we both made our wishes," he murmured, almost as if he talked to himself. "It will not be full again for thirty days." He threw her a sideways look. "I am not quite sure what you wished for, and I beg leave to keep my desires private, but I cannot help wonder if they did not have a commonality which in some strange way brought us together." He cleared his throat and reached for his tea. "Speculation, of course. We may never know." He met her eyes briefly over the edge of his cup and looked away.

"So, are you suggesting that on the next full moon—in a month—we both make a wish for me to return?"

William set his cup down and clasped his hands in front of his stomach. He nodded.

"That is correct. At exactly ten-thirty in the evening."

Mattie rested her chin on top of her knees. A month. Too long? Not long enough? She gazed at William with an inward sigh. Not long enough, she thought.

"Do you have any idea what I should do until then? Is there

somewhere—"

"You will stay here, of course. I have had little time to form a plan, but I have some rudimentary thoughts. It would be disastrous should anyone discover that you have come from the future. We will have to acquaint my mother and sister with our...secret"—his lips twitched again—"so that they may assist us in finding you suitable clothing and a plausible story for your presence here in the house. My mother has scheduled several parties and at least one rout during the month." He gave her a wry smile. "She wishes to see me married and is going to great lengths to achieve that end."

Mattie's heart dropped to her stomach. Nowhere in her fantasies did her dream man marry someone else!

"I see," she murmured. "Well, I really don't need to be much trouble. If there is a small room, maybe where the servants sleep? I could stay out of the way." She offered him a helpful smile, though it wavered at the end.

"That is out of the question, Miss Crockwell. I do not think you are a servant. If I may ask"—William hesitated—"what is your station? You mentioned you work in a bank. Do you assist your father, perhaps? Some male relative? I am not familiar with women in banking."

"My station?" she repeated as her smile broadened. "This is straight out of a Jane Austen novel, I swear. I really didn't think people talked like that." She pressed her wayward lips together at the narrowing of his eyes.

"I'm sorry." She winced at the severity of his look. "Yes, my station. Well, I work for a living. No, my father doesn't own the bank. I am just an employee there."

"An employee," he repeated thoughtfully. "And your family? Are they landowners?"

"Well, my parents owned their home in Nebraska, but they both passed away several years ago. They were older, and I was an only child."

William brought his eyes together in a frown and inclined his head.

"My condolences, madam. I am afraid I have not heard of this...Nuhbrasska...but assume it is in America. And with whom do you reside at present?"

"I live by myself...in an apartment."

He quirked a surprised eyebrow.

"Alone? In your own apartments? Without a companion? How unusual!"

Mattie grinned. William was definitely having a hard time wrapping his head around her lifestyle, and she didn't blame him. She'd read enough Georgian- and Victorian-era literature—even the good stuff—to know that most young women did not live on their own, and certainly no women of the upper classes.

"No, William. No companion. Just me."

He shook his head.

"Perhaps we could avoid sharing that bit of information with my mother and sister. The former would be shocked, and the latter would no doubt pounce upon such a notion as an excellent idea." He gave her a quick bow. "I certainly do not mean to impugn your customs."

"Of course." Mattie nodded with a smile.

William checked his watch once before stowing it away in his vest.

"Well, Miss Crockwell," he said heavily, "I think it is time I go to see my mother. We must enlist her aid if I am to keep you safe over the coming month."

Mattie watched him rise, admiring the long, lean lines of his legs and thrilling to the words "if I am to keep you safe." She stood to follow him to the door. He turned before he opened the door, looking down into her upturned face.

"You would do well to finish your breakfast, Miss Crockwell. You will need your strength, for my mother will surely wish to interview you at length, and much more rigorously than I."

Mattie's heart thumped with anxiety, and it must have shown in her face. William softened his voice and regarded her kindly.

"Do not worry, Miss Crockwell. You will remain here at the house under my protection. I am master here."

"Thank you, Mr. Sinclair. Good luck," she murmured as he slipped through the door.

****

William tapped on his mother's door and entered on hearing her response.

"Good morning, Mother. How are you?"

Lucy Sinclair relaxed on a small sapphire-blue velvet sofa sipping hot chocolate, a fetching lace cap perched on her blonde curls, a confection of white lace and pink satin covering her from neck to toe.

She looked at him in surprise and offered up her cheek for a kiss. William obliged and straightened. He dropped down into a matching blue velvet wingback chair.

"What brings you here so early, William? I would have thought you to be riding this morning. It looks to be a fine day." His mother's crystal blue eyes strayed toward the open window.

"I have a matter to discuss with you, Mother, and it cannot wait."

His mother lifted a well-groomed eyebrow. "Indeed. Good news, perhaps? Did you meet someone last night after all?" She set her cup of chocolate down on a mahogany side table and eyed him with interest.

William, who had been staring at the floor, jerked his head up at her words. He stared at her for a moment.

"One might say that." He could not help but smile. His mother seemed to have a sixth sense about many things, but had no inkling how close she was to the truth—and yet how far.

"And who is the fortunate young woman?" She seemed almost to hold her breath, if one could ever witness her doing such a common thing. William hated to disappoint her, but disappoint her he must.

He jumped up restlessly. "If you have no objections, Mother, I think Sylvie must be here. It would be foolish to discuss the same matter twice. With your permission, I shall call her in."

"William? Is something wrong?"

He had reached the door when he turned to see her staring at him with an expression of alarm. He thought to allay her fears but realized he really could not.

"That remains to be seen, madam."

He strode across the hall in three steps and tapped on his sister's door.

"Enter," she called in a voice husky with sleep.

William opened the door to find the room in darkness, Sylvie still drowsing in bed. He crossed the room to open the heavy velvet drapes, ignoring the subsequent protests.

"Out of bed, sister. I need you to come to Mother's room."

Sylvie shot up with a look of alarm matching his mother's face. "Is something wrong? Mother?"

"No, no. She is fine. I have a matter of some importance to discuss with both of you, and it cannot wait for long."

Sylvie slid nimbly out of bed and grabbed a shawl from a nearby chair while William waited at the door. When she came within arm's length, he ruffled her hair as he had done when they were younger. She tried to tousle his as well, but failed to reach his head, even on tiptoes.

"So, what is this important matter?" she mumbled through a yawn as he opened the door to allow her to precede him.

"You must wait until we reach Mother's room. I feel I can only explain this once, therefore I wanted to speak to you both at the same time."

Sylvie paused to stare at him. "This sounds serious, brother. Need I be concerned?"

With a hand on his mother's door, William cocked his head and gave her a small half-smile.

41

"I am not sure, my dear. Perhaps," he murmured, his smile broadening despite his best intentions to remain grave. Interspersed with moments of gravity at the implication of Miss Crockwell's presence were moments when he felt an unexpected giddiness. He supposed it was from lack of sleep.

They stepped into the room to see their mother seated on the settee in an alert manner.

"Good morning, Mother. What do you suppose our Will is about this morning?" Sylvie mumbled as she shuffled across the room, kissed her mother's cheek and settled next to her in a corner of the settee.

"I have no idea, dear. We so rarely have these 'family' meetings and almost never at this hour." Mrs. Sinclair turned a pointed look toward the Ormolu clock on the mantle.

William ignored her look and leaned against the mantle, regarding the women of his family. Fully aware he was making matters worse by prevaricating, he was uncertain as to how to proceed.

"Well, William?" his mother prompted. "What is it? I admit to being quite intrigued, although somewhat concerned about the frown upon your brow. Somehow, I feel that you cannot have felicitous news to impart."

William made a conscious effort to smooth his brow.

"I apologize for intruding upon you both so early this morning. If I felt the matter could wait, I would certainly have allowed you to take breakfast before approaching you, but as it is, I think I need your immediate assistance."

"Whatever is wrong, William? The matter sounds urgent." Sylvie straightened and leaned forward, her mother's blue eyes mirrored on her own face.

William regarded the two women on the settee, so alike in appearance and temperament. Intelligent and gracious with impeccable manners, as befitted their station and training. His sister possessed a natural kindness, which his mother shared—albeit with somewhat more reserve.

He drew in a deep breath, depending on their graciousness.

"Last night, I stepped outside and took a short stroll in the garden."

"To which I expressed my displeasure," Mrs. Sinclair murmured.

"Yes, I am afraid I needed some air, Mother. The dinner parties can be so...stifling at times."

"The caged bird sings," she responded with a sardonic half-smile.

"Go on, William," Sylvie urged. "You went outside..." she prompted.

"I found myself wishing on the moon..." He paused and raised a hand to his mouth to cough slightly, wishing he had left that detail out as his mother's eyebrows quirked once again and her smile widened.

"Ah, the moon," Mrs. Sinclair interjected in a faintly acerbic manner.

"William! How sweet!" Sylvie chuckled.

"Yes, well, that is beside the point," he added hastily. "As I was saying, I was in the garden for only a few moments. When I turned to return to the house, I stumbled over something—a fairly large something." A vision of pink fluff brought an involuntary twitch to his lips.

"Well, what was it, Will?" Sylvie prompted.

"A woman." A gasp and a rustle of silk wrappers warned him to hurry through his explanation before the expected barrage of questions came his way. He clasped his hands behind his back and began to pace, avoiding their eyes for the moment. "I am not yet sure how she came to be there, but she had fainted. I picked her up and brought her into the kitchen, where Mrs. White saw to her until I was able to return after the dinner party to see if she would require a doctor."

"William!" his mother predictably remonstrated. "This is most irregular. You should have sent for a doctor at once."

William paused and faced his mother.

"I doubt you would say that had you been in my situation, Mother. You see, she was in her...em...well, she was in her sleeping garments."

"Out on the lawn? Our lawn? Surely you jest, William," Mrs. Sinclair said incredulously.

"Who is she? Did you send for the physician? What happened?" Sylvie perched on the edge of the settee, her eyes sparkling.

"I do not know who she is," William replied with a shake of his head. "She did not appear to need a physician, as she appears to be quite well." He resumed his pacing to give himself time to parry his mother's inevitable questions.

"Appears?" his mother said sharply. "William! Is she still in the house?"

He paused and nodded.

"Yes, she is—"

"But, Will, who is she?" Sylvie interrupted with wide eyes. "Does she not have a home of her own? How could she wander about in her sleeping garments in someone's garden? Is she a guest of one of the servants?"

William shook his head and held up a hand.

"Be patient, Sylvie, and I will finish the story."

His sister sealed her lips and waited. His mother's mouth was closed as well, but her lips seemed to be pressed together as if to bite her tongue—for the moment. He knew the look well.

"You will believe me to be crazy or you will believe her to be crazy, so I will just say this as best I might. She is clearly not from England and states she is from America. She is not staying with anyone and has no idea how she came to be in the garden except that"—he hesitated, dreading his next words—"she also wished on the moon at the same time…from her own home in America." He looked away from his audience's confused expressions. "We believe some phenomenon has occurred, that in fact, she may very well have"—another cough behind his hand to clear his throat, which threatened to seize—"traveled through time."

Instead of the expected onslaught of questions, his words were received with acute silence. He had halted his pacing and turned to face his mother and sister, whose expressions could be called comical if he were in such a fanciful mood. Even his elegant, usually unflappable mother had allowed her jaw to slacken as she stared at him. Sylvie matched her expression.

He took a deep breath and exhaled deeply as he dropped into the blue chair near the settee. What was the worst that could occur? They would laugh at him? Scream?

Surprisingly, it was Sylvie who first broke the silence with a whisper.

"Is that possible?" she whispered as she leaned forward.

William, grateful for such a muted response, shrugged.

"I do not know, but I have no other explanation for her presence. When you meet her, you will know that she is…not one of us." He pressed his lips together. He could have phrased that in a better manner. "That is to say, she seems…different."

"Where is she, Will?" Sylvie scooted to the edge of the settee once again. "I am anxious to meet her."

"She is down the hall in the green bedchamber, Sylvie," said William, his eyes on his mother, whose cheeks were unusually red. "I shall introduce you in good time."

"You put a stranger on the same floor as your sister? Was that wise, William?" William was not surprised to see his mother stiffen.

"I had no other suitable room for her, Mother. I did not want to pique the servants' curiosity by putting her in their quarters. Mrs. White is the only one who knows she is here. She seems harmless, albeit as confused as I about her current circumstances." He gave a slight shake of his head.

Mrs. Sinclair rose swiftly.

"Is she awake? We shall dress and go to meet her at once."

William jumped up.

"Well, you see, that is part of the problem. She does not have any clothing with her except what she would normally wear to…bed."

His mother turned a narrowed eye on him. "Ah, yes, so you said. Sylvie, run back to your room and put on a morning frock. I will dress as well. Return in twenty minutes, and we shall go to meet our 'guest.' Since she will not yet be dressed, perhaps it would be better, William, if we visited her alone."

"No, Mother, that will not do. I intend to be present when you meet her. She is frightened enough and is depending on me."

He was aware that Sylvie jumped up and watched the battle of wills between them with rounded eyes.

"As you wish," his mother murmured with a slight inclination of her head.

William held the door open for Sylvie, who dashed across the hall with unbridled excitement. He checked his watch and returned to his own room, there to pace while he waited for his mother and sister to finish dressing. He studied the closed door of the green room as he passed, wishing he could pop in and reassure Miss Crockwell, who undoubtedly thought she had been abandoned by now, but he thought it best to keep his mother and sister from the knowledge that he had already seen her in her undressed state that morning, let alone slept in her room.

He heard the creak of a door opening in the hallway and poked his head out. Sylvie, now dressed in a light blue silk day dress and busily trying to pin her unruly golden curls atop her head, dropped the effort and beckoned to him.

"Will!" she whispered as he approached. "This is so exciting. How lucky you are to have such an adventure."

William grinned and shook his head. He took his sister by the shoulders and turned her around to pull the drawstrings of her dress tight in the back and tie them, a task he had performed more than once during their youth.

"I am not certain that is the case, my dear. Mother seems less…enthusiastic than you, I am afraid."

"Thank you, Will. I know I look a fright, but I did not wish to wait for the maid to help me dress," Sylvie murmured as she took his hand. "Come, Mother must be dressed by now." Sylvie dragged him across the hall and tapped on their mother's door.

Upon the sound of Mrs. Sinclair's voice, Sylvie opened the door and stepped in. Their mother, lovely and elegant in a cream-colored frock, sat on a stool at her dressing table and adjusted a few curls as they peeped out from her frothy lace cap.

"Thank you, Mary. That will do," Mrs. Sinclair said to the older, gray-haired woman who gathered up her mistress's discarded nightclothes.

"Yes, mum." Mary, a plump, motherly woman, dipped a quick curtsey and worked her way out of the room with a swipe at an imaginary dust speck here and there, and a beaming smile for her mistress's two children.

"Good day, Master William, Miss Sylvie."

William gave the long-time family retainer who had once held the duty as nanny the same familiar grin he reserved for Mrs. White and Mrs. Bailey.

"Good morning, Mary. I hope you are well?"

"That I am, Master William. Thank you for asking."

"Oh, Mary," Mrs. Sinclair called out.

Mary turned. "Yes, mum?"

"Please bring tea to the green bedchamber. For four."

"Certainly, mum." Too well trained to ask, Mary bobbed another short curtsey and slipped out through the door with only a quick glance in William's direction to betray her curiosity at the unusual activities of the morning.

Mrs. Sinclair rose and turned, one graceful eyebrow lifting as she surveyed her children.

"Sylvie! Did you attempt to dress yourself this morning? It certainly seems that way."

Sylvie, unabashed, appeared as if she would hop from foot to foot in anticipatory excitement if she could.

"Yes, Mother, I did. I did not wish to waste time on my toilette as I am anxious to meet our new guest." She flashed William an impish smile, and he responded with a grateful curve of his lips at her use of the word "guest."

"Our guest," Mrs. Sinclair murmured dryly. "Of course. Shall we?"

William opened the door and allowed his sister and mother to precede him. They moved down the hallway and came to stand in front of the door leading to the green bedchamber.

"I think I shall just step in and prepare her for your arrival." Again, he blithely ignored their startled looks as he tapped on the door and slipped into the room.

Miss Crockwell jumped up from the sofa and turned to stare at him with wide eyes. He could not help but notice the sleek shine of her russet hair as a streak of sunlight from the open window danced across it.

"Forgive me for not waiting to enter," he said as he executed a small bow. "I thought you might simply remain silent on the chance that someone other than myself might be knocking on the door. My mother and sister are waiting to meet you. The situation is most irregular in that you are not dressed to receive anyone, and yet we need their assistance to find clothing for you."

"What did you tell them?" she whispered, her eyes fixed on the door as if some terrible beast lay in waiting outside.

William shrugged.

"The truth," he said simply. "As you and I understand it."

She swung a wide-eyed gaze toward him.

"Really? How did they take it?"

William's lips twitched.

"My sister, an adventurous spirit, is most anxious to meet you. My mother is as well, though I am afraid she is somewhat skeptical."

Miss Crockwell pulled the sash of her robe tighter around her and seemed to square her shoulders. She nodded toward the door.

"I'm ready, but William..."

With a hand on the door, he paused, her unexpected use of his first name intimate—and somehow alluring.

"Yes?"

"You promised me. Don't let anyone take me away. If things don't...uh...work out, I'll leave. I'll be fine."

"You will be safe, Miss Crockwell. My mother may appear inflexible at first meeting, but she has a kind heart. Do not be afraid. There will be no need for you to leave until it is time."

He pulled open the door and ushered his mother and sister in. Both women came to an abrupt halt as they eyed the oddly dressed woman in the room, who gave them a tentative smile.

William moved forward and came to stand by Miss Crockwell's side.

"Mother, Sylvie, may I present Miss Matilda Crockwell?" William determined to observe the niceties as if he could infuse the situation with respectability, no matter how extraordinary the circumstances. "Miss Crockwell...my mother, Mrs. Lucinda Sinclair, and my sister, Miss Sylvie Sinclair."

CHAPTER FIVE

Mattie watched the two women dip into small curtsies, albeit Mrs. Sinclair inclined her head more than curtsied. Empire waist, ankle-length dresses adorned with lace and ribbons swished. Mattie bent her shaking knees and tried a curtsey herself in response.

The younger one, a blonde beauty with lily-white skin and a warm smile—William's sister—glided toward her with hands outstretched.

"Miss Crockwell, how delightful to meet you," she murmured in a musical voice. Crystal blue eyes sparkled and her cheeks glowed pink. So, this is what they called an English rose, Mattie thought, as Sylvie caught her hands. Sylvie's silky-soft skin was cool and dry, and Mattie cringed as she realized her own palms were cold and sweaty.

"Thank you," Mattie mumbled.

Mrs. Sinclair moved forward, and Sylvie released Mattie's hands to stand to the side.

Mattie threw William a quick, panicked look. Was she supposed to curtsey again? She wasn't certain. Surely not! William gave her a reassuring smile that failed to reassure her one little bit.

"Miss Crockwell, how do you do?" Mrs. Sinclair murmured in a measured tone of elegance and reserve. She inclined her head again, and Mattie nodded in return.

"Fine, thank you," she murmured in a low voice.

"I see that William has had tea brought to you this morning. How thoughtful of him."

A tap on the door startled Mattie. Who else, she wondered?

William strode to the door and pulled it open.

"Please allow Mary to enter, William. No one can keep secrets from her. She will know soon enough," Mrs. Sinclair directed.

William hesitated, and Mattie craned her neck to see this Mary. A small, rounded woman dressed in serviceable dark cotton with an unadorned cap on her head struggled under the seemingly heavy load of a silver tea service, though she deftly carried it to the small table in front of the settee. She stilled for just an instant when she saw Mattie, but recovered nicely and set the service down, picking up the other tea tray.

"Thank you, Mary. Sylvie will pour. Mary, I know I can count on your discretion."

"Yes, of course, mum." She bobbed another quick curtsey, threw another quick look in Mattie's direction and left the room.

"Please sit down, Miss Crockwell," Mrs. Sinclair said serenely. "Forgive our intrusion on your privacy this morning, but William indicated there was some urgency to the matter."

Mrs. Sinclair settled on the settee and indicated Mattie should sit beside her. Mattie, suddenly cold though the room had been comfortably warm, unlocked her knees and obediently sat down. Sylvie perched on the chair that William had vacated earlier, the toes of her dark boots peeping out from under the hem of her skirt.

"Did you find the room satisfactory, Miss Crockwell?" Sylvie asked with a scan of the bedchamber as she reached for the tea service. "It is quite one of my favorite rooms in the house." Her gleaming smile seemed genuine and bore a striking resemblance to her brother's rare smiles.

"It's beautiful. Thank you," Mattie answered, keeping one wary eye on Mrs. Sinclair and the other on William, who returned after following Mary out into the hallway. He moved back into the semicircle of furniture in front of the hearth and settled himself into the chair opposite Sylvie.

"Do you take milk or sugar, Miss Crockwell?" Sylvie poured tea into delicate porcelain cups with some expertise.

"None, thank you," Mattie murmured. In fact, she wasn't even sure she liked tea.

"Here you are." Sylvie handed her a cup with a warm smile.

Mattie noted the young blonde's eyes often traveled to Mattie's robe with frank curiosity. She dared not turn to look at Mrs. Sinclair, the close proximity to her on the small sofa necessitating a meeting of the eyes, something Mattie was hardly ready to do.

"Is the tea not to your liking, Miss Crockwell?"

Mattie, who had fixed her eyes on William's dark shoes, jumped at the sound of Mrs. Sinclair's silky voice. Her cup clattered in the saucer, and she lifted it quickly.

"Oh, no, it's lovely. Thank you," she mumbled, and took a sip. When was someone going to come to the point? Surely, they didn't intend to sip tea all morning and ignore the large pink elephant—or rabbit—in the room? Namely her?

Out of the corner of her eye, Mattie saw Mrs. Sinclair set her tea down and fold her long, slender hands in her lap.

"I hardly know where to begin, Miss Crockwell. To say I am astounded would be an understatement. Although William has told us of your…meeting, I feel I need to hear a recount of events from you. Would that be agreeable to you?"

Mattie raised her eyes and met the unconvinced blue gaze of William's mother. She looked toward William, wondering what he had told his mother. He gave an imperceptible nod of encouragement. She set down her teacup and took a deep breath.

Ten minutes later, Mattie reached for her cup with a shaking hand. Even to her own ears, her story sounded utterly ridiculous. And that was without adding William's wild theory that the moon had somehow been a catalyst for her time travel. Nor had she actually used those words. *Time travel.* Far-fetched in the twenty-first century, the notion would certainly land her in some sort of lock-down facility in the mid-nineteenth century.

She sipped her cooling tea and reluctantly raised her head to look at her audience.

Sylvie's eyes sparkled even more brightly blue, if that were possible. She beamed as she met Mattie's eyes, seemingly young enough to believe anything was possible. She remained silent, however, turning toward her mother to await her comments.

William watched his mother with narrowed eyes. Mattie followed his gaze toward Mrs. Sinclair who, other than a pale face and compressed lips, showed little emotion as she directed Sylvie to refresh everyone's tea.

Mattie bit her lip and had to content herself with holding her breath just a little bit longer. It seemed decorum and civility would rule any situation in the Sinclair household—even one so bizarre as the arrival of a time traveler. Mattie had assumed such etiquette was only the stuff of romance novels of the Regency and Victorian eras, but there she was—smack in the midst of a family gathering where the proper serving of tea and suppression of genuine spontaneity were of the utmost importance.

"Miss Crockwell," Mrs. Sinclair began ominously. "I cannot state with truth that I begin to understand what you are saying. I admit to having my doubts about your origin, but in the absence of any other explanation, I must accept your version of the events of last night." She sipped her tea with deliberation. "In the absence of any other proper course of action, I believe we must allow you to stay with us—as our guest—until such time as you and William are able to find a way for you to…return home. William suggested your arrival, and possible departure, may have something to do with the moon's cycle." She gave a slight shake of her head, dislodging a tight curl, which dropped down below her cap. "I fear I am somewhat skeptical at such a…dreamy notion, but I am not so rigid that I cannot grasp new ideas."

"I think the idea is absolutely romantic," Sylvie sighed aloud when her mother paused.

Mattie's face flamed at Sylvie's words, and she avoided looking at William, who shifted in his seat and re-crossed his legs.

"Romantic is not a word I would use in this instance, Sylvie," Mrs. Sinclair said sharply. Sylvie grinned and took an unrepentant sip of her tea, with a speculative look in her brother's direction.

"This is now William's house, and he will decide whom he has to stay. I believe it incumbent upon us, Sylvie, to attend to more practical matters such as finding Miss Crockwell some appropriate clothing and devising a plausible story to account for her arrival and stay with us for the servants as well as our neighbors and friends."

"Thank you, Mrs. Sinclair, but I really think if I just stay out of sight for the month—"

"I believe I can speak for Miss Crockwell when I say how appreciative we are, Mother, for your attention in this matter. I understand this may be an awkward time for all, most especially Miss Crockwell, who is far from home in a strange land." William threw her a half-smile. "As it happens, I have given the situation a great deal of thought and have hopes of devising a believable story within the hour. It will involve a fabrication that Miss Crockwell is the distant cousin of a cousin who traveled to America. That will prevent the usual questions about her family, who were, I am certain, of excellent character." He went on to explain. "Miss Crockwell's mother passed on a year ago, and her father the year before that."

"Oh, Miss Crockwell, I am so sorry," Sylvie murmured with a sympathetic blue gaze.

"My condolences, Miss Crockwell. Have you other family?" Mrs. Sinclair's face softened for a moment.

Mattie stiffened. It hadn't occurred to her that her parents hadn't even been born yet. How odd! At the moment, she felt completely and utterly alone. She blinked back unexpected moisture.

"No, I'm afraid not. I'm an only child. My parents were older when they married. They did not plan on having babies. I was a bit of a surprise to them."

"Oh, dear. I see." Mrs. Sinclair's cheeks took on a pink tinge, and she picked up her cup once again. Sylvie's eyes widened and she turned to look at William. Mattie threw William an uncertain glance. Was it something she said? William looked as surprised as Sylvie, but rose to the occasion.

"Miss Crockwell will not be used to our customs, Mother. Whether or not one believes she has come from another time, it seems very clear—to me, at least—that she has a refreshing candor about her that bodes well for our own future." He favored Mattie with a warm gaze that generated a thrill which started in her toes and made its way up her spine.

"I'm sorry if I said something...improper. Wil—Mr. Sinclair is right. I am not used to your customs, though I have read several books which seem to be true to life," Mattie murmured.

"Books? About us?" Sylvie piped up. "What kind of books?"

Mattie blushed, wishing she could name a wonderfully literary title. She gave a self-deprecating shrug.

"Novels, really."

"Novels?" Sylvie cried. "I love novels. William, you must allow her to read some of your books in the library." She turned to Mattie. "William has an extensive collection, including some novels." Sylvie's cheeks flushed becomingly, though Mattie had no idea why.

Mrs. Sinclair eyed her daughter with a frown.

"I think my daughter refers to some recently published works by a lady whose name remains anonymous. William bought a copy of each and added them to his library, though I must say I have never read them myself."

"A lady?" Mattie repeated, her mind racing through every tidbit of historical information she could remember. Surely not... They weren't talking about...

"Oh, yes, Miss Crockwell. One of my favorite books is called *Sense and Sensibility*. You probably will not have heard of it, but it is absolutely entrancing. You read it, did you not, William?" Sylvie turned a happy smile on her brother, who seemed to hide the lower half of his face behind the ruffled cuff of his right hand. A *Mr. Darcy* look-alike if ever Mattie had seen one. He coughed and cleared his throat, dropping his hand to expose bronzed cheeks.

"Yes, Sylvie. I do admit to reading the lady's works, though I find them more suitable to the female taste than to mine. Still, they are well written and very entertaining."

"Perhaps the books do not exist in your time...that is...where you come from, Miss Crockwell. I am sure you would enjoy them. Please do read them while you are here."

Mattie nodded and bit the smile from her face. She was in no position to reveal Jane Austen's identity.

"That would be lovely, thank you." Mattie couldn't wait to hold a first-edition copy of *Sense and Sensibility* in her hands.

"Unfortunately, Miss Crockwell will not be able to visit the library if we do not make some arrangements to see her properly dressed." Mrs. Sinclair's acerbic tone brought a damper to Mattie's visions of holding an authentic first edition copy of Jane Austen's *Sense and Sensibility*. "Fortunately, I believe you and she are of a size, Sylvie. You may pick out a few gowns for her, and I will ask Mary to bring them over to Miss Crockwell directly."

"Oh, how lovely, Mother! I know just what will suit you, Miss Crockwell, with your lovely auburn hair."

Mattie blushed and tried to retreat into her robe much like a turtle would its shell.

"I'm so sorry to be trouble," she murmured.

"Oh, no, this will be great fun! Just like having a sister. I have always wanted one." It seemed likely that if Sylvie could have gotten away with bouncing in her chair, she would have, but her mother's pointed look gave her pause...just. Sylvie tapped her toe slightly and beamed at Mattie.

"Very well, then." Mrs. Sinclair rose. "William, if you would be so good as to provide us with Miss Crockwell's...er...background as soon as possible. I will send Mary to you at once, Miss Crockwell."

William rose when his mother did, as did Sylvie. Mattie jumped up as well, unwilling to be the only one still sitting.

Mrs. Sinclair moved with a swish of skirts toward the door, followed by Sylvie. She paused with her hand on the door and turned back to eye William, who stood beside his chair with his hands behind his back.

"William?"

"I will join you shortly, Mother. I need to discuss a few more matters with Miss Crockwell."

"William, my dear, I do not think... The bedchamber..." She pressed her lips together, her eyes flickering toward Mattie.

"I understand the delicacy of the situation, Mother, but Miss Crockwell may rely upon your superior parenting to see that I behave with the utmost discretion in these most unusual circumstances." He inclined his head with a twitch of his lips.

Mattie watched the exchange between the two and wondered who would win. She wasn't quite sure, but she thought she saw an answering lift of Mrs. Sinclair's elegant mouth.

"Do not be long, William." She nodded in Mattie's direction. "Miss

Crockwell."

William moved forward to pull the door open for his mother. Sylvie reached up to give him a quick peck on his cheek before following her mother out.

Mattie sank back onto the couch with weak knees, feeling as if she'd somehow survived an ordeal by fire. William returned to his seat to perch on the edge of it.

"Quickly, Miss Crockwell, let us compare notes and fabricate a story such that will satisfy all concerned. You are Matilda Crockwell...of..."

"Nebraska?" she offered.

"I still do not know where this Nuhbrasska is. Could it be in New York? Virginia? The Carolinas?"

Mattie shook her head, wishing she'd paid more attention in history classes. When did Nebraska become a state, a territory?

"Forget Nebraska," she said hastily. "I don't live there anymore. You've heard of Seattle, right?"

He shook his head. "No, I am afraid I have not."

Mattie felt another rise of panic. Who hadn't heard of Seattle? Hadn't it been there forever?

"In the west?"

"Do you mean in the new Columbia country? With Indians?" He straightened and eyed her with something akin to awe.

"What? Indians! Well, sure, there are plenty of tribes, but..." Mattie thought fast. Did he think she was traipsing around in the forest picking roots and hiding from shooting arrows? Good gravy!

"Okay, never mind. So, what cities have you heard of? I'm sure I can pretend to be from one of those."

"New York?" he offered.

"Okay, the Big Apple...New York it is. I've never been there, but at the rate we're going, no one else you know will have been there either." She nodded with satisfaction.

"I am afraid I do not understand your reference to an apple, but what you suppose is most likely true. I do not imagine that any of our acquaintance whom you might have occasion to meet during the next thirty days will have been to New York."

"Good." Mattie breathed a sigh of relief. One shouldn't travel through time if one didn't know one's history—that was for sure.

"Miss Matilda Crockwell of the Crockwells of New York City. Very good. And you are related to us through my late father's aunt's brother through marriage. Does that sound a complicated enough relationship?" A rare smile lit his face.

Mattie found herself chuckling. "That sounds just fine. I won't worry about having to explain it."

William stood, impossibly tall.

"Very well, then. I am sure Mother has sent for Mary, and Sylvie will be waiting anxiously to help you select a garment for today. I will see you again shortly at breakfast."

"More breakfast?" Mattie murmured.

William bowed. "Certainly. What I brought you was simply a small refreshment." He turned to move away, and Mattie watched his lean, fluid movements, so well emphasized by the snug fit of his trousers.

William paused with his hand on the door.

"There can be no further occasion for you and I to be alone as we are now, Miss Crockwell...in your bedchamber. As a result of the unusual circumstances of your... em...arrival, it has been necessary to make some allowances, but propriety dictates that as an unmarried woman, you must be chaperoned when in the company of an unmarried man."

Mattie swallowed hard.

"But what if I need to talk to you...about..." She raised her hands as if to encompass the room, the situation, her "arrival" in his time.

"I will watch you closely, Miss Crockwell. Should you have need of me, I will make myself available to you. You have only to signal me with your expressive hazel eyes, and I will be instantly at your side."

He pulled open the door and left the room, closing it silently behind him. Mattie stared at the closed door with a gaping jaw and a desire to run to the nearest mirror and study her "expressive hazel eyes."

CHAPTER SIX

Within moments, a light tap on the door heralded the return of Sylvie with Mary. Mary carried an armful of garments, which she laid out on the bed. She dipped a small curtsey in Mattie's direction upon hearing that Mattie was a "distant cousin" from America.

"I think this frock would do very nicely for today, don't you, Mary?"

Sylvie held up an eggshell-white dress of some sort of muslin. Bright red ribbons decorated the small puff sleeves and ran across an empire waist. Mattie stared at the lovely gown with a growing sense of unease. She wasn't wearing a bra. Just her underwear, pajamas and her robe. Could she possibly get by for thirty days without a bra or a change of underwear? She thought not.

"Um…Sylvie, I don't have any…uh…fresh underwear."

Mary's eyes widened, and she turned away hastily to sort through the garments on the bed.

Sylvie took it in stride. "I suspected not. Certainly, I never sleep in my unmentionables, so I have brought some of my own for you to use." She held up several odd-looking bits of cotton and lace, including something that looked suspiciously like bloomers. Mattie winced. Surely, the fabulously dressed cover model on her favorite paperback never sported bloomers under her silk gowns, did she?

"Shall we help you dress?" Sylvie handed the underclothing to Mary and reached for the sash of the robe. Mattie forced herself to submit, wondering how long it would take before she ran screaming from the house. What was she going to do?

"What a soft dressing gown," Sylvie murmured as she pulled it from Mattie's shoulders. "It is most luxurious. How lucky you are. I do not think we have a garment such as this." She cast a quick glance toward

Mary. "Here in England, that is." Sylvie laid the robe down carefully on the chair beside the bed and turned to survey Mattie.

Though her eyes flickered uncertainly toward Mattie's pajamas for a moment, she only murmured.

"May I call you Matilda? As we are cousins?"

"Mattie. People usually call me Mattie."

Sylvie beamed, golden curls bobbing at the side of her face.

"Mattie, then. Is this what women wear to bed in America? How utterly charming."

Mattie regarded her pink nylon pajamas, unable to imagine Sylvie in such casual clothes. The girl was born to wear dresses—in more ways than one.

"They're called pajamas. A lot of women wear them to bed. Others wear nightgowns. And others—" Mattie brought a halt to her chatter, aware that Mary, standing by with the undergarments, seemed to be listening intently though she kept her face averted. Sylvie was an unmarried young woman in 1825. It wasn't likely she would ever sleep in the nude, so there was no point in bringing it up.

"Puh-ja-muhs," Sylvie repeated slowly. Mattie smiled in response. "I should like to have a pair. Perhaps we could have the dressmaker make a pattern from yours."

Sylvie reached for the top button, and Mattie decided she'd had enough.

"Sylvie… Mary… I'm not used to…that is…I'm awfully shy. Do you mind if I try to dress myself?"

"But Mattie, it is not possible to dress oneself without assistance. There are ribbons to tie and laces to tighten. It always requires two people."

Mattie eyed the various dangling bits of material hanging from the clothing in Mary's arms.

"Well, let me try at least. I could call you if I get into a bind."

Sylvie's sparkling laugh caught Mattie by surprise.

"You will no doubt get yourself into a bind, but I will honor your wishes. Mary and I will await you in my room, which is the next door to the right."

Mattie nodded gratefully and took the undergarments from Mary, who eyed her curiously before she followed Sylvie from the room.

With a sigh of relief, Mattie dropped the garments on the bed and slid out of her pajamas, folding them neatly and hiding them under one of the pillows— just on the off chance someone might decide to take them. If nothing else, she was determined to keep one thing from her "real" life to help keep her grounded through the coming days or weeks.

She picked up the top garment and held what appeared to be some sort of linen shift with short sleeves up to the light from the window. A slip? Not a nightgown?

Mattie slid the shift over her head and allowed it to settle on her shoulders. The material felt unexpectedly soft against her skin. She found a drawstring at the front just above her breasts and pulled it tight. The shift fell to just above her ankles.

The next item in the pile was another white garment with straps at the shoulders, laces at the back and an inflexible front. It appeared to be some sort of corset, and Mattie's eyes widened. Surely, she didn't have to wear a corset, did she? And if she did, should she have put it on first?

With a sigh, she undid the lacing at her neck and pulled the shift back over her head. She grabbed up the corset-like garment and slipped it over her shoulders with the lacing in the front. Something seemed wrong. Mattie closed her eyes and thought back for a moment to the books she'd read. Images of some hapless maid pulling the strings of a corset at the back of some long-suffering gentlewoman came to mind. It must have been a movie she once saw. She pulled it off and put it back on, laces to the back. Some sort of long, restrictive, unbendable ruler-like affair ran down the middle of the front of the corset, and the silly thing only came to just below her breasts, pushing them up in an unnaturally perky position.

Mattie grimaced, fairly sure she wasn't going to be wearing the bizarre contraption. She didn't really have to, did she? Would anyone even know? She gave the garment one last valiant try as she reached awkwardly for the laces at the back and pulled. As if taking on a life of its own, the corset stiffened and forced her body upright into a ramrod-straight position from which she was unable to bend forward, a necessary task if she were going to tie the darn thing.

At a complete loss, Mattie sidled over to the full-length mirror near the dressing table and gazed at her reflection. Her body seemed taller, her posture considerably improved, but her breasts appeared particularly prominent—pushed up as they were by the rim of the corset and separated by the long, rigid piece of wood which ran down the middle of the garment. She knew without a doubt she wasn't going to be able to wear the contraption.

She loosened the ties in the back and wriggled back out of the thing. She slid the shift back over her head and tried to remember the names of the garments. Shem... Shemmy... Chemise! That was it! A chemise. And the corset was called a stay. She remembered a line from her book. *She loosened her stays.* Hah! Well, stays or not, she wasn't wearing the darn thing.

She picked up what she'd thought of as pantaloons and held them aloft, noting with narrowed eyes that the middle seam was missing. It seemed as if the two legs of the garment were separate objects, to be tied around the waist and leave one's personal areas open to the breeze.

Not going to work! Mattie tossed them down and thanked her lucky stars for her cotton panties. She would just have to wash them out every night.

A tap at the door caught her attention.

"Mattie! Are you in a bind yet?" A gurgle of laughter came from the other side of the door. "I did not like to leave you so long, fearing you would be quite unable to cope with your stays without assistance. May Mary and I enter?"

"Come in," Mattie murmured. She watched as Sylvie sailed in, her hair now neatly groomed—no doubt by Mary. Sylvie stopped abruptly, her blue eyes wide.

"But Mattie! You have only just donned your chemise! What have you been doing since we left?"

With a quick look in Mary's direction, Mattie shrugged and waved a helpless hand toward the clothing on the bed.

"Trying to figure out which garment goes where. I thought I could figure it out, but I can't. And there are just some things I can't wear."

At this, Sylvie turned to Mary.

"Mary, thank you. I will help Miss Crockwell dress this morning."

Mary bobbed a quick curtsey and left the room while Sylvie bustled forward.

"Which of the garments are troubling you, Mattie? Is it the stays? I cannot imagine trying to lace them without Mary's help." She picked up the delicate-looking, though surprisingly unyielding corset.

"I can't wear that thing, Sylvie. Please say I don't have to wear it."

Sylvie turned surprised eyes on Mattie and then slid a thoughtful gaze to the stays. "Our mothers used to wear true corsets—with stiff, brutal whalebones throughout designed to enhance tiny waists. We are so fortunate not to have to wear such old-fashioned clothing." She eyed Mattie curiously. "Do you not wear stays at all in your time? No undergarment to mold the feminine figure to advantage?"

Mattie shook her head, then paused. "Well, there are girdles and body shapers. I think my mother used to wear a girdle every day." She shivered. "I can't imagine wearing anything that confining."

Sylvie dropped the stays onto the bed.

"Then you shall not wear them during your visit with us. I do not want you to be unhappy."

Mattie nodded gratefully and gazed down at the assortment of clothing on the bed.

"So, what do I put on next?"

"Have you put on your stockings yet?" Sylvie grabbed up two long, white, opaque stockings that appeared to be made of silk. Mattie grimaced. They were exquisite, but she was reluctant to wear them, too. Still, she had to make some concessions to the era. Who knew during the long nights of dreaming about meeting a man from the Georgian period that she'd be so resistant to wearing the clothing?

As if on cue, a tap sounded on the door, followed by William's voice.

"Sylvie? Miss Crockwell? Breakfast is waiting."

"We will be down presently, William. Beauty cannot be rushed," Sylvie murmured with a broad smile that Mattie suspected would not translate through the door. She sat down and pulled the stockings up, attaching them to a garter belt that Sylvie found among the pile on the bed.

Another petticoat on top of her chemise, and at last, the gown. Sylvie turned her around to tie the red ribbons in back while Mattie lowered her head and stared in dismay at her chest. Way too much of her cleavage showed, and she really couldn't leave the room looking like a...well, with her breasts exposed.

"Sylvie! I can't... Do you have...? Isn't there something to cover...?"

Sylvie turned Mattie around to face her once again and dropped her eyes to Mattie's hands, which covered her extensive cleavage. She smiled sympathetically.

"I understand your reservations, Mattie. I will admit to some anxious moments when fashion decreed we must lower our necklines. Here is a fichu you may wish to wear during the day." She draped a length of white gauze around Mattie's shoulders and tucked the ends inside the neckline of the dress. "But you will have to learn to tolerate baring your...shoulders when we have a dinner party or a dance. You would seem such a fuddy-duddy if you were to wear a fichu for evening."

Sylvie laughed and pulled Mattie toward the mirror.

"Now, your hair. I do not possess Mary's gift with hair, but I think I can fashion it well enough to make you presentable for breakfast. No adult lady wears her hair down outside of the bedroom."

Mattie admired the opaque nature of the fichu covering her cleavage while Sylvie attempted to dress her hair. She hoped claw clips would come soon to this era, rendering hairdressing a feat any child could perform. Mattie kept her eyes innocently wide and fought back a grin as Sylvie struggled with a mass of curly hair in one hand and a red ribbon in the other. But Sylvie prevailed at last and pronounced herself satisfied with her performance as a lady's maid.

"Thank you so much for all your help, Sylvie. I can see I couldn't have done this without you," Mattie murmured, thankful she didn't at least have to wear a feather headdress or some other such foolishness.

"I am delighted to know that if ever my brother should banish me from the house and my mother turn her back on me, I can make a suitable living as a lady's maid," Sylvie said with a laugh as she headed for the door. "Come. I am famished for my breakfast. Remember now, the servants will be curious about your...late-night arrival, and will listen to every word you utter, so it would be in all of our best interests if you were to...em...speak as little as possible for the moment."

"Mum's the word." Mattie smiled. Sylvie, her hand on the door, turned with a curious expression, but a renewed knocking on the door startled her. She swung the door open.

"William. Patience, please. We are ready." She pulled the door wide and signaled for Mattie to precede her. Mattie felt the carpet under her feet, and realized she had no shoes. Sylvie tsked.

"Why do we wear so many clothes?" Sylvie fussed. "I am certain I brought a pair of slippers for you. Where have they got to?" She turned to search through the pile of clothing.

Mattie, standing at the door, turned to look at William with an uncertain smile. William stared at her, his eyes widened, a disconcerting light in them. Frantically, she dropped her eyes to her chest to reassure herself nothing showed. The fichu did its job.

"Miss Crockwell. I hardly recognized you," William murmured with a faint smile.

Mattie's cheeks flamed, and she averted her face to see Sylvie rush toward her with a pair of white slippers, which resembled those of a ballerina. Mattie slipped them on awkwardly, fully aware William continued to watch her. Fortunately, she and Sylvie appeared to have the same shoe size.

"At last," Sylvie sighed as she moved through the doorway and into the hall. "Lend us your arm, William."

William extended his arm, and Sylvie slipped her hand beneath it.

"Mattie? Will you take William's arm?" she urged. Mattie stepped forward and reluctantly slipped her hand beneath William's left arm. They moved down the hall toward the stairs, Mattie feeling like a complete bumbling fool lost in a Jane Austen movie. Her dreams had not addressed Mattie's innate feelings of inadequacy but had apparently glossed over her character flaws in favor of some image of a competent, beautiful woman—the "voluptuous redhead with masses of flowing curls, impossibly long dark eyelashes, and a graceful swan neck," who had "luxuriated in the capable embrace of Lord Ashton" from her book.

As a matter of necessity, and much to Mattie's relief, they dropped William's arms when they reached the dining room, since all three would not fit through the doorway at the same time. Sylvie stepped in first, and when Mattie would have hung back, William bowed and extended a graceful hand to indicate that Mattie should follow.

"Mother," Sylvie said. "I am sorry we are late to breakfast. I am afraid Miss Crockwell was hesitant to use Mary's services, and I was a poor substitute."

"Why ever not, Miss Crockwell?" Mrs. Sinclair presided at the far end of a long, well-polished mahogany table topped with a large vase of colorful, fresh-cut flowers and several candelabras. Several place settings flanked her. William pulled out a chair to his mother's left and indicated Mattie should sit.

Mattie slid into the golden velvet chair, but found the fine sprig muslin of her dress hung up on the material of the seat and bunched to the left side. As William moved to push her chair in, she popped to her feet again and grabbed her skirts to adjust them. The chair struck the back of her knees, and she plopped back down onto the seat ungracefully as William apologized.

"Forgive me, Miss Crockwell! How clumsy of me." His cheeks bronzed, and he looked taken aback.

"Oh, no, sorry, my fault. My dress..." She let her voice trail off as she saw a serving maid holding a platter stop to watch her with curiosity.

Mrs. Sinclair threw a quick look toward the scullery maid. "Susie, please be so good as to serve now. Thank you."

Susie, a small, thin, youngish woman of indeterminate age, blinked and moved forward rapidly to set a tray of hot rolls on the table in front of Mrs. Sinclair.

"Sorry, mum," Susie murmured.

William took a seat next to Mattie, and Sylvie slid effortlessly into the chair on her mother's right. She threw Mattie a bright smile, and Mattie responded thankfully to the twinkle in Sylvie's eyes. Surely, someone at some point in the history of time had found their long dress uncomfortably bunched up under their rear ends, hadn't they? She glanced at Mrs. Sinclair from under her lashes. No, perhaps not. Mrs. Sinclair's skirts had never bunched up. It wasn't possible.

Another serving girl, who appeared to be about eighteen, as plump as Susie was thin, poured tea for the newcomers. Mattie scanned the room, noting a high ceiling with massive olive-green silk drapes framing a set of large windows. The walls were papered in a minute yellow indistinguishable print. A white-mantled fireplace presided at the opposite end of the room from Mrs. Sinclair's position, and a lovely painting depicting a restful country scene, complete with stream and fields, hung above the mantle. Several gleaming mahogany sideboards flanked the walls on either side of the dining table.

"Thank you, Emma. Please leave the pot on the table. We will refresh ourselves. You and Susie may leave."

Emma bobbed her blonde curls, dipped a curtsy and left the room with Susie in tow.

"I thought it best the servants leave the room for the present," Mrs. Sinclair offered.

Mattie stared at the meager food on the table, consisting of dry toast and hot rolls. Since Mrs. Sinclair sent the girls away, she assumed the food on the table comprised the entirety of breakfast...what one might call a "continental breakfast." Was this really all folks in the Georgian era ate for breakfast? No wonder everyone was so slim! Mattie, a fan of hot breakfasts with loads of potatoes and pancakes, wondered if she were going to lose weight during her stay in the past.

Mrs. Sinclair startled her by holding out her hand for Mattie's plate. Mattie handed it over, and Mrs. Sinclair placed one of every item on the plate.

"Will you take some orange marmalade, Miss Crockwell?"

"Yes, thank you." Mattie took the plate Mrs. Sinclair proffered and waited until William and Sylvie served themselves. She kept an eye on William and followed his lead as he spread marmalade on his roll and bit into it.

"At the risk of discussing matters best left to the dressing room, please tell me, Miss Crockwell, why you refused Mary's services. Our gowns are sewn such that the owner is not able to fend for herself. Hence, the need for a lady's maid." Mrs. Sinclair quirked an eyebrow in Mattie's direction.

"Well, I've never...that is...I'm not used to..." Her cup rattled as she set it down. "I hated gym in high school," Mattie murmured with an apologetic shrug. She reached for a piece of toast and bit into it, hoping Mrs. Sinclair wouldn't pursue the matter, hoping William had ignored the entire conversation. But neither of those wishes was realized.

"Jim? High school?" Mrs. Sinclair repeated. "I am afraid I do not understand your meaning."

"Mother, I think these are references to things in her present life. I do not think Jim is a man's name, is that correct, Miss Crockwell?"

With a look of gratitude toward William, Mattie shook her head. "No, I'm sorry. A gym is a...an athletic facility where one exercises or performs sports? One often bathes there after exercising?" She raised hopeful eyebrows in William's direction. Could he interpret for her?

Surely, they could find some common language in a span of less than two hundred years, couldn't they?

"Ah, sports! Yes, of course..." William coughed behind his ruffled sleeve. "Though I was not aware women...em...participated in such activities."

Mattie grimaced. Her excuses seemed feeble and best left to the conflicted memories of high school. Besides, no one understood her anyway, and the conversation had the potential of evolving into discussions of football, soccer, NASCAR racing and the Olympics.

"It's not important," Mattie said. She turned to Mrs. Sinclair. "I apologize for refusing Mary's help, and I'm more than happy to ask for her assistance in dressing in the future."

"Very sensible," Mrs. Sinclair murmured.

"Mattie," Sylvie interjected. "Can you tell us about your time? Already you have used words we have never heard of...this Jim and athletic facility. It must be so fascinating!"

"I don't know how to explain it all, Sylvie," Mattie said. "I'm afraid much of it would seem shocking to you in your time, much as some of your customs might seem shocking to people during the seventeenth century. These necklines, for instance." She studiously avoided looking at William.

"You are correct, Miss Crockwell. Some of your customs will seem shocking to us, including discussion of...*necklines*...in mixed company." Mrs. Sinclair directed a look in William's direction.

"Nonsense, Mother," William said with a broad smile. "I have not lived with two women most of my life to suddenly become affronted or offended by discussions of women's clothing." He turned to Mattie, whose cheeks continued to burn.

"Miss Crockwell, please do not hesitate to speak your mind when we are in private as you would in your own time. It is refreshing." He smiled ruefully. "In public, however, Sylvie and my mother must be your best guides. There are many, many social niceties which must be observed in this day and age, all of which I consider particularly oppressive. Would that I could visit your age to experience some enlightenment." He sighed and sipped his tea.

"William!" Mrs. Sinclair protested. "You present a grim picture for Miss Crockwell indeed. Our customs, which you disparage, serve a valuable purpose and provide a guide for proper living. Without them, we would simply live as barbarians."

"I fear I must agree with William, Mother. I am certain every society boasts strictures they must obey, but I find ours rather onerous as well." Sylvie chimed in with a decided opinion.

"Goodness gracious, my children! Will you both abandon me now in favor of another world in which you cannot live?" Mrs. Sinclair directed a disapproving look toward Mattie, who would have crawled under the table if she could.

"Tell us then, Miss Crockwell. How does your society compare to ours? Mind you, I am not fully convinced of this theory of time travel," Mrs. Sinclair asked.

Responding to the challenge in the older woman's eyes, Mattie stiffened her spine.

"I might have an advantage in that I've read many books written during this time period, and have some knowledge of the restrictions of the upper class." Mattie furrowed her brow, wishing she could say something truly profound, but nothing came. She forged ahead. "Our customs are different—especially concerning women. In my time, women have equal rights to men—the right to vote, to own property, to marry and divorce whom they will, to choose to have children or not, to seek gainful employment no matter what their social class." She wavered at the shock in Mrs. Sinclair's widened eyes but pressed on. "Children have rights and are protected under the law—from abuse, from their parents if need be, from performing labor. All children must attend school no matter what their income level—at least in the United States...and in England."

A little handclap from across the table caught her attention. Sylvie fairly jumped up and down in her seat.

"Mattie! How delightful! I join you, William, in wishing that I too could visit Mattie's time. Would it not be fabulous to live such a life of freedom?" Sylvie's eyes sparkled.

Mrs. Sinclair directed a narrow-eyed stare at her daughter. "I am afraid that is not possible, Sylvie. Not only do I struggle to accept Miss Crockwell's concept of traveling through time, I too can hardly believe such a utopia exists. School for all children? As wonderful as that sounds, it hardly seems possible." She turned back to Mattie. "You say these things will come to England, Miss Crockwell? When?"

"In about eighty years here in England, I think. It took the United States much longer to insist on mandatory education for all children." Mattie awed herself, marveling that she was able to come up with this information. Who knew the research for a term paper in an obscure college history class would have lingered in the recesses of her memory?

"Truly?" Mrs. Sinclair stared at Mattie, her face lightening inexplicably. Mattie nodded.

"Ah, Miss Crockwell, you may have endeared yourself to my mother," William said with a grin. "Education of children is one of her pet projects. All the children on the estate attend classes with our former governess, Miss Whipple."

"That's very forward thinking of you, Mrs. Sinclair," Mattie said.

"Nonsense, William. Pet project indeed! It is the only sensible thing to do. One cannot have children running about the estate all the day with no direction and no function. The classroom is a pleasant place to while away one's time while one matures to become a productive adult." Mrs. Sinclair's cheeks glowed as she dropped her eyes and picked up her cup of tea.

A chuckle from William made his mother sniff, and Mattie met Sylvie's twinkling eyes across the table.

Mrs. Sinclair set her cup down sharply. "Enough of this chatter. We need to plan. As you know, I have planned a rout tonight. I leave it to you, Sylvie, to ensure that Miss Crockwell has something suitable to wear this evening, and to you, William, to ensure that she is acquainted with our guests and customs."

Mattie's heart raced. A social function? She thought not.

"I can just stay upstairs, Mrs. Sinclair," Mattie said. "Please don't go to any trouble."

"You will do no such thing, Miss Crockwell. We cannot have you skulking about above stairs like a wraith in some Gothic novel." She caught Mattie's surprised eye. "Yes, I read novels as well." A slight lift of Mrs. Sinclair's lips lightened her face, and Mattie thought she could see shades of lighthearted Sylvie in her mother's expression.

Mattie took a deep breath. "Thank you. I would be happy to come to the rout tonight," she acquiesced, unwilling to remove the smile from Mrs. Sinclair's face.

Mrs. Sinclair called for the maids, and the Sinclairs and Mattie rose from the table in unison. Mattie, unsure where to go or what to do with herself, opted to return to her room, but Sylvie grabbed her arm.

"Come, Mattie. Let us take a turn in the garden together. The air is fine, and I long to be out of doors."

"Do not tire yourself, girls. I must consult with Mrs. White on the menu for this evening," Mrs. Sinclair threw over her shoulder as she followed the maids through a door.

William lingered. "Do you ride, Miss Crockwell?"

"Ride? Horses?" Mattie asked. "Um...no, I don't. Well, not since I was a little girl. And only stable horses. I'm sure I wouldn't remember how."

He cocked his head and regarded her thoughtfully. "Perhaps we can remedy that during your stay here. This afternoon, we shall endeavor to refresh your memory if that is agreeable with you."

"What? Oh, I don't know." Mattie looked down at the fine muslin of her gown. "In these dresses? How does one...?"

"Do not worry, Mattie," Sylvie intervened. "I will lend you my riding habit. It is in excellent condition since I do not like to ride." She made a face at her brother. "William will select a gentle mount for you. You will be quite safe. A groom shall escort you to act as chaperone."

"It is settled, then. Two o'clock at the stables." He executed a small bow, turned on his heel and left the room.

Mattie watched him walk away, wondering how she'd managed to get herself invited on a horseback ride. She bit her lip. This never happened in her Georgian novels. Where was the chaise and four—whatever that looked like? Could the day be shaping up any worse?

CHAPTER SEVEN

William leaned back in his chair and stretched his arms overhead. An hour-long examination of the books revealed Mr. Jenkins had taken his usual care with the estate records, and all seemed to be in order. His father's steward continued to serve with excellence. William closed the books and rose, crossing the study to stand before the floor-to-ceiling windows which faced the front lawn. A check of his pocket watch indicated it was one o'clock. He longed to be outside, trotting across the fields on Ajax, with the strange creature who was Matilda Crockwell at his side. Impatiently, he turned away from the view and left the library, taking the great staircase two steps at a time up to his room.

A ring of the bell brought James, his valet, within moments.

"My riding clothes, James."

James, a small, slight man with a well-groomed thatch of sparse gray hair, hurried to the tall mahogany dresser and withdrew several pairs of breeches and a pair of riding boots.

"Which will you wear today, Master William?" James offered up a dark gray pair of riding breeches and a lighter tan pair.

William cocked his head and pointed to the dark gray pair. He shed his beige pantaloons and donned the sturdier clothing. James grabbed the boots, bent down on one thin knee and pushed them up over William's stockinged feet, adjusting the length of his breeches so that they fit seamlessly.

"The dark blue jacket over the gray waistcoat, I think, Master William?"

William, somewhat distracted by his upcoming excursion with Miss Crockwell, gave a vague nod.

"Yes, thank you."

James, the smaller of the two, reached up to slide a waistcoat over William's broad shoulders. He whipped around to the front to button the vest, before picking up a finely tailored cutaway coat to ease onto William's back.

William waved James away when he reached for the buttons.

"That will do. Thank you, James." William grabbed his pocket watch from the top of the nearby bureau and eyed it for a moment with a sigh. Still only half past one.

He grabbed his top hat and riding stick from James, nodded and left the room. Taking the stairs two at a time once again, he paused at the landing, listening for the sound of female voices, but heard nothing. Another check of his watch—only one minute had passed since last he checked it.

William turned to make his way to the stables at the rear of the house when he heard the sound of hooves near the front door. He paused for a moment as John, the footman, hurried to the door.

"Well met, William!" Thomas Ringwood entered the foyer. "You appear to be dressed for riding. Join me! I am just partaking of the pleasant fall afternoon."

William eyed his friend with not a small amount of misgiving. They often rode together, and today should not be any different, but it was. He had already asked Miss Crockwell to join him, and he could not withdraw his invitation. In fact, he had no desire to cancel the outing, and had indeed looked forward to an opportunity of spending more time with her—out of earshot of his mother and Sylvie.

"Thomas! Good afternoon." William recollected himself and jumped forward to grasp Thomas's hand. "Yes, as you see, I was just about to set out. We have a guest staying with us, Miss Matilda Crockwell, and I had already made arrangements to take her on a short ride through the estate. She is an inexperienced rider, and the pace may be too tame for you."

Thomas cocked an eyebrow and grinned. "And who might this Miss Crockwell be, William? Am I, as is usual, the last to be informed of some momentous event in the Sinclair household?"

"I understand your insinuations, Thomas, and no, there is no news of any sort. You begin to sound as hopeful as my mother," William said with a pointed look. "Miss Crockwell is a distant cousin from America."

"America?" Thomas exclaimed. "How delightful! I must meet this Yankee at once. You will invite me to join you and Miss Crockwell, will you not?"

"If I must, Thomas." William turned just then at the sound of voices near the top of the stairs. Mattie and Sylvie descended slowly, Mattie becomingly dressed in a royal blue velvet riding habit of Sylvie's. The top hat crowning her russet curls was a miniature version of his own.

"Thomas," Sylvie exclaimed. "I did not know you were riding today."

William watched Thomas bow elegantly to the women descending the stairs, his normally tanned face taking on a bronze tinge. When would his sister and his best friend simply give in and declare themselves, he wondered for the hundredth time?

"Sylvie, how nice to see you," Thomas murmured as they reached the landing. He took Sylvie's hand in his and kissed the tips of her fingers lightly.

William turned away from the childhood friends turned awkward suitors and looked down on the top of Mattie's hat. Such a tiny woman. He had long had a penchant for taller women to whom he could speak face to face, but something about the fragile bob of the hat caught at his heart. He cleared his throat.

"Miss Matilda Crockwell, may I introduce my friend, Mr. Thomas Ringwood. Mr. Ringwood lives on the estate bordering our property to the east."

Thomas dropped Sylvie's hand and bowed smartly.

"Miss Crockwell! I am delighted to make your acquaintance. I understand you have come from America. How exciting! I trust the journey was not overly long. I have every hope of traveling there myself one day soon, and I must ask you all about it."

Mattie opened and closed her mouth and threw a look at William, who jumped in to assist.

"Perhaps later tonight, Thomas. You attend my mother's rout, do you not?"

Out of the corner of William's eye, he noted Sylvie's cheeks burned brightly. Surely, she was not jealous of Mattie, was she? Then he remembered Thomas's reference to traveling to America. His friend's frequent travels and adventures away from England boded little promise of a marriage between them.

"Yes, yes, of course." Thomas beamed. "I would not miss it for the world. Your cook serves such exquisite fare, I daily anticipate any invitation to your home if refreshment is being served."

William grinned. Mrs. White was a marvel with food, of that there could be no doubt.

"You are always welcome here, Thomas, on your infrequent stays in the area." Sylvie's pointed look in Thomas's direction served only to heighten the color in his face.

William, deciding that everyone clearly wore their hearts on their sleeves at this point, offered his arm to Mattie.

"Shall we, Miss Crockwell? Mr. Ringwood has asked if he might join us this afternoon, and I have no plausible reason with which to deny him." He threw a pained look across the top of her head toward Thomas, who flashed him a bright smile.

"Indeed not, Miss Crockwell. And why should he?" He turned to Sylvie. "You do not join us, Sylvie? Never fond of the horses, eh?" His voice held a challenging note.

"No, thank you, Thomas. I will do well enough here. I have things to see to." She turned a shoulder on him. "William, please take care of Mattie. Remember…" Sylvie did not finish her sentence.

"I'll be fine, Sylvie," Mattie said with a rueful smile. "As long as the horse is docile, I'll be all right. I can hang on. If not, I'm sure I can throw myself from the horse and not hurt a single thing through the thickness of this riding habit."

Sylvie chuckled, but William sent her a warning look. Mattie followed his eyes to Thomas, who stared at Mattie with widened eyes.

"Miss Crockwell teases us, of course," William said with forced nonchalance as he offered Mattie his arm. "They have such interesting speech in America, do they not?"

With his arm dangling uselessly in midair in such an unaccustomed fashion, William reached for Mattie's hand and placed it on his arm.

"Oh," she mumbled as she glanced up at him in confusion. "Sorry."

She turned to Thomas. "I should watch what I say, Mr. Ringwood. We do speak differently. I hope I don't offend, but if I do, please write it off to my American ways." She flashed everyone a smile, and William was pleased to see that Thomas seemed to relax.

"But of course, Miss Crockwell. I have met several Americans in my travels and never fail to find their speech and mannerisms refreshing."

William intercepted Sylvie's warning look and turned away. There was little he could do, short of stuffing a cloth in Miss Crockwell's mouth. Even were it possible to do such a thing, he rather thought he might mourn the loss of her eccentric speech.

"We shall see you at the stables, Thomas." William guided Mattie away to the back of the house where they descended the stairs and walked across the lawn toward the stables.

"That was awkward," Mattie murmured. "I've read enough historical novels to know how to speak in some semblance of formal English, but I can't seem to remember to actually *do* it."

William chuckled. "You would be simply another young woman staying at a country manor if you did, Miss Crockwell. I find your modern speech amusing and would not wish you to change it…in private."

"In private," she repeated. "But try to put a lid on it in public, right?"

William laughed outright. "If I infer the meaning of your expression, then yes, I really think that would be best unless you can remember, as you say, 'formal English.'"

"This is going to be a long thirty days," Mattie sighed, completely unaware of the pang William felt at her words.

"Surely, you are not ready to return to your own time just yet, are you, Miss Crockwell?" William stiffened and awaited her response.

She threw him a startled look. "No, no. I'm fine. Really! I'm sorry. I didn't mean to sound rude. I appreciate everything you've done for me. It's just that…"

"Yes?" he prompted as he bent to look into her face beneath the brim of her hat.

"It's just that I really love to talk, and I don't know how I'm going to keep my mouth shut for the whole month."

The forlorn note in her voice caught at his heart. She sounded very lonely…and lost.

William paused. His first impulse was to take her in his arms and comfort her, but they were now within view of the stables, and he saw Thomas awaiting them.

"Give us time, Miss Crockwell. Perhaps we will grow on you." He grinned. "And perhaps you will grow on us. I think that might already be the case." He threw another look toward Thomas, who walked his bay back and forth while throwing them odd glances. "I do not ask you to remain mute, but only to be careful what you say. I ask this to protect, not because I do not enjoy your voice."

Mattie followed his eyes toward the stables.

"I'll try, William. I'll try."

They turned for the stables.

"At last you are come." Thomas eyed them with curiosity. "I think my horse is fair worn out with pacing. Some familial matters to discuss, perhaps?" The broad smile on his genial countenance belied any serious query.

"If it were a familial matter, it would not concern you, would it, Thomas?" William favored him with an affectionate look of scorn.

"Touché!" laughed Thomas as he turned his horse over to a groom and followed William and Mattie into the stables.

William caught Mattie's confused look at the exchange and hastened to explain.

"Thomas, Sylvie and I have known each other ever since we were children. Our banter rarely has any significance." He couldn't resist quirking an eyebrow toward Thomas. "And how *did* you find Sylvie today, Thomas?"

Thomas had stopped to fondle the nose of a dark gray horse. He turned to them with a rueful grin. "As well as ever, William. As well as ever." He sighed heavily. He gave the horse one last pat and hurried to catch up with them. "Which horse will you seat Miss Crockwell on today, William? I am reminded of Sylvie's words of caution." He turned an engaging smile to Mattie. "Are you also timid of horses, Miss Crockwell?"

William would have answered for her, but he bit his lip and held back. Mattie threw him a quick look for guidance, but he only gazed at her passively. She turned back to Thomas.

"No, I am not afraid of horses, but I have not ridden since I was a child."

William did not miss the quick peep of her hazel eyes in his direction, but thought it best she begin to form some of her own responses—within reason. He beamed approvingly.

"I am thinking of having the groom saddle Marmalade for her." William nodded in the direction of a stall, where a lovely roan poked her head out curiously. "A gentle mare."

Thomas nodded. "I remember her. Yes, she would certainly be a suitable ride." He directed a glance to Mattie. "I believe you will enjoy her, Miss Crockwell."

"Thank you. I am sure I will."

William called for a groom to prepare Marmalade with Sylvie's saddle, and the threesome returned to the fresh air outside to await the horse. Another groom brought his horse, a black beauty named Ajax, and William laid a hand against the horse's sleek neck, absentmindedly smoothing his coat as he watched Thomas talk to Miss Crockwell about the weather. It appeared she could indeed curb her idiosyncratic speech into a more acceptable form, but the light faded from her eyes when she concentrated, and he did not like to see her struggle.

William refocused his eyes and caught Mattie watching him as he stared at her. Embarrassed, he straightened abruptly, unsettling his horse, and gave her a small bow as he turned to watch the groom bring Marmalade out.

A small mare, no more than twelve hands, she seemed a perfect fit for the small mystery known as Matilda Crockwell, who had taken the halter and now murmured soft words to the horse. William turned Ajax's reins over to a waiting groom and moved to Miss Crockwell's side to assist her in mounting as a groom held the horse's head.

"Will you put your foot in my hand?"

Mattie looked at his cupped hands and threw a hasty glance over her shoulder.

"Don't you have a mounting block or something?" she whispered. "I don't want to put my dirty shoes in your hands."

William chuckled and inclined his head. "It would be my honor, Miss Crockwell. Please allow me."

Mattie gave Marmalade's neck a swift pat and reached for the horn. She put her left boot in William's cupped hands and swung her right leg over the horse's back.

"What the..." Mattie hissed with a look down at the saddle. "Oh, for Pete's sake! This is a sidesaddle, isn't it?"

William stepped back the moment she threw her leg over the horse's back and stared. He threw a look toward the groom at Marmalade's head, who had lowered his head discreetly. A quick glance over his shoulder revealed Thomas engaged with mounting his own horse.

"Quickly," William hissed, "bring your right limb over and hook your knee behind the horn."

Mattie followed his eyes toward Thomas and bent down to whisper.

"I can't. I don't think I can lift it that far. This is ridiculous. I can't ride sidesaddle without a lesson. Do *you* know how to ride sidesaddle?" Her eyes flashed for a moment as she leaned close to William.

"No," he muttered. It was too late. Thomas had mounted and angled his horse toward them.

"I say, Miss Crockwell, I knew Americans rode different in the colonies, but you have a mighty fine seat there," he said with seemingly genuine admiration. "Would that our English ladies could ride so comfortably."

William stepped back and attempted to accept yet one more change to his normally structured world. The groom moved away and went to mount his own horse.

"Miss Crockwell informs me that she has never ridden sidesaddle, Thomas. I was not aware of that."

"No, I'm sorry. I don't know how to ride a sidesaddle. It didn't even occur to me to tell you. Maybe I should just forget about this and return to the house."

"Not at all, Miss Crockwell," Thomas said. "We would not hear of it, would we, William? We ride only on the grounds of William's estate today, is that not right? There is no one to see us."

William caught Thomas's pointed look in his direction, expecting him to reassure Mattie, but he didn't know if he could. He raised his eyes to her. She actually looked quite charming riding the horse astride. Thomas was right. Why did not more women ride in such a way? It seemed a sight more comfortable than balancing upon one's...

He resisted finishing the thought.

"Yes, of course you must ride with us, Miss Crockwell. We are quite private on the grounds here, with no gossipmongers to spoil the day." William forced a smile. "Are you comfortable? Do you need any adjustments to your saddle?"

"No, I'm fine," she mumbled. "Please go slow, though. I really haven't ridden in years and years."

"Certainly," William murmured. He returned to his horse and swung himself up in the saddle, waiting for Mattie to urge her horse forward. Marmalade, a true lady, stepped forward with a kindly amble, and Thomas led the way out of the stable area. William allowed Mattie to precede him and threw one last look toward the house with a fervent hope that his mother did not watch from the windows.

****

Mattie followed Thomas's horse, acutely aware of William behind her, no doubt watching her "seat." Honestly! If these men realized how risqué half of their comments would be considered in future societies, they would die of embarrassment. She knew William would. He seemed a bit more straight-laced than his charming friend, Thomas Ringwood. Mattie was thankful he had joined them, if only to ward off a potentially disastrous situation at the stables.

Relaxing into Marmalade's gentle gait as they moved along a dirt lane bordered by a tall grove of elm trees, Mattie threw a quick glance over her shoulder toward William. He did indeed watch her, and dipped his head in acknowledgement before she turned hastily forward, certain that the blush on her face extended to the back of her neck.

Thomas fell back as the lane widened a bit, and maneuvered his horse next to Mattie.

"Miss Crockwell, are you finding England to your liking?"

Mattie grinned. He seemed absolutely charming. Why hadn't some young gal caught him by now? She opened her mouth, reminding herself to avoid contractions.

"I have only been here for a short while, so I am not sure how I feel about it yet. It is very beautiful." Mattie exhaled, with the thought that her speech sounded just about right.

"Yes, it is," he agreed, looking across the fields as if trying to see them through her eyes. "I must admit, though, to being anxious to see your country. Tell me, how was the voyage? Was it long? Tempestuous seas? Calm?"

Mattie tightened her grip on the reins. Uh oh! Her response called for an out-and-out lie, didn't it? What did they say? Stick to the truth as much as possible?

"The…voyage was very short, actually. Much shorter than I suspected. I would describe it as calm. In fact, I think I slept much of the way."

He threw her a sympathetic glance. "Ah! Seasick, were you? Of course, sleep is the best medicine for a long, tedious journey across the water."

"Yes, I found it so," she murmured with a half-smile.

"And where are you from in America?"

Mattie bit her lip. What had she and William agreed on? She remembered he said something about Indians. Ah! She remembered.

"New York. Yes, New York City," she murmured with a satisfied nod. But his next words wiped the smile from her face.

"New York City! How wonderful! I cannot wait to visit New York City. Tell me, Miss Crockwell, is it as grand as they say? Tell me everything you know about New York."

Mattie thought frantically. New York City in 1825! Had it even been a city then? She was going blank, couldn't think straight. Surely it was. She tried to remember any movies she'd seen set in nineteenth century New York. They all seemed to have Irish characters, some boxing, mostly poor. Was that accurate? She had no idea. She came from Irish ancestry and wasn't about to malign her ancestors.

"Miss Crockwell?"

Mattie threw Thomas a hasty smile.

"Oh, well, you know, it's New York…home. How does one describe home?" She shrugged her shoulders and cursed herself for using a contraction.

He nodded. "Yes, I understand. I suspect New York City is much like London, although not as old. But still, it must be so exciting to live in such a city. Have you seen Indians?"

Mattie nodded. It would be much better if he just asked her questions.

"Yes, I have. Very nice people. In fact, I work with a girl who is Native American. Cherokee, I think."

"Indeed? Native American? Is this another term for Indian?"

At the widening of Thomas's eyes, Mattie realized her mistake. She threw a harried glance over her shoulder toward William. At that moment, her sweet mare took a sidestep, and Mattie tightened her grasp on the reins. A glance to her right rear showed William gently nudging his large horse in between Thomas and herself. Luckily, the path had widened enough to accommodate the three horses side by side. The groom remained to the rear.

"William!" Thomas's voice held a hint of amused reproof. "Either your horse is displaying extremely bad manners or you are. You have

MOONLIGHT WISHES IN TIME

come between Miss Crockwell and I just when we were having the most delightful conversation about New York City and Indians." He leaned forward and threw Mattie a conspiratorial smile. "If I may, Miss Crockwell? Did you know, William, that she has a friend who is Indian...em...Native American? I had not heard America's Indians referred to in such a way before, have you?"

Mattie leaned back in her seat, keeping William's broad shoulders between her and the insatiably curious Mr. Ringwood. She looked skyward and rolled her eyes. How could the past be so difficult?

Out of the corner of her eye, she caught William looking at her. She met his eyes and responded to the twitch of his lips.

"No, I have not. But then, I am not American. Knowing you as well as I do, Thomas, I am sure you bullied Miss Crockwell mercilessly for information about America. Would that be an accurate depiction, Miss Crockwell?"

Mattie laughed with relief. William realized her mistake and had set himself to the task of distracting Thomas.

"No, no, Mr. Sinclair," she replied. "Mr. Ringwood did not bully me, but was merely interested in my country."

William turned an approving look on her. "There, Thomas! Miss Crockwell is only newly arrived from the colonies and already she begins to sound English."

Mattie blushed.

"But, William, I find her American 'drawl' quite charming. Let us not try to turn her into a proper little Englishwoman too fast, eh?"

"There isn't much chance of that, I'm afraid," Mattie chuckled, lapsing back into the "drawl."

She caught William's gaze once again, delighting in the sparkle of his dark brown eyes.

"You are right, Thomas. Miss Crockwell's American ways are very refreshing. We must take care not to try to change them." William's soft voice seemed to wrap itself around her in an intimate caress.

Mattie, her face burning brightly, turned away to look across the rolling fields to the left of the path.

"I think it is best we begin our return," William murmured. "No doubt Miss Crockwell will require a rest before dinner this evening."

Mattie threw William a grateful look. She was ready to return to her room and bolt the door for some much-needed privacy, and perhaps a little screaming into a pillow.

"Yes, of course, Miss Crockwell," Thomas said as he turned his horse along with William. Mattie tugged and tugged at the reins until her little mare decided she wanted to turn. Unfortunately, she soon found herself sandwiched between William and Thomas once again, and made herself a solemn promise that she wouldn't ride with men again unless Sylvie came to help amuse them.

Thomas continued to ply her with questions while William tried to come to her aid with plausible answers. Mattie desperately hoped that William remembered his responses, since she was not likely to.

"And I believe I heard you say 'I work with a girl,' Miss Crockwell?" The stables were in sight and Thomas had time for one last question. "And are you using the word 'work' as in employment?"

"She is, Thomas," William interceded hastily. "She has assisted her family in their banking business on occasion in a clerical capacity. I believe that is what you told me, Miss Crockwell. Is that correct?"

"Yes, that is correct," she murmured. Exhausted from making up a world which didn't exist and unable to imagine an entire night of more of the same mental gymnastics, she wondered if she could get out of the evening's dinner party by saying she had a headache. Surely, she'd read enough books where the heroine "begged off" from something by "pleading a headache."

Relieved to touch terra firma again, she gave Marmalade one last pat on the neck and wondered if she dared ask for a man's saddle next time...if there were a next time.

Thomas dismounted and approached her to say goodbye. He bowed and kissed the back of her gloved hand.

"Until we meet again this evening, Miss Crockwell," he said with a wide grin as he straightened.

"Goodbye," Mattie murmured in bemusement as she turned away and stared at the back of her glove. So, they really kissed the backs of hands? Just like in the movies? Did William? She glanced at him. He watched her with a quizzical expression she couldn't quite decipher.

"Shall we, Miss Crockwell?" William held out his right arm and gave Thomas a wave with his left hand. Mattie placed her hand on his arm and followed William back to the house, waddling slightly from the horseback ride.

"You did very well, Mattie. I think that went smoothly."

Mattie raised her eyes to his face, inordinately pleased with the compliment.

"I worry so much about what to say. I can't believe I made that mistake about my friend. He asked if I'd met any Indians. They're all over the place. Who hasn't?"

"But they are mostly wild, are they not? Marauders, thieves and heathens?"

Mattie, who had dropped her eyes to watch her steps in the ungainly, long skirt, looked up, startled. His expression appeared grave with no hint of a smile. He wasn't kidding!

"Oh, no, William! That was a long, long time ago. Well, not to you, of course," she added with a wry smile. "Much of that history is yet to come, but you have to know that the British, Americans, French and Spanish were also extremely brutal in their treatment of Indians." Mattie gesticulated expressively with her free hand as they walked. "Native Americans today live anywhere they want, though many live on land called reservations. They're productive members of society, and lots and lots of people are of mixed Native American descent." She wound down, out of breath and surprised at her vehemence on a subject she had never discussed before. But, of course, she'd never explained history to someone from the past before either.

William laid his left hand over hers for a moment before he lowered it.

"I cannot conceive of such a world," he said in a bemused voice. "Although I am not as openly enthusiastic as Thomas, I, too, share a great curiosity for this New World." He gave her a diffident smile. "Especially as you describe it to me." He cleared his throat and pulled his eyes from her to look toward the house. "I cannot help but wonder, Mattie, if meeting you will not be the single most influential event of my life."

Mattie's hand jerked on his arm, and he reached for her hand once again but kept his eyes straight ahead. The angles of his high cheekbones bronzed. She stared at his handsome profile and took a breath.

"Well, William. I know that meeting *you*...and coming here to your time," she added hastily, "will definitely be the highlight of my life."

A muscle worked in William's jaw, and he turned his head in her direction.

"We are agreed, then," he murmured with a faint smile.

"Yes," Mattie whispered. "We are agreed."

CHAPTER EIGHT

"You are no more nervous than any new girl just emerged from the schoolroom for her first dinner party, Mattie. You will manage. We all do. And perhaps you will enjoy yourself." Sylvie tugged at Mattie's hand as Mattie lay prostrate on her bed, pretending to have the world's worst headache. "Come, our guests will be anxious to meet you. And once they do, they will be charmed." Sylvie tugged again. "Rise, Mattie."

"Rise and shine," Mattie mumbled as she allowed Sylvie to pull her to a sitting position. She slipped off the bed and wandered over to the chair to survey the bevy of garments Mary had dropped off for her to consider for the evening.

"Pick something, Sylvie," Mattie muttered. "What do I know about fashion? What are you wearing?" The latter question was rhetorical, of course. Sylvie would wear an empire-waist gown of a certain color and certain fabric.

Sylvie clapped.

"Wonderful! I am so pleased I shall not have to drag you from the room unchanged and present you in that riding habit," she said with a grin. She turned to sort through the garments on the chair. "I am wearing a blue silk dress with lace trim about the sleeves and hem of the skirt. It is new, and I think the blue will match my eyes nicely."

"I'm sure it will," Mattie said with sincerity. Sylvie would look beautiful in anything. At the moment, she wore an afternoon tea gown of a soft yellow, which matched her hair. And she looked beautiful, of course. Mattie sighed. She could never hope to achieve Sylvie's natural good looks any more than she could hope to attract a man as handsome as William, who could probably have his pick of hundreds of women.

"This is perfection!" Sylvie said enthusiastically as she held up a rose-colored silk gown trimmed with antique lacing around the high waist and neckline.

Mattie took a step back.

"Oh, Sylvie! I couldn't wear that. It's so beautiful. Everyone would stare at me."

"Yes, of course, they will, silly!" Sylvie cried with delight. "That is the point. You want to be looked at."

Mattie shook her head firmly.

"No, no, I definitely do *not* want to be looked at. People will already be staring at me, wondering where I'm from."

"Is it not wonderful?" Sylvie smiled brightly as she held the dress up against Mattie's form. "Imagine all the eligible bachelors who will want to dance with you." She pretended to sigh, and, clutching the dress in her arms, turned to search for undergarments.

Mattie felt the blood drain from her face.

"Oh, no, Sylvie, I can't dance. Is that what a rout is?" she whispered. She stepped backward and sagged against the bed. She shook her head vehemently when Sylvie turned to stare at her. "I don't know how to do your dances. They're complicated—with steps and everything, right? People dipping and standing in lines and curtseying and stuff?" Mattie tried to remember every Jane Austen movie she'd ever seen.

Sylvie's smile drooped, and she sighed as she laid the clothing back onto the chair. She crossed the short distance between them and joined Mattie on the bed.

"Yes, a rout is a dance, albeit smaller than a ball. The quadrilles do involve certain steps, and I cannot teach you in less than one hour," Sylvie said with a downcast expression.

She sighed again, as if in disappointment, but Mattie sighed with relief. No dancing for her, thank goodness, she thought! Never in her wildest fantasies did she ever imagine herself trying any of the intricate steps of Georgian-era dances.

Both young women gazed at their feet for a moment, which stuck straight out before them on the high four-poster bed. Sylvie's dainty feet were encased in pale, bone-colored slippers, and Mattie had disposed of her boots and stuffed her feet into her fuzzy slippers, though she still wore the blouse and skirt of the riding habit.

"How do you dance in your time?" Sylvie asked, turning toward Mattie with a curious smile.

"We just stand around with our partner and move individually for the most part," Mattie said with a wry smile. "Or we dance slow...kind of like a slow waltz."

"Waltzing?" Sylvie said. "We dance the waltz and have done so for several years now!" She beamed and slipped off the bed, suddenly revitalized. "That settles it, then. You shall dance during the waltzes and plead fatigue during the quadrilles! I will inform William of our plan and enlist his aid in partnering you so that you do not have to concern yourself with a plethora of young men seeking to dance with you."

Sylvie bustled over to the chair and snatched up the rose-colored dress and undergarments once again. She held them out to Mattie, who sat frozen on the bed.

"And behold, I will not insist that you wear stays, as you have expressed such an aversion to them," Sylvie said. "I am very envious of your…freedom. Would that I could dispense with them as well. Come, Mattie. It is time to get dressed." For a moment, Mattie saw the shadow of Mrs. Sinclair in Sylvie's determined expression, and she gave in and jumped off the bed in response.

"Okay, okay," Mattie muttered as she took the clothing from Sylvie. "But I'm really, really nervous about all this. It would be much better to leave me upstairs." Mattie couldn't believe what she was saying, that she was willing to give up witnessing her first Georgian-era dance— something she'd dreamed about every time she read her romance novel. But at the moment, she would have given up every fantasy she'd ever had if she could just be a footman who served drinks and whom no one ever noticed.

Sylvie smiled in sympathy and patted her arm.

"I imagine you are frightened, Mattie, but you will do very well, I think, and I believe you will enjoy yourself." She eyed Mattie askance. "Do you wish me to remain to lace you up, or shall I have one of the maids come assist? I think Mary must be with my mother."

Mattie nodded, still chastened by the morning's efforts to dress. "Yes, please. I think I'm going to need help."

"Good." Sylvie beamed. "I shall send a maid right away. Now, I must run to my room and complete my own toilette. I will return shortly."

Sylvie sailed out of the room, and Mattie dropped into an empty chair, holding the rose dress carefully across her lap as she stared at it with misgiving. The silk was exquisite, unlike any material she'd ever felt. She suspected the color would suit her coloring, but she never wore such festive colors as a rule. Roses, pinks and reds simply screamed "Look at me! I'm a girl!" and she liked to keep a less flamboyant profile.

She looked toward the door and wondered what William was doing. Was he in his room across the hall dressing? Had he already dressed and gone down to his study to drink port or some such other manly Georgian thing? How she wished she were with him at the moment. Inexplicably, though her heart raced whenever he was near, she still felt more comfortable in his company than away from him.

William had said he would not be able to be alone with her in the future, but they had walked to the stables alone. What had he meant? That he couldn't come to her room as he had last night? Could they take walks together? Or was that out of the question as well? Would she need a chaperone every time? How could she possibly communicate with him when she needed to? Her throat tightened, and she knew a moment's anxiety as if she'd been told she couldn't talk to her best friend. She gave herself a shake. William was hardly her best friend, but he was the only friend she had at the moment. Well, besides Sylvie.

A knock on the door heralded a young maid, who said she was named Jane. Of course, Mattie thought. She was in the Georgian era. There had to be a Jane somewhere.

"Miss Sylvie sent me, miss," Jane said with a short curtsey. "She said I am to help you dress and not to ask you any questions."

Mattie smiled shyly and nodded her head. She would have held out her hand, except that she still carried the clothing.

"It's nice to meet you, Jane. I appreciate you coming to help me. I'm lost with these garments. We don't have these in...New York." Mattie told the first lie of what she suspected would be many throughout the night. Or maybe everyone would ignore her, she thought. She hoped.

"Yes, miss." Jane, a tall, thin girl, hardly more than a teenager, bobbed another curtsey with an unreadable expression and stepped forward to take the garments from Mattie's hands. She laid them out on the bed and turned back to Mattie.

"So, where do I start?" Mattie sighed as she moved toward the bed to survey the clothing.

Jane picked up a chemise and eyed it for a moment.

"Well, miss, I think since you are already wearing your chemise and petticoats, you need only to slip on the dress."

Mattie shuddered.

"I can't wear these, Jane. I already wore them today when I went horseback riding, and I'm sure I smell like a horse." She attempted a feeble chuckle, suddenly longing for the simplicity of her pink fuzzy robe, slippers, her easy chair and a romance novel.

"It's bad enough that I can't take a shower—that is...wash up after being outside," Mattie muttered almost to herself.

"Would you like me to bring some hot water from the kitchen, miss?" Jane asked quietly. "We always have hot water ready. I could bring some to you." She tilted her angular face and regarded Mattie with a serious expression.

Mattie stared at her with something like adoration on her face.

"Could you?" she breathed. "Is there time?"

"We will have to make haste, miss, but yes, I think there is time to wash." Jane turned and moved swiftly to the door. "I will return as soon as I can."

"Thank you, Jane! Thank you," Mattie said to Jane's departing back as she slipped through the door.

Mattie paced the room for the next ten minutes, keeping an eye on the ornate clock on the fireplace mantle. She heard a knock and trotted over to the door to press her ear against it. She held her breath, hoping it wasn't Sylvie coming to see if she was dressed and ready.

"Miss," Mattie heard a low voice on the either side. "It's Jane."

Mattie pulled the door open, and Jane stepped in carrying a large pitcher of steaming hot water, several linen towels and a bar of soap. Over Jane's shoulder, Mattie saw William's door open. William, apparently in the act of dressing, wore only a pair of pale gold silk pantaloons and a white shirt unbuttoned at the neck.

Mattie caught her breath as he paused in his doorway, a question on his face. His state of undress gave him a relaxed, casual air that seemed boyishly charming.

"Is all well, Miss Crockwell?" His speech was contrastingly formal.

"Oh, yes, Mr. Sinclair," she replied airily, while she closed the door behind Jane so that it was open just a crack. She stuck her face around the corner of the door. "Just getting dressed," she said.

William raised one dark eyebrow.

"It grows late, Miss Crockwell. I had planned to escort you downstairs when you were ready. Will that be soon?"

Mattie blushed. She had hoped William wouldn't come up with such a plan. There was no doubt everyone would stare at her if she showed up on his arm. Oh, to be a scullery maid, she sighed.

"Well, I'd get dressed a lot faster if I could close this door." She smiled slightly to soften the words.

William's lips twitched, and he nodded.

"Thirty minutes, Miss Crockwell?"

"I'll be ready," Mattie squeaked before she shut the door and turned to face the room.

"Hurry, Jane, I only have half an hour to get ready."

"We will be ready, miss. Here is your water."

Jane had gone into the "room" that Mattie had dubbed the bathroom. An oil lamp lit the room enough for Mattie to see that Jane had poured steaming hot water into the basin on the dresser. Mattie threw a longing glance at the tub before approaching the dresser, where Jane had laid out the towels and soap.

"How does one get to use the bathtub?" Mattie asked.

Jane turned. "A bath would take much more time than you have available, miss. Had I known you wished to bathe earlier, I could have had footmen bring enough hot water up to the water closet to fill the tub."

Mattie chewed her lip. "Did everyone else bathe?"

"No, miss, I do not believe so."

"Okay, I guess I'm good with a sponge bath."

Jane had taken one of the towels and dipped it into the water to moisten it when Mattie realized what the young maid was planning.

"Oh, no, Jane!" Mattie exclaimed, and held up her hands as if in defense. "I'll wash myself. Why don't you wait for me out there?" Mattie nodded toward the bedroom with a red face.

Jane bobbed a curtsey.

"As you wish, miss."

She left the "water closet" and closed the door silently behind her.

Mattie sprung into action and pulled off the rest of her clothing, taking care to lay it over the rim of the tub. She dipped the towel into the hot water, rubbed the lavender smelling soap into it and began the process of giving herself a sponge bath as if she were camping out. Not one romance novel that she'd read had covered this aspect of Georgian life, she muttered silently.

Moments later, scrubbed and feeling a little bit better, Mattie pulled the door open a crack and peeped out. Jane was straightening the covers on the bed.

"Jane," she whispered, though she wasn't sure why she instinctively kept her voice down. William seemed to have excellent hearing, and she wondered how much he could hear from just outside the doorway—if he were there.

"Yes, miss," Jane said as she turned and approached the door.

"Could you hand me the clean drawers? I think I'll slip those on while I'm in here. Oh, and the chemise as well," Mattie added with a self-conscious smile.

"Yes, miss," Jane said without expression as she handed the garments to Mattie through the crack in the door.

"I'll be right out," Mattie mumbled. She closed the door and pulled the towel from around her as she bent to step into the drawers. She slipped them on over her own underwear and tied them in back, wondering why on earth women bothered with the silly things if there was no protection from drafts. She promised herself that if she made it back to her own time, she would do as much research on the era as possible. There was only so much she could share with William about the difficulties she was encountering in the Georgian era, and having to wear drawers so she could hide her modern-day underwear from the maid wasn't one of them.

She slipped the soft cotton chemise on over her head and grabbed up the habit and dirty clothes before stepping back into the bedroom.

Jane, now dusting furniture with a rag she must have had stowed in the pockets of her voluminous gray skirt, turned and hurried up to take the clothing from her.

"We must hurry, miss. We still need your stays, stockings, garters, shoes, and I need to do your hair," Jane said as she laid the worn garments over the arm of a chair.

Mattie sighed.

"No stays for me, Jane." She leaned in to whisper conspiratorially. "I broke a rib recently and find it too painful to wear them." Mattie beamed with pride as her imagination seemed to soar to new heights.

Jane's face registered surprise, then sympathy.

"Oh, miss, however did you break a rib?" Jane cried. Then her eyes narrowed, and she cocked her head to the side. "How do you know it's broken?" She began to tie Mattie's chemise, which barely covered anything as far as Mattie was concerned. Mattie submitted to the intimacy and raised her eyes to the ceiling—the better to think of a quick answer for the intelligent maid.

"Ummm... I fell last winter on some ice," Mattie said. "And the doctor said I broke a rib."

"Raise your arms, miss. The petticoat," Jane murmured, and Mattie obeyed as the taller Jane effortlessly slipped a shift-like, sleeveless cotton garment over her head that settled to her ankles in a froth of delicate lace. Jane stepped around to Mattie's back and began to fasten the petticoat. Mattie was beginning to relax when Jane spoke again.

"Well, now, miss, I think it is very interesting that a doctor knows when a rib has been broken. How could he know?" Jane asked persistently.

"Ummm... I think he just felt around and decided it was broken," Mattie said ineffectually. If she couldn't even fool a young maid, what chance was she going to have in a public setting with well-educated and traveled people?

"I was just asking, miss, because my father was a doctor." Jane smiled diffidently as she reached for the rose-colored silk dress. "I assisted him on occasion."

"Really?" Mattie asked. "But why—" She bit her tongue as she nearly blurted out a rude question, but it was too late.

"Arms, miss."

Mattie obediently raised her arms as Jane slipped the dress over her head. It slid down over Mattie's body in a swath of sleek material.

"You wondered why I am in service, miss? My father died, and I was forced to seek employment." Jane's face remained composed in a neutral expression, but two bright spots on her cheeks gave her away.

"Oh, I'm so sorry, Jane," Mattie said as she grasped Jane's hands.

Jane smiled slightly and pulled her hands away.

"It was a year ago, miss. Time passes."

"How did you come to work here?" Mattie asked over her shoulder as Jane moved around to button the back of the gown.

"Our housekeeper knew of a position open here."

Mattie thought hard. "But…" She stopped, reminding herself to tread lightly. This was not some fiction novel. "I mean, did you ever want to be a governess or a lady's companion?" Surely, the daughter of a doctor had been educated, Mattie thought.

"No, miss." Jane's voice came from behind Mattie. "I wanted to be a nurse."

"Can you?" Mattie asked.

"If I went to nurse's school," Jane responded in a matter-of-fact tone. She came around to the front.

"We must see to your hair, miss." She led the way to the small dressing table, where an oil lamp burned bright. Mattie sat down on the small bench in front of the table, keeping her eyes on Jane in the mirror.

"And do you plan to go to nurse's school?" Mattie pressed as Jane picked up a silver-backed hairbrush and began to brush her hair.

"No, miss. I do not want to leave Ashton House."

Mattie blinked. "Why ever not?"

Jane stilled for a moment, and met Mattie's eyes in the mirror. Delicate color spread across her cheeks.

"Well, miss, there is a boy…" She sighed. "I have known him all my life, and some day, we wish to be married. He is a footman now, but…"

"John!" Mattie exclaimed, as she recalled the handsome young man who had opened the door to Thomas earlier in the day.

"Yes, miss, John," Jane said with a bright smile that lightened up her face.

"He's very handsome, Jane."

"Yes, miss," she replied evenly. "And now, I must attend to your hair." Jane flashed Mattie one last smile before she sobered and began to dress Mattie's hair.

Mattie tore her eyes from the maid and stared at her reflection in the mirror.

"This neckline is very, very low, Jane. Can I wear one of those fichu things with this dress?"

Jane's lips twitched, but she remained solemn. "No, miss, not for evening, not unless you are a dowager."

Mattie sighed and tugged at the neckline of her dress to pull it up.

"But," Jane said with emphasis, "you may pretend to be chilled and wear a shawl."

Mattie brightened.

"Oh, really?"

"Yes, miss. I am sure Miss Sinclair has something she could lend you."

"That would be great!" Mattie breathed. Jane worked wonders on Mattie's hair in a matter of minutes, pulling and twisting it into a chignon with loose curls cascading around her face and down to her shoulders.

"There, miss. Now, it wants only a headdress. Perhaps some feathers?"

Mattie scrunched her face and shook her head.

"No feathers! Oh, no, not for me," she said emphatically. "I don't have to wear anything in my hair, do I?" She gave Jane a pleading look over her shoulder.

Jane allowed herself a small, patient heave of her chest, which could be construed as a sigh, and to Mattie's dismay, she nodded in the affirmative.

"Yes, miss, you do. But I think we might make do with some ribbons. I will just run to Miss Sinclair's room and ask her maid for a shawl and some ribbons...and some slippers." Jane's idea of "running" was to bob a curtsey and walk with purpose to the door, slipping through it and closing it quietly behind her.

Mattie set her elbows on the dressing table and stared at herself, wishing she at least had some lipstick—never mind mascara, eye shadow and foundation—to help brighten her face. Her pale features hardly did justice to the dazzling rose of the dress. She rose restlessly.

A knock on the door startled her, and thinking it was Jane, she rose to open the door.

William stood on the other side, resplendent in formal dress, and looking much more masculine than she would have thought in the golden satin knee-length breeches, stockings and black-ribboned shoes of the time. His dark blue velvet coat was cut to perfection, emphasizing his impressive broad shoulders and narrow waist.

He stared at her with his mouth half open—not something she was used to seeing from the confident man.

"I'm not ready yet," she said hurriedly, throwing a look down the hall toward Sylvie's room. She straightened and crossed her arms in front of her chest. "I don't have any shoes on...or a shawl."

William seemed to recover himself, though the color in his cheekbones was high. He looked down at her feet.

"Will you be wearing shoes this evening, Miss Crockwell? Not having had the good fortune to meet many Americans—and certainly none from the twenty-first century—I am unclear as to whether shoes are considered a necessary article of clothing."

Mattie narrowed her eyes and stared at him as his eyes traveled back up to her face, pausing momentarily on her tightly crossed arms.

"Are you finished?" She tapped one bare foot.

"I beg your pardon?"

"Checking me out? Are you done?"

William's face flamed.

"I have no earthly idea what that means, Miss Crockwell, but it seems to have offended you." He dipped his head. "And for that, I apologize." He raised his eyes to her face again, and Mattie saw not one hint of remorse in his sparkling dark brown eyes. Nor did it appear as if he failed to understand her meaning.

Under her crossed arms, she managed to tug at the top of her bodice once again, and William's eyes dropped to the movement. His lips twitched.

"Perhaps I might fetch you a shawl?"

Mattie blushed. How had he managed to see such a slight movement, she wondered?

"Jane has gone to get me one, and here she is," Mattie announced with relief as Jane came out of Sylvie's room, followed by a fully dressed Sylvie, stunning in a white satin gown that draped about her body in the manner of a statue of a Grecian goddess.

Jane dropped a curtsey in William's direction and stepped past Mattie to enter the room.

William pulled his watch from his vest and consulted it.

"Oh, do not be so stuffy, William," Sylvie said as she sailed past him to enter Mattie's room. "Jane assures me that Mattie will be ready within minutes." She surveyed Mattie with a smile of pride. "She looks breathtaking, does she not, William?"

"And very comfortable, I might add," William said with a solemn face which barely concealed his amusement. Sylvie followed his eyes to Mattie's bare toes and laughed.

"Well, William, if you will give us just a few more minutes, Mattie can don her slippers, and we will be ready to take your arm. Mother has gone downstairs to speak with Mr. Smythe to ensure that all is ready."

William bowed formally.

89

"I await your pleasure," he said with a twinkle in his eyes, which Mattie didn't miss as Sylvie closed the door.

Jane pulled her hastily into one of the chairs and slipped the little satin shoes over her feet. She handed Mattie a paisley shawl in hues of gold and rose.

"You look wonderful, Mattie, as if you were born to this era," Sylvie sighed. "That dress is exquisite on you and suits you much more than it would have me."

Jane silently gave Mattie's hand a tug and pulled her to her feet, guiding her to the small bench in front of the dressing table again. She began to weave bright satin ribbons the color of the dress throughout Mattie's hair while Mattie clutched her shawl.

"Would have?" Mattie asked. "Are you saying you haven't worn this dress before?"

Sylvie was twirling about in the middle of the room as she waited for Mattie. She paused.

"No, I have many dresses I have not yet worn. I had my first season in London last winter, and Mother bought me more dresses than I could ever hope to wear."

She approached the bench and stood next to Jane, watching her dress Mattie's hair.

"Mother would be most pleased if she could see me married alongside William." She smiled. "You would think she must be planning to pack her bags and sail off to France or some such thing once she has seen her children settled."

Mattie laughed.

"How funny! That is exactly what our senior citizens do." She saw Sylvie's eyes widen. "Not that I'm saying your mother is a senior citizen—far from it—but once children leave the home, people in my time often move to warmer climates...especially Florida."

Sylvie chuckled. "Florida. I think this must be part of the Spanish colonies." She nodded. "My mother would dearly appreciate a small cottage somewhere on the Spanish Mediterranean. My parents traveled extensively when my father lived."

Mattie nodded, wondering exactly what Florida's status was in 1825. How she longed for a good internet service with a decent search engine.

"There, miss," Jane said as she gave Mattie's hair one final pat. Mattie stared at the elegant hairdo and sighed, wishing she had a camera. Her hair looked gorgeous, even if she did say so herself. Parted in the middle, Jane had managed to make little ringlets out of what was normally nothing more than a natural wave. Glimpses of satin rose peeped out from the curls as the ribbon wound its way around her head and through the chignon.

"Thank you, Jane, it looks beautiful." Mattie rose, clutching her shawl to her chest.

"You have outdone yourself, Jane." Sylvie beamed. Jane bobbed one of her ubiquitous curtseys and moved across the room to pick up the discarded clothing from the chair.

"Mattie, you cannot clasp your shawl so." Sylvie gave a short laugh. "Let me show you how it is draped thus." Sylvie demonstrated how she carried her own lovely periwinkle blue silk shawl lightly about her elbows as an accessory.

"Yes, but Sylvie, I'm not wearing this shawl because it's pretty." Mattie saw Jane's shoulders shake ever so slightly out of the corner of her eye as she bent over the clothing. So Jane could laugh.

"I'm wearing it to cover us this...cleavage," Mattie said brazenly, watching Jane's shoulders shake as if she were about to erupt into hysterics.

Sylvie laughed outright.

"Oh, Mattie, you say the most droll things. Cleavage indeed," she repeated as she draped the shawl above Mattie's elbows. "If you must refer to that area of your figure, we call it a décolletage."

Jane coughed and turned to face them, sporting a bright red face and suspiciously shiny eyes. She held the discarded clothing.

"If that will be all, miss, I will just take these downstairs to have them cleaned." She curtsied and fled the room, though with Jane, that meant walked swiftly. As she pulled the door open, William could be seen leaning on the banister of the staircase overlooking the floor below. He turned as Jane exited the room and came toward the open door.

"Come, Mattie, we have kept my brother waiting long enough," Sylvie said as she took Mattie's free hand and pulled her toward the door. Mattie's other hand was taken up with holding one end of her shawl over her chest in what she hoped looked like a natural posture. She wasn't surprised at the next comment.

"Mattie, release the shawl," Sylvie whispered as they moved toward William.

Mattie thought the handsome William might see her heart pounding against the skin of her "décolletage," just about where her collar line ended. Oh, for some double-sided sticky tape—the favorite accessory for Hollywood award show ensembles.

"Miss Crockwell must do as she wishes," William said in an even voice, though Mattie could swear one corner of his mouth turned up for an instant. "No doubt, she will let loose of her shawl when she finds it difficult to dance or dine with both hands so occupied."

"William!" Sylvie scolded as she smacked her brother with her fan in a most unladylike gesture that Mattie envied. "Do not speak to Miss Crockwell so. Apologize," she demanded.

William inclined his head regally.

"Please forgive me, Miss Crockwell, yet once again. You must think me quite boorish," he murmured as he extended his arms.

Sylvie took his right arm and Mattie slipped her hand into the crook of his left arm, requiring her to switch hands as she struggled to keep the shawl "casually" across her chest.

They descended the carpeted stairs to the hallway below, where an elderly man in a dark cutaway jacket and black breeches above white stockings and black boots bowed to them. Lined up behind him were several footmen, John among them.

"Mr. Smythe. Where is our mother?" Sylvie asked as they reached the bottom floor.

"She is in the kitchen and should return directly," Mr. Smythe answered as he consulted his watch. "I hear the sound of a carriage arriving. It is time."

Mattie's stomach rolled over. Why, oh, why couldn't she just wait up in her room until everyone had arrived and then slip unnoticed into the throng of people? As it was, the first few guests would wonder who the strange woman was, especially if she didn't manage to pull her arm out from William's elbow. However, her hand seemed to be locked against the side of his ribs, and he didn't appear to have any intention of loosening his grasp. She knew, because she'd already nonchalantly tried to pull away once or twice.

She found herself being guided toward a set of large, gold-toned ornate double doors leading off from the foyer. John sprang forward to push open the doors, and William paused just outside. Sylvie released his arm and took up a position on his right, and Mattie had no choice but to stand next to him.

"William!" she whispered. "Is this a...a receiving line? Don't make me stand in a receiving line, for goodness' sake! Everyone is going to wonder who I am!" She tried pulling her hand from his arm again, but he placed his free hand over her cold one. His hand was warm, and she almost felt reassured by his touch...almost.

"Have courage, Miss Crockwell." He kept his voice low as he bent his head to hers. "It is customary for visiting family members to receive our guests along with the family. And we are planning on introducing you as a distant cousin from America, are we not?"

Mattie had forgotten about the distant cousin thing. She supposed he was right. At the moment, it hardly seemed to matter as she was completely distracted by his close proximity and the feel of his strong hand over hers. She tugged at her hand.

"Well, you don't need to keep my hand anymore, do you? People will definitely notice that!" she whispered as she forced herself to meet his eyes.

"You are right, Miss Crockwell. Your hand under my arm will most certainly be noticed, since you would be considered an eligible young woman and I am closely watched to see if I will pick a bride." He maintained a grave face, but his lips twitched. "I choose to hold your hand because it pleases me," he added as he looked down at her.

"William!" Mrs. Sinclair approached in a swish of lavender silk and gauze with a hint of a frown around her lips. "Miss Crockwell will need her hand to greet our guests, who enter as we speak." She came to stand before William and glanced toward the door, which was opening to admit the first guests.

Mattie's face flamed and she pulled her hand, but William refused to let go, though he held her carefully.

"In good time, Mother. Miss Crockwell is understandably nervous, and I seek only to reassure her that she is among friends...and family," he said as he squared off with his mother.

"Family...yes. I must remember." Mrs. Sinclair took a place at the head of the line on the left side of Sylvie, who watched the interaction between mother and son with interest. "And what is the connection once again?" Mrs. Sinclair whispered behind her fan.

"She is from New York City and a cousin through Father's aunt's brother by marriage," William edged out quickly just as an older couple sailed across the foyer and hailed Mrs. Sinclair.

Mattie felt William give her hand one last squeeze before he released her. Her arm dropped to her side, and it was all she could do, perversely, not to grab him once again and cling as the new arrivals worked their way down the receiving line. She plastered a smile on her face and locked her shaking knees.

CHAPTER NINE

William straightened from bowing toward Lord and Lady Kilgore, and he turned to watch Mattie greet the elderly couple. She had done remarkably well over the past half-hour, maintaining a bright smile on her face and curtseying gracefully, though for the first few moments, he'd had to steady her with an unobtrusive hand when she faltered. He was inordinately pleased with her presentation that evening. None of their guests suspected anything out of the ordinary. Miss Matilda Crockwell was quite the surprise, William thought in bemusement. Quite the surprise...

"Shall we join our guests?" his mother announced as the first wave of arrivals dwindled. She ran a quick hand to her hair and turned toward her children and Mattie.

"You were very gracious, Mattie," his mother said in a quiet voice. "You could not have done better had you been born in this era."

Startled at his mother's unexpected words of praise, William quickly raised his arm as she extended her hand toward him.

"Yes, she did do rather well, I think," he murmured with a glance in Mattie's direction. She blushed and clasped her hands in front of her, clearly discomfited. If he'd had his preference, he would have offered Mattie his arm, so nervous did she appear.

"Sylvie," he said in a quiet voice, directing his gaze toward Mattie.

Sylvie complied happily. She linked arms with Mattie.

"Come, Mattie, you did so well! I agree with Mother. One would never know you had not been born in this century." She whispered the last word as they followed William and their mother into the ballroom.

William escorted his mother down the center of the room and saw her delivered safely into the company of several of the ranking women in the room. Sylvie and Mattie followed and stood by while the orchestra struck up the first notes of a quadrille. William saw Mattie throw several looks his way, but he could not interpret her expression. Her eyes seemed bright, perhaps overly bright, and her cheeks bloomed a rosy hue, which matched her gown. She leaned in as Sylvie whispered something in her ear. Her responding smile of even teeth made him catch his breath for an instant.

She was absolutely stunning, whether she wore a rose ball gown or a pink fuzzy robe. William did not care to contemplate whether she was the most beautiful woman in the room, for she was certainly the most beautiful woman in the room to him. He could not quite decide whether it was the vivid green and gold flecks of her eyes or the red highlights in her dark hair which attracted him the most. Perhaps it was her odd American turn of phrase or the undecipherable expression on her face when she looked at him.

Two young dandies approached Sylvie diffidently, both acquaintances from neighboring estates. At any other time, William would have thought nothing of their greeting to Sylvie, but it appeared as though they had the express intent of obtaining an introduction to Mattie.

"Sylvie...Miss Sinclair," the tall, slim, dark-haired one said, his youthful face red. "Will you not introduce us? My family has only just arrived, and we were not able to meet your new cousin earlier."

Sylvie grinned with the familiarity of a childhood friend.

"But of course, Reggie. Miss Crockwell, may I present Lord Reginald Hamilton and his brother, the Honourable Samuel Hamilton? We have been friends since childhood. They are our closest neighbors. Their father is Lord Jonathan Hamilton."

Both young men, similar in appearance, executed graceful bows. William watched with narrowed eyes as Mattie blushed and curtseyed when Reggie took her hand and kissed it.

"I am delighted to meet you, Miss Crockwell. I wonder if you might honor me with the next dance," Reggie said with a flash of white teeth.

William reacted quickly. Having set himself as Mattie's protector, he had not thought to share her with anyone, and he was unprepared for the visceral reaction which now made him grit his teeth.

"Miss Crockwell has been so kind as to give me her hand for the next two waltzes, gentlemen." William smiled evenly as he moved closer to Mattie. "And I am afraid she has informed us that she does not dance any of the country dances. Is that not correct, Miss Crockwell?"

Mattie blushed as she looked uncertainly from William to Sylvie and then to the Hamilton boys. She seemed to force a smile.

"Yes, Mr. Sinclair is right. I actually do not know how to dance very well at all. I-I did not pay attention to my dancing lessons."

Sylvie laughed. "Miss Crockwell! How brave you are! You must have had the good fortune to have a governess who did not withhold your dinner until you executed your steps flawlessly." Sylvie sent William an amused look, but he could not force his lips into a responding smile at the moment.

"I'm afraid I didn't have a governess," Mattie said with a tentative smile.

"No governess?" Reggie exclaimed. "How fortunate for you!" He grinned. Samuel nodded in enthusiastic agreement. "You must tell us how you managed to avoid such a fate! Would that we could have escaped our lessons!"

Mattie bit her lip and threw William a quick look, and he wished the Hamilton boys to the devil. Sylvie seemed indisposed to provide any assistance whatsoever, and had resorted to pressing her amused lips together while she favored him with an innocent look.

"Miss Crockwell tells us she had a nanny until her education was turned over to the care of a tutor. Her father did not feel dancing and drawing were particularly necessary. I think that is not uncommon in America." He surprised himself with his ease of fabrication, having had no previous need in the past to prevaricate on this level.

"Well, I certainly had *some* education," Mattie returned with a show of force that took William by surprise, as did the sparks in her blue eyes...directed at him. "Just not dancing!" She turned a bright smile on the boys.

"Quite right," William coughed behind his hand and nodded.

"Gentlemen, Miss Crockwell and I are parched." Sylvie fanned herself with grace. "Would you consider getting us a glass of ratafia?"

"At once, Sylvie! It would be our pleasure," Reggie said with enthusiasm as he and the shy Samuel bowed and hurried away. Sylvie covered the lower half of her face with her fan and chuckled.

"You have already made an impression, Mattie! I sent them away for a few moments to give you time to collect yourself. You seemed somewhat taken aback by William's inexpert attempts to explain away your lack of a governess."

"I'm so sorry, you guys," Mattie said with a look of remorse. "I don't know why I snapped like that. I know you were only trying to help," she said as she looked at William. "It's just...I sounded so...uneducated."

William was about to proffer his apologies for his inept excuses when Mattie sighed heavily and attempted to cross her arms over her chest. Sylvie intercepted the movement and tapped one of Mattie's arms with her fan and a whispered comment regarding ladies with arms hanging gracefully at their sides. Mattie turned a startled eye on Sylvie and dropped her arms to clasp her hands in front.

"That is better, Mattie."

William watched in amusement but kept quiet. Mattie had quite enough coaching from Sylvie, who seemed to be emulating their mother more and more every day. As if he conjured her up, Mrs. Sinclair approached.

"My word," she said, "Lord Hamilton's sons can be seen racing each other across the room in the most unbecoming way to procure you a drink. Can I hold you responsible for their exuberance, Sylvie?"

"Why, yes, Mother, I think you can." Sylvie smiled.

William watched the two of them—so much alike—challenge each other affectionately. He noted that Mattie watched as well, clasping and reclasping her hands. She seemed somewhat uncertain around his mother—and with good reason, he thought. Although his mother had been civil and gracious to Mattie given the unusual circumstances of her arrival, she seemed somewhat aloof, which was out of character for her as a rule. She was not normally a haughty woman, yet he feared that was the impression Mattie must be receiving.

He looked down at Mattie who, omitted from the women's conversation by his mother, gazed around the room as if committing it to memory, which she no doubt was. He longed to be able to touch her cheek and reassure her that she was not alone, but he could not—not in the ballroom filled with guests. He clasped his hands behind his back to prevent himself from reaching for her.

"Mrs. Sinclair. Miss Sinclair. Miss Crockwell! William." Thomas Ringwood bowed in front of them. "What a fine gathering you have here."

"Thomas," Mrs. Sinclair murmured with affection. "Thank you for coming. Your parents accompany you, I trust?" She looked beyond him.

Thomas bent over her hand, and straightened. "Yes, Mother and Father are with me. They are over there, exchanging greetings with Lord Hamilton, I believe."

William watched his mother's cheeks take on color. When would she agree to consider the man's repeated offers of marriage? She continued to try to hide the matter from Sylvie and he as if they were small children. Was she truly waiting for him to take a wife before she would consent to wed and leave Ashton House?

"I must say good evening to them," his mother said. "It is lovely to see you as always, Thomas. I trust you are staying home for a length of time?"

William watched Sylvie's lips tighten. The lovely flush on her face paled when his mother spoke. Mattie looked at him uncertainly, and he gave her a reassuring smile. He supposed he ought to find a few moments alone with her to explain that the women in his family were both involved in affairs of the heart at the moment, however complicated those affairs might be.

Thomas bowed. "For some time, madam," he murmured with a sideways glance at Sylvie. His mother moved away in the direction of Lord and Lady Ringwood.

"Miss Crockwell! How delightful to see you again!" Thomas bowed over her hand, and she offered him her first genuine smile of the evening.

"Sylvie, you look beautiful," Thomas murmured as he turned to her, holding her hand a trifle longer than was necessary.

"Make haste, Thomas, and ask Sylvie to dance. Lord Hamilton's boys are intent on courting this evening, and are almost upon us." William took Mattie's hand in his arm. "I believe I hear a waltz, Mattie. Shall we?" he asked with a grin as he guided her toward the dance floor and past the crestfallen face of Reggie and Samuel Hamilton as they returned, holding two glasses of ratafia.

William took Mattie in his arms and guided her across the floor. He looked down into her face, but she kept her eyes averted, holding her lip between her teeth. He could feel her hand tremble in his. He was not absolutely certain his own hand did not tremble as well.

"Are you well, Miss Crockwell?" he asked quietly. "I know this must be extremely taxing for you." He waited for a response. She seemed so unnaturally subdued, and he allowed, even to himself, some concern about her.

"I'm fine," she said with a small smile. She peeped up at him with her dazzling eyes. William thought his heart must certainly have missed a beat. "I'm glad you asked me to dance. At least with you I can take a break from pretending to be a proper young lady." She gave him a sheepish smile.

"I am not quite certain that was particularly flattering to me," he murmured with a lopsided grin. "I would have you know that many young women would consider themselves fortunate to be in my arms." William tried to pretend he was teasing, but he was certain the effort fell short when Mattie smirked and lifted a pointed eyebrow.

"Many young women?" she repeated softly as she cast her eyes about the room. "Which young women, William?"

William blinked and met her eyes as she returned her gaze to his face.

"It would not be gentlemanly of me to say," he countered.

"Oh, I see," Mattie said. "Well, I'm sure I can find a spot to sit down and rest if you think there are *many young women* who want to dance with you." She sighed mournfully. "I wouldn't want to keep them from you...or you from them."

William tightened his jaw for a moment as he tried to think of something clever and profound. He cleared his throat as he played for time.

"Now, there's a young woman who looks like she has her eye on you." Mattie nodded toward a pale young woman with demure brown hair who stood with several other ladies. "Oh, no, wait. It looks like she's going to dance with Reggie."

"Had her eye on me?" William repeated in a baffled tone.

"You know, William. She was watching you?" Mattie's eyes sparkled as she gazed at him. "But I'm sorry. I must have been mistaken. I think maybe she was just looking at Reggie after all."

William barely noticed Reggie taking the young woman's hand in preparation for the next dance.

"I think you must be mocking me, Miss Crockwell." He looked into her upturned face.

"Mocking you? Why, I do declare, sir! Why would I do a thing like that, especially to my host?" Mattie's speech had taken on a distinct accent, somewhat like a drawl.

"Perhaps because I sounded so arrogant and conceited just a moment ago?" William felt the heat on his face, but he gritted his teeth and willed it away.

Mattie laughed, a warm, full-bodied sound that caused several befeathered heads to turn in her direction.

"You did, William. You definitely did," she said with a grin.

"I apologize. I think I meant only to impress you, and I did it badly." He looked down at her, wishing he could touch a lock of her hair to see if it was indeed as silky as it appeared as it gleamed under the bright candlelight of the ballroom. She favored him with a delightful smile, and he felt his lips curl in response.

The dance ended all too soon to suit William, and he escorted Mattie back to the end of the room, where Sylvie waited with Thomas. Sylvie's face was severe, and Thomas waited only until William returned before he bowed and walked away.

"That man!" Sylvie seethed. William was not surprised. His sister and his friend rarely spent much time in each other's company of late without arguing over Thomas's wanderlust and Sylvie's desire to see him settle down...and preferably ask for her hand in marriage, though she would never admit to the latter.

"What's wrong, Sylvie?" Mattie asked with genuine concern.

"It is of no significance," Sylvie muttered as she stared at Thomas's retreating back. Mattie threw William a confused look, and he could only give his head an imperceptible shake to try and reassure her.

"Let me hazard a guess. Thomas is planning another adventure," William murmured, probably more for Mattie's edification than from any surprise on his part.

Sylvie threw him a sharp look but softened her expression when she saw Mattie's worried face.

"Yes," she sighed. "He wants to embark on another journey...again! He just returned from the continent only days ago." She watched him as he stopped to visit with a group including their mother, Lord Hamilton and his parents. "I do not think Thomas will ever learn to stay in one place," she murmured.

"Is that a problem?" Mattie asked innocently.

Sylvie returned her attention to her companions.

"No, certainly not," Sylvie responded with forced gaiety. "It matters not in the least. Not to me." She gave Mattie an overly bright smile and tapped her closed fan rapidly in her other hand before turning to look in Thomas's direction again.

William felt it was time to intercede on Mattie's confused behalf.

"Sylvie and Thomas have had...an understanding since they were young, Miss Crockwell."

"And I am not getting any younger," Sylvie muttered. "Come, Mattie. Let us go find something to drink. I do not know where Reggie and Samuel could have disappeared to with our ratafias."

"Well, I think we passed them on our way to the dance floor," Mattie said just before Sylvie took her by the arm and whirled her off in the direction of the dining room. William saw Mattie throw him a look over her shoulder, but he could not decipher her expression. He was aware of a growing desire to keep her in his sight at all times. Had he seen regret in her downturned face? That they were walking away from him? He fervently hoped so.

He took a step forward.

****

Mattie tried to drag her feet when Sylvie towed her away, thinking that for a slender girl, Sylvie certainly was strong. Mattie threw a look over her shoulder toward William, hoping that he would rescue her, that he would demand Sylvie leave her in his care, where she wanted to be. William looked at Mattie with a question in his eyes, and short of screaming for help—which seemed a tad extreme in her formal surroundings—there was nothing she could do. She turned to face forward, propelled by the strength of Sylvie's will.

"Allow me to accompany you, ladies," William said almost

immediately behind Mattie. She swung her head to look up at him with gratitude…and some surprise. He had certainly crossed the room quickly. Almost as if he'd sprinted.

"I am in need of some refreshment myself." William extended his arms for both women.

"William! Surely you do not intend to monopolize Mattie all evening?" Sylvie hissed as she placed her hand on his left arm. Mattie leaned in to listen while touching William's other arm lightly with her fingers. Even the feel of his coat seemed magical at that moment, she thought.

"I most certainly do, Sylvie," he said with a glint in his eye and a smile in Mattie's direction. "That is, if Miss Crockwell does not mind." He raised a questioning brow, and she shook her head.

"No, I don't mind," she murmured, unable to control the flush that sprang to her face.

They proceeded into the dining room, now transformed into something resembling a buffet line. Those guests who weren't dancing milled about talking and visiting, now undeterred by the muted sounds of the otherwise loud orchestra in the ballroom.

"What will you have to drink, ladies?" William asked. "And do not think to fob me off as you did Reggie and Samuel. I will find you." His grin took the censure from his words.

Sylvie laughed, and Mattie chuckled. She had certainly read about young women sending unwanted admirers off in search of refreshment while they themselves found other more attractive company, but she didn't know she would actually see the maneuver in action.

"William!" Sylvie chided, a sparkling smile returning to her face. "I cannot imagine what you are on about. I had no intention of 'fobbing' Reggie and Samuel off. I do not understand how you can say such a thing of your beloved sister."

Mattie watched the exchange between Mrs. Sinclair's gorgeous adult children, wondering what Mr. Sinclair had looked like. Did William resemble his father?

William lifted a dark brow. "It is because you are my beloved sister that I know you so well. Stay here," he ordered. "Or if you wish to wander away, deliver Miss Crockwell to my side." He dropped his eyes to Mattie's face with a broad grin. Mattie blushed but kept silent. She couldn't believe he'd actually "lifted a dark brow." How had she ever thought she could fit into one of her romance novels and belong?

"William, you are being so tiresome. Mattie will be in good hands with me. Allow her to enjoy herself."

Mattie, quick to protest that she was enjoying herself, stopped when

William spoke again. He dropped his smile.

"Nevertheless, I think I must keep vigil over her," he said quietly.

Mattie thought she might just keel over from his words. He could certainly "keep vigil" over her anytime he wanted. Forever might be too short, she sighed inwardly.

"And I would hope that she is able to enjoy herself, despite my companionship," William continued. His face took on a diffident look.

Mattie's eyes widened at the expression on his face, and she stepped in. He was probably worried she'd say something and be found out.

"I'm fine to stay with William, Sylvie. You don't have to babysit me," she said quickly. "And I appreciate that William wants me to stay out of trouble. I really do."

"Babysit?" they both repeated with puzzled faces.

"What a strange term," Sylvie said. "Do you mean as if one cares for a child?"

Mattie nodded. "Well, yes," she said ruefully. "In my time, we might also use the term to mean watching out for an adult—as if that adult was a child."

William straightened. "I would not presume to treat you like a child, Miss Crockwell."

"Yes, you would, William," Sylvie murmured. "It would seem Mattie feels so, otherwise, she would not have used the term, would she?"

"Is that true, Miss Crockwell?" William looked down at Mattie, and she could have sworn she saw hurt in his eyes. She shook her head. That hardly seemed likely. She'd only known him for a little less than twenty-four hours.

She put a bright smile on her face.

"No, William. I didn't mean to imply that you or Sylvie treated me like a child. It was a poor use of the expression, I think."

"I think I must say hello to Louisa," Sylvie said, suddenly distracted as she waved to someone across the room. Mattie turned to see a dark-haired, fair-skinned beauty in a gown of lilac satin approaching them with a perfect smile. Mattie didn't miss the way the newcomer looked her up and down, although it was done quickly and discreetly. A flicker of Louisa's dark eyes in William's direction summed up the situation.

Mattie caught her breath and looked up at William, who watched Louisa cross the room with a welcoming smile.

"Louisa! I was not aware you had arrived," Sylvie said as she leaned in to kiss Louisa's cheek. Louisa took Sylvie's hands.

"We only just arrived," Louisa said in a warm voice. "And this is your cousin, I think?" she asked, turning her sweet smile on Mattie.

"Louisa, may I present our cousin from America, Miss Matilda

Crockwell," William said with a small bow. "Miss Crockwell, Louisa and her family are friends and neighbors. Sylvie, Thomas, Louisa and I spent many an afternoon playing together as children."

"Indeed we did," Louisa said as she dropped a curtsey in Mattie's direction. "It is so lovely to meet you, Miss Crockwell."

Mattie returned the curtsey, certain she would never be able to emulate Louisa's graceful dip. She wanted to like Louisa, but the look in the beauty's eyes as she glanced at William made Mattie grit her teeth.

"It is lovely to meet you as well, Miss...?" Mattie quirked an eyebrow.

"Please call me Louisa. And may I call you Matilda?"

"Mattie."

"Mattie. What a wonderful name."

"Thank you," Mattie mumbled, wondering how Louisa got her impossibly brilliant hair to shine like it did.

"Isn't this a crush?" Sylvie leaned in to ask Louisa.

"It is a lovely turnout, Sylvie. So many people. You must surely have invited the entire county." Louisa laughed.

"Mother did, Louisa. You know she is trying to find a wife for William."

"I am afraid it is true, Louisa. Mother is matchmaking with unparalleled enthusiasm." William let loose a pretend sigh.

"Well, you *are* growing long in the teeth, William. It is time you settled down." Louisa's eyes sparkled, matched only by the gleam of her beautifully straight white teeth.

William's face bronzed, and he dropped a sideways glance in Mattie's direction. She met his eyes with a neutral expression. Would Louisa be the match, she wondered?

"In good time, ladies. In good time," he murmured with the air of a man who had no immediate plans.

Louisa turned her smile on Mattie.

"Forgive us, Mattie, if we seem boorish. Having lived in such close proximity all our lives, we have few secrets from one another and will always tease without mercy."

"It is true, Mattie. This is not how we speak to others in polite society," Sylvie said. Though she laughed, Mattie saw the warning in her eyes.

"But I am sure Mattie understands the manner of civil address, Sylvie. Surely, it cannot be so different in America?" Louisa cocked her head and regarded Mattie with a soft lift of her lips.

"We are a bit more casual, I would say," Mattie said with care.

"Yes, I believe that is the case," William noted. "And how are your parents, Louisa?"

Mattie breathed an inward sigh of relief as William steered the conversation away from her. She threw William another sideways glance. He continued to beam in Louisa's direction, and she was sorely tempted to either kick him in the shin or stomp off. Since none of those actions seemed quite the thing to do, she opted to paste a serene smile on her face and stare around the room while Sylvie, Louisa and William talked.

A dark-haired man at the far end of the room caught Mattie's eye. Tall and slender, he struck an intriguingly handsome pose as he leaned an arm against the white mantle of the fireplace. She reddened when she realized that he was looking at her, and dropped her eyes, but not before she saw him move in their direction. She turned to face the conversation once again, acutely aware that he approached. She wasn't sure why, but something told her this man might not be easily fooled. She hoped he was just a passing acquaintance of the family.

"I hope I'm not interrupting?" the newcomer said with the air of one who assumed he was not. Mattie swallowed hard and kept her face down, focusing her eyes on the tips of his black, well-shined boots. His baritone voice was deep, cultured, with a hint of amusement, and his accent was...American.

"Stephen," Louisa murmured. "Are you back from America, then?" She didn't wait for him to answer. "Permit me introduce you to our newest American, Miss Matilda Crockwell. Mattie, Mr. Stephen Carver, a fellow countryman of yours. You will have much in common."

Mattie heard her name, and raised her eyes to Stephen's penetrating blue gaze. While she should have been elated to find another American in the crowd of very and sometimes unintelligible British accents, she had a sickening feeling that she might not be able to deceive this man.

She felt William's touch at her elbow, and she looked up at him quickly.

"Welcome back to England, Carver. Are you visiting your aunt again?" William's tone sounded less welcoming than his words. His hand remained under her arm, and she felt more secure at his warm touch.

Stephen executed a small bow before Mattie. He raised his head, his eyes lingering for an instant on William's hand, before he fixed her with his startlingly blue eyes.

"Miss Crockwell, I am delighted to find a fellow American here in the English countryside." He reached for her hand and brought it to his lips. William could do nothing but release her.

"How do you do, Mr. Carver?" she enunciated, sounding for all the world like Eliza Doolittle in *My Fair Lady* practicing her elocution.

Stephen turned to Louisa and Sylvie and bowed to them before addressing William.

"Yes, I have returned, Sinclair. My aunt asked me to help her with some matters of estate. Since my uncle died, she's been anxious to turn the estate over to a manager and move to London." His handsome face wore a friendly expression that lessened Mattie's anxiety. Maybe he wouldn't be a problem after all, she thought.

"Have you recently arrived, Miss Crockwell?" Stephen asked. "What ship did you sail on? I can only hope that your journey was less prone to storms than mine."

Mattie swallowed hard. Ship? The USS Enterprise? The USS Missouri? No, those were aircraft carriers, weren't they? She was fairly sure she couldn't just wing it. So much for Stephen Carver not being a problem! She turned instinctively to William, hoping he would come to the rescue.

"Miss Crockwell arrived on the Daniel Webster only a few days ago, Carver. She is a distant cousin who has come to visit with us for a short period."

Mattie fought the urge to throw William a grateful glance. She nodded mutely and waited with bated breath for Stephen to announce that he too had sailed on that very same ship.

Stephen nodded. "Yes, of course, the Daniel Webster. I heard it had arrived. And was it a smooth sailing?"

He directed the question to Mattie once again, and she threw herself out there, hoping the answer would be right.

"Yes, very smooth, thank you, Mr. Carver. I'm—I am sorry to hear that yours was not."

Stephen smiled ruefully. "I have had several pleasant sailings, so I was due to have a poor one. At the risk of alienating our British hosts with boring talk of America, perhaps we could talk again? If I may call upon you tomorrow?"

Mattie choked on something. Air? Saliva? Impossible. Her mouth had gone dry. She covered her mouth with a gloved hand and threw a panicked look to William. His face darkened, and he gave an almost imperceptible shake of his head in her direction as if to warn her. Not that she needed warning. She might be able to fool English aristocrats who knew nothing of the United States, but she wasn't sure she could bamboozle the intelligent-appearing American in front of her.

"I-I…" She coughed again, trying to stall while she thought fast.

"That would be delightful, Mr. Carver," Sylvie chimed in. "We would be happy to receive you tomorrow. At two o'clock?" She smiled graciously, ever her mother's daughter. Mattie could have hugged her.

Louisa unwittingly helped distract Stephen's attention.

"I am sorry to hear that your aunt intends to return to London permanently, Stephen. We will miss her presence here in the country." She smiled warmly at Stephen. "How long do you propose to stay in England this time?"

Mattie regarded Louisa and Sylvie with admiration. These young women, not older than twenty to twenty-two, were superbly poised and polished, displaying gracious manners beyond their years. Mattie felt clumsy and tongue-tied next to them...and old. Even at twenty-eight, she had still not mastered the social skills that Louisa and Sylvie effortlessly demonstrated.

Stephen's smile, when he answered Louisa's question, was warm and friendly, showing even white teeth. Mattie hadn't realized that most of the people she'd met in the last twenty-four hours since her "arrival" in the Georgian era rarely showed their teeth when they smiled. Every smile appeared to be somehow thin-lipped, as if it were impolite to show one's teeth.

"I am not sure, Louisa. I am quite content to delay here in England as long as possible, but I do have responsibilities back in New York."

Mattie's eyes widened. New York? Oh, why hadn't she said she was from San Francisco or even Boston? She stole a glance toward William. He studiously ignored her, keeping his attention on the exchange between Stephen Carver and Louisa. Mattie tried to read his face. Was he jealous? Her heart skipped a beat as she watched Stephen and Louisa. They certainly seemed to know each other well. They were even on first-name basis, which she thought wasn't really common in the Georgian era between men and women who weren't married.

"Yes, of course," Louisa murmured. She turned to Mattie with her beautiful smile. "Stephen is a philanthropist, Mattie. He sits on the board of many charities."

"Louisa seeks to put me in a good light, perhaps in honor of my fellow American, Miss Crockwell. I do not contribute as much as I should, I fear." Stephen bowed his head deprecatingly.

"But of course, I would wish for Mattie to think the best of her compatriot, Stephen," Louisa said. "Do not believe him, Mattie. I believe he recently oversaw the building of something called City Hall in New York City, did you not, Stephen?" Louisa turned to William, Sylvie and Mattie. "Mrs. Brookfield has been boasting on his behalf. She is very proud of her American nephew."

Louisa's lips curved into a playful smile, which Stephen mirrored. Mattie eyed them both with blatant admiration. Everyone really was quite beautiful in her Georgian novel metaphysical experience. They really were. Never again would she look at the cover of a romance novel without seeing Stephen's brilliant blue eyes or Louisa's burnished brunette curls.

"Ah, yes, my aunt has placed me on a pedestal from which I will undoubtedly fall one day. But let us talk of more interesting matters." To Mattie's dismay, Stephen turned to her again. "And where do you reside in America, Miss Crockwell?"

Mattie threw another look in William's direction, but he had turned to listen to something Sylvie was saying.

"Oh, uh, New...New York," Mattie stuttered ungracefully. She interlaced her gloved fingers together.

"New York! What a wonderful coincidence," Louisa exclaimed.

"We are practically neighbors, Miss Crockwell. How delightful," Stephen said. "We must talk further tomorrow. I look forward to meeting with you again." He bowed to the group. "For now, I see my aunt beckons to me so I must attend to her."

Mattie swallowed hard as she watched his elegant figure move across the room toward a plump, elderly woman in a purple satin gown.

"William, I..." Mattie began anxiously as she turned back toward the group. She caught sight of Louisa and clamped her lips together. Louisa appeared not to notice. William caught Mattie's words and flashed her a nod of understanding.

"I must mingle as well, I am afraid," Louisa said, to Mattie's relief. "My mother will be pleased to know that Stephen has returned so soon. She seems to be inordinately fond of him." Louisa laughed. She leaned forward to kiss Sylvie on the cheek, and turned to William. "You have been very silent this evening, William. Are you well?"

"Quite well, Louisa," William said with a smile not evident in Stephen's presence. "I was content to listen to you and Mr. Carver exchange pleasantries. At the risk of annoying you, I must say that not only is your mother inordinately fond of Mr. Carver, you seem to harbor some great regard for him as well."

"William!" Sylvie chided. "Do not tease her."

"Tease me?" Louisa laughed. "Whatever do you mean, Sylvie?" Louisa ran a hand to several perfect curls at the nape of her neck. "I am only acquainted with Mr. Carver through his aunt."

"Mr. Carver, is it?" William snorted. "I am certain I heard you call him Stephen...more than once."

"Stuff!" Louisa murmured. Her lovely white cheeks took on the faintest pink hue. Mattie was surprised to see the break in her composure, infinitesimal as it was.

William bowed in Louisa's direction with a teasing smile. "Please give your mother my regards."

"And mine as well," Sylvie said.

"Mattie, you and Sylvie must come and call on me soon. My mother would enjoy that."

"I'd—I would love to," Mattie ventured, unsure if that was a good idea or not. However, failing to answer would be noticeably rude, and she could only stall for answers by coughing into her gloved hands so many times before someone carted her away to a tuberculosis sanitarium.

"Lovely. Perhaps you would be so kind as to bring them around, William." Louisa allowed William to kiss her hand before she moved off, a vision of elegance in lilac satin.

"Well, William," Sylvie said with a chuckle. "You certainly are fast on your feet. Did the Daniel Webster really arrive a few days ago? You know that Mr. Carver is quite likely to discover whether that is so."

William's lips twitched as he looked from Sylvie to Mattie.

"Yes, it did, my dear sister. Though how the voyage went, I do not know. Perhaps Miss Crockwell can embellish that portion of the tale, should the need arise." He cocked his head to the side as he regarded her. "Although Miss Crockwell appears to be remarkably tongue-tied at the moment."

Mattie raised a hand to her cheek as if to unlock her tense jaw. She released a deep breath.

"I can't thank you enough, William. I didn't know what to say. I have no earthly idea how long it takes to sail from New York to London, or—"

"The voyage is from New York to Southampton. London does not have ports deep enough for seagoing vessels."

Mattie wrinkled her brow.

"See? That's exactly what I mean. How would I know that?" She hugged herself, looked down at the tips of her small slippers and shook her head. "I have no idea how I'm going to get by. Perhaps we should have introduced me as your mute cousin." She raised her eyes and gave them a crooked smile.

"Dear ones," Mrs. Sinclair murmured in a low voice as she approached. "Please do not allow Miss Crockwell to cross her arms in that unbecoming fashion. People will begin to talk of our strange American cousin."

Mattie dropped her arms as if they were on fire. No, of course, young women in the Georgian era didn't cross their arms at dances. Sylvie had already said so.

Mrs. Sinclair came to stand beside them. "Take her to dance, William.

She will be less conspicuous on the dance floor amongst other young women. I have had several inquiries about her already, and I am quite beside myself trying to remember what story we agreed upon."

"I would be honored, Mother," William said as he held his arm out to Mattie with a reassuring smile. "We are also finding that it has been difficult to remain true to the narrative we fabricated. However, any alternative is quite out of the question." Mattie put her hand on his arm, grateful that he always seemed ready to defend her from his mother's sharp tongue.

What alternative, Mattie wondered?

"Mother, I am sure William is happy to oblige you, but he has already danced with Mattie once. If you want her to be inconspicuous, perhaps dancing two dances within one half-hour with the most eligible bachelor in the county is not quite the best way to achieve that." Sylvie's smile bordered on a smirk.

Mrs. Sinclair threw a sharp glance in William's direction.

"Sylvie is right, William. I had not realized. I think it is best if Miss Crockwell remains with me. You should mingle with our guests."

Drat the woman! She was probably right. Mattie remembered reading some such nonsense in her novels. Not that she minded keeping William all to herself, but she wouldn't be here forever, would she? Mattie sighed inwardly and attempted to pull her hand from William's arm, but he covered her hand with his own, subtly but firmly disallowing her retreat.

"Nevertheless, I believe I shall dance with Miss Crockwell, Mother. It would be poor manners to withdraw my arm after I have offered it." He softened his words with a smile in his mother's direction. "I do not concern myself with the gossipmongers. You know that. Let them enjoy themselves."

With a short nod of the head in the direction of his mother's slightly flushed face and Sylvie's broad grin behind her mother's back, he turned to guide Mattie toward the ballroom.

On the dance floor, he bowed toward Mattie, who hoped her responding curtsey was an improvement over the last. Several sets of female eyes, probably more than several, bored into her head, and she faltered slightly as she placed her hand in William's. The music began, and William placed his right hand around her waist once again.

"I'm sorry, William. Your mother looks angry," Mattie said as William moved her across the dance floor. She kept her eyes on his chest and concentrated on not embarrassing him by stumbling.

"She will recover, Miss Crockwell. She is not used to being thwarted."

Mattie took a second to peek up into his face. He looked down at her and met her eyes. A smile played on his mouth, and his eyes twinkled.

"I see," Mattie murmured, fixing her gaze upon a button on his shirt. "You're enjoying this. Making your mother mad."

"Not at all, Miss Crockwell. I presume by 'mad,' you mean angry, and not insane." He smiled. "I most certainly do not enjoy angering my mother. But you are correct about one thing. I am enjoying this." His fingers tightened against hers.

Mattie caught her breath and met his eyes. His smile broadened, and he whirled her away. Somehow, the feminine eyes boring into her back didn't seem quite as frightening as they had only a few moments ago.

CHAPTER TEN

Mattie awakened in the morning to a soft gray light filtering in through the crack in the curtains. She turned her head quickly to locate the wing chair, but William wasn't sitting in it, keeping watch over her. She had begged William to let her sneak upstairs after their second dance. Anxiety had taken its toll—anxiety about being discovered, anxiety about her future, anxiety about being in William's presence—and she had been desperate to relax.

She turned on her side to stare at the chair—William's chair, as she thought of it now. Where was he? Was he awake? Had he gone off to work? Did he work? She couldn't remember. The last thirty-six hours had been hectic.

One moon down, only twenty-nine more to go, she thought. Twenty-nine more days. How would it happen, she wondered? Would she go to stand on some balcony at midnight? Would she put her robe and slippers on and traipse out into the garden again, waiting to be taken up in a light? Or faint? Would she be in the middle of a conversation with William and suddenly fade away? Or even lying in his arms?

Mattie shivered, and then she chuckled. Fat chance she'd ever end up in William's arms. He was way too romance-novel-cover handsome for her to handle.

A tap on the door brought her out of her pleasant daydream.

She sat up. "Come in," she called out. William?

The door opened slowly, and Jane peeped in, pushing the door wider with her foot while she balanced a silver tray.

"Good morning, miss. I hope you slept well."

"I did, thank you, Jane."

Jane closed the door behind her with a hip and moved toward the bedside table with the tray of what looked like hot chocolate and some sort of biscuit on a saucer.

"What's that, Jane?" Mattie peered at the biscuits, which resembled biscotti.

"Biscuits, miss. You're to drink your chocolate, miss, and dress quickly. Master William asks for the pleasure of your company in his carriage this morning. Miss Sylvie will be joining you. Master William sent me to tell you." Jane's lips twitched becomingly in her otherwise passive expression.

"Carriage!" Mattie cried. "Are we going for a ride?"

"Yes, miss. I believe Master William and Miss Sylvie have planned an outing to the lake." Jane headed for the wardrobe.

"You're kidding! That sounds great!" Mattie said as she jumped out of bed. She grabbed a biscuit. "I've never been in a carriage before. How exciting!" Mattie crossed over to open the curtains on a softly lit day.

Jane pulled her head out of the wardrobe to stare at Mattie.

"Never been in a carriage? But how is that possible, miss?"

Mattie bit her lip. "Well, I mean, we didn't have a carriage," she mumbled lamely. She turned away to head for the bathroom.

"Oh," Jane murmured as she returned to selecting garments. "Even *I* have been in a carriage. My father owned a conveyance, and I rode with him to visit his patients."

Mattie mumbled an acknowledgement and stepped into the bathroom, not looking forward to the cold water left over from the night before. To her delight, a pitcher of steaming hot water rested by the bowl, and fresh linen had been laid beside it.

She pulled open the door.

"Did you sneak in here earlier and bring this hot water?"

Jane, her hands full of clothing, closed the cupboard, and turned with a smile.

"Yes, miss."

"Oh, Jane, thank you." Mattie's voice broke and unexpected tears sprang to her eyes. "You take such good care of me. I would be lost without you." Mattie embarrassedly dashed a hand across her cheeks. She must be tired, she thought.

Jane paused in the middle of the room, her smooth forehead creased.

"Oh, miss! It's nothing. You sound so sad. Are you homesick, then?"

Mattie thought of her dull life back in the States, back in her own time. Not homesick. Then what? Why the unexpected moment of grief?

"No, I'm not homesick," she said with a small shake of her head. "I'm probably just tired," she murmured with a last quick swipe of the back of her hand across her cheek. "Don't pay any attention to me.

Thanks for the hot water. I'll be out in a few minutes."

Ten refreshing minutes later, Mattie opened the door and stuck a hand through.

"I'm ready for the undergarments," she sang out. The mirror showed her cheeks were rosy, and her eyes sparkled. Amazing what hand-delivered hot water and the prospect of time with a handsome nineteenth-century man could do for a gal's expression, she thought. Everything seemed just a little more precious here than it did in her time.

Jane dropped the drawers and chemise into Mattie's outstretched hand, and she quickly slipped into them. She opened the door and stepped back into the bedroom.

"Is Mrs. Sinclair going as well, Jane?" Mattie had to ask the nagging question.

Jane shook her head as she helped Mattie into her stays and turned her around to lace her.

"I do not know, miss. I have not heard. I think Mrs. Sinclair is expecting Lord Hamilton to pay a call this morning."

"Oh, really?" Good, Mattie thought. Then she wouldn't be coming. Mattie wished she could like William's mother, but the arrogant woman wasn't making it easy.

Mattie reached for the petticoat in Jane's hand, but Jane extended her other hand—the one holding the stockings and garter belt.

Mattie made a face, and Jane raised an eyebrow. Again, the corner of her otherwise placid face twitched.

"I take it miss does not like to wear stockings?"

Mattie sighed, shook her head and took the stockings gingerly from Jane. She trudged over to the chair to sit down heavily.

"No, Jane, miss doesn't like to wear these things," Mattie murmured as she bent over to thrust her foot into one stocking and then the other. "I don't mind the dress, or the petticoat, but I don't like the stockings, and I definitely don't like the corset."

"Stays, miss. They are called stays," Jane murmured with a smile. She discreetly laid the stays down on the end of the bed before holding the dress up.

Mattie slipped into the white muslin gown decorated in small rose ribbons. Jane stepped around to tie Mattie's dress.

A knock on the door startled her, and she spun around and out of Jane's hands.

"William?" she asked in anticipation. Jane shook her head in inquiry and crossed the room to pull open the door.

"Thank you, Jane. If you could leave us for a moment, please. I will ring when I need you." Mrs. Sinclair stepped into the room, crisply dressed in an elegant moss green silk gown, accented with ribbons in a darker shade of green. Jane didn't turn around, but bobbed a curtsy and left quietly, pulling the door shut behind her.

Mattie's mouth went dry, and she clutched at the untied dress, which threatened to fall from her shoulders.

Mrs. Sinclair eyed her narrowly.

"I hope you do not mind the interruption, Miss Crockwell. I wished to speak with you briefly concerning..." She paused as her eyes took in Mattie's struggle with her gown. "Whatever are you doing, Miss Crockwell?" she asked in an amused tone, somewhat reminiscent of William. "Ah! My arrival prevented Jane from completing your toilette." She turned toward the door as if to call Jane, and then turned back. "Perhaps I may be of assistance. That will allow us time to talk."

Mattie nodded mutely while Mrs. Sinclair expertly tied the back of her dress.

"There," Mrs. Sinclair announced with an air of satisfaction. "I will have Jane return to dress your hair shortly. Please join me." She led the way to the settee near the opposite end of the room.

Mattie followed, uncertain of what was to come, and wishing William was with her at the moment. He had thus far managed to stand up to his mother.

Mrs. Sinclair sat on the edge of the settee with a straight back and inclined her head, effectively commanding Mattie to sit, which she did, albeit with much less grace than Mrs. Sinclair due to the fact she accidentally stepped on the back hem of her dress and essentially plopped onto the settee. Mrs. Sinclair pretended not to notice. Mattie's face flamed.

"Miss Crockwell," Mrs. Sinclair began. "Perhaps you can imagine how perplexed I am by this situation." She gave a gentle shake of her head. "At the risk of sounding quite impolite, I must reiterate that I simply do not understand how you have come to be with us." One eyebrow lifted hopefully as she looked at Mattie. Mattie opened her mouth to say something, anything, but Mrs. Sinclair went on.

"I now believe that you are as perplexed as I am regarding your presence in...this time, Miss Crockwell." She refolded her hands in her lap, and Mattie had the distinct impression that she was nervous. Ill at ease. Perhaps she wasn't used to feeling out of control. *Welcome to my world, Mrs. Sinclair!*

"What I wished to discuss with you is the...em...your connection with my son. With William."

Mattie shook her head vehemently.

"Oh, Mrs. Sinclair, there's no—I mean, there is no connection. Not like you mean." Mattie shook her head once again for emphasis. "William is just trying to help me until I can return..." Mattie left the last word hanging. Return how? Mrs. Sinclair wondered the same thing.

"And how do you plan to return, Miss Crockwell? Is there a mechanism by which you arrived here? A spell? A chant?" Mrs. Sinclair refolded her hands once again.

Mattie almost smiled.

"No, Mrs. Sinclair. I don't think there is a spell or a chant. William and I..." Mattie paused at the tightening of Mrs. Sinclair's jaw. "That is, I believe I will be able to return on the next full moon. At least, I hope so."

Mrs. Sinclair faced her directly. "Then you *do* wish to return? Is that correct, Miss Crockwell?"

"Yes, of course," Mattie replied airily. *And never see William again. Sure! Who wouldn't want that?* "Of course," she murmured, as she looked down at her own fingers clutched together.

"I must admit that I am pleased to hear you say so, Miss Crockwell. Under any other circumstances, I would be pleased to have you visit, but..." Mrs. Sinclair paused, and Mattie looked up. A delicate rose stained her cheeks, giving her a vulnerability Mattie did not know she possessed.

"William must marry, Miss Crockwell," Mrs. Sinclair stated with a sigh. Her shoulders softened just a little, with what in other people might have been described as a sag, but Mrs. Sinclair did not "sag."

"The estate is entailed to him," she continued. "He must produce an heir, or the estate will pass out of our hands and into the hands of some distant cousins. My husband would not have wanted that. This estate has been in his family for over one hundred years."

Mattie wasn't surprised to hear the details of William's inheritance. Mrs. Sinclair paused and looked at Mattie.

"I understand," Mattie said, more to fill an uncomfortable silence as Mrs. Sinclair seemed to study her.

"I would like to be frank with you, Miss Crockwell. William seems...quite taken with you."

Mattie opened her mouth to protest, but Mrs. Sinclair held up a graceful hand.

"No, Miss Crockwell. I can see that you will attempt to deny it, but it is true." She smiled unexpectedly. "You have a certain...mystery to you, Miss Crockwell. An air of...candor, of informality that we do not practice in our time. I can see why William would be fascinated by you."

Mattie's face burned, and her heart thumped loudly against her chest. Really? William fascinated? By her?

Mrs. Sinclair's face sobered.

"But William must stay here, Miss Crockwell, in this time. And if you are to return to your time—to your home—then I think it best you dissuade him from his attentions to you." Mrs. Sinclair gave Mattie a direct look. "For his sake. I do not want to see my son cast down by a romance without future."

A lump formed in Mattie's throat. It seemed obvious by the softening of Mrs. Sinclair's face that she really loved her son. And Mattie wasn't sure she herself hadn't fallen head over heels for the tall, dark, handsome hero of her romance novels as well.

"No," Mattie murmured with a faint shake of her head. "Of course not." She forced herself to meet Mrs. Sinclair's brilliant blue eyes. "Please do not worry. William is only trying to help me until I can go home. He is not interested in me." Mattie gritted her teeth to ensure that her face remained neutral, though she felt very near to tears. She forced herself to face reality.

Why would someone as handsome and perfect as William be interested in her when he could have his pick of any woman in the county? Louisa, for instance.

The memory of William and Louisa as they danced together the night before brought a renewed lump to her throat. The smiles on their faces as they linked arms in a waltz, shining dark heads complementing each other as they twirled in unison, the perfection of their pairing, both gorgeous specimens of their gender.

Mattie brought her eyes back into focus to find Mrs. Sinclair studying her. Mattie blinked and smiled. To her surprise, Mrs. Sinclair reached over to brush a lock of hair off her forehead before rising.

"I fear you might be mistaken, Miss Crockwell," she sighed as she paused to look down at Mattie. Mattie jumped up hastily, her forehead tingling where Mrs. Sinclair had touched her.

"I hope for both of your sakes that neither of you has designs upon the other, in light of your impending return to your own time." She moved to the door, and Mattie wavered between following her to hear every word or standing her ground in some symbolic way. She stood still and held her breath.

Mrs. Sinclair paused again at the door and turned back, allowing Mattie to see her softer side once again as she smiled ruefully.

"Please take care in how you proceed, Miss Crockwell. I think you must be stronger than William. I do not think he can resist you. Although he comports himself with an air of seeming indifference, he is a soft-hearted romantic."

She left the room quietly, and Mattie slumped down onto the settee, unsure of what just happened. She raised a hand to rub her forehead absently. One could say she was "warned off," but that hardly described Mrs. Sinclair's words or behavior. Mrs. Sinclair seemed as confused by events as she was.

I do not think he can resist you. Did she really say that? Mattie could only dream of someone like William falling in love with her. In fact, she *had* dreamt of such a thing, night after night.

Jane knocked quietly and stepped in.

"Master William is waiting, miss. We must comb your hair."

Mattie allowed Jane to guide her over to the dressing table, where she stared at her wide eyes and bright red cheeks.

"Master William was not pleased to hear that madam was with you," Jane murmured as she pulled Mattie's hair into some sort of wonderful creation with the help of some red ribbon and a few curls allowed to float on her right shoulder.

Mattie met Jane's grave expression in the mirror.

"I can imagine," she murmured. "Mrs. Sinclair appears to love her son very much, and she is worried about him."

"Yes, miss," Jane said.

"She wants me to leave him alone, I think."

Jane nodded sagely. "Yes, miss, I can imagine." She repeated Mattie's words with a faint smile. "And what is your desire?"

Mattie turned and tilted her head to look at Jane standing above her.

"Oh, Jane!" she sighed. "My desire…" Afraid she would start crying, she blinked and dropped her eyes from Jane's searching gaze to pluck at an imaginary crease in her dress.

She raised her eyes, and rose to face Jane's sympathetic expression.

"William," she said simply. "My desire is William."

****

William paced restlessly in front of the barouche with his hands clasped behind his back as he waited for Mattie and his sister. He was unaccountably eager to take Mattie to the lake, feeling much like a young boy in short pants as he anticipated her arrival.

The large wooden and brass door opened, and Sylvie and Mattie stepped out. William had eyes only for Mattie, who was a vision in a fetching straw bonnet of rose ribbons. He sprang forward to take her hand. One groomsman stood by the open door of the carriage while the other held the horses.

Mattie's cheeks colored becomingly as he handed her up into the carriage.

"Thank you, William," she murmured. He held her hand a moment longer than necessary, and would have continued to do so had not Sylvie brought him to his senses by clearing her throat. With reluctance, he let go of Mattie's gloved hand and watched as she settled into a corner of the barouche. He reached for Sylvie's hand to help her into the carriage when Mattie stood up abruptly to straighten her dress in the most unbecoming and endearing fashion before gingerly taking her seat again.

"Are you quite comfortable, Miss Crockwell?" he quizzed, unable to keep the amused smile from his face.

"My...uh...skirt was bunched." Mattie colored. "I mean, I couldn't move. It was pulling at my neck." She shrugged her shoulders faintly.

"I cannot imagine how you ladies wear those garments day in and day out. You have my earnest sympathy." William hoped he understood her words.

"Would that I had the courage to make the necessary adjustments, Mattie," Sylvie said as she sat on the same bench as Mattie, albeit in one fluid and graceful movement. "However, I must perch myself on the bench with nary a visible concern for my comfort. Not a twitch. Not a wriggle. Not a grimace."

William looked at his sister in surprise as he climbed into the barouche and seated himself opposite Mattie and Sylvie. He struggled to keep from staring at Mattie.

"I had no idea of your struggles, sister," William murmured. He tapped the side of the coach to signal the coachman.

The carriage began to move with a jolt, and Mattie grabbed the calash.

"Good gravy," she cried out. William reached to steady her but pulled back as Sylvie patted Mattie's free hand.

"Do not worry, Mattie. You will not fall out." She chuckled.

"Miss Crockwell, have you never been in a carriage before?" William asked. Mattie continued to cling to the retracted hood with a set face.

"No," she shook her head. "No, never."

"But how do you travel?" Sylvie asked.

"By car," Mattie responded. She loosened her grip as the carriage rolled smoothly down the long drive from the house.

"Car?" Sylvie queried.

"Well, they're a bit like carriages, I suppose," Mattie said, "but without the horses. In fact, they used to be called horseless carriages."

"No horses?" William exclaimed. "I cannot imagine. How do they move, your cars? How are they propelled?"

"By gasoline," Mattie responded. "And electricity," she added. "I'm not sure I can explain gasoline or electricity to you." Her face brightened as she shrugged once again. "I should have done more research before I left my time, but I didn't know I was coming here." She looked down at the red velvet seat and ran a hand along it, appearing to grow more comfortable with the swaying motion of the carriage.

"Gasoline is a fuel, a liquid that's derived from oil, which comes from fossil fuels deep under the earth. Electricity is an energy source, and I really cannot describe where it comes from. Water, the sun." She pointed up. "All I know is I flip a switch, and the lights come on."

William nodded. "We have heard of this electricity, although it is still in the experimental stages and not available to the common man."

"Pray, what do you mean, flip a switch, Mattie?" Sylvie asked.

"A button on the wall. We have buttons on the walls called switches, and we flip them so"—Mattie demonstrated with her free hand—"and the lights come on."

"No candles?" Sylvie asked.

"Some people use candles, but only for ambience. We don't need them for light unless the electricity goes out."

"How might the electricity go out?" William noticed that Mattie let go of the calash and appeared to enjoy herself now as she swayed with the coach.

"Something is interrupted in the circuitry or the lines delivering power to homes. Perhaps a storm."

"I think I understand," William murmured. "You seem very knowledgeable about these things, Miss Crockwell. More than is usual for a woman." He ignored Sylvie's look of affront. His sister already affected an expression of long suffering at the scientific turn in the conversation.

The severity of Mattie's countenance, however, alarmed him. Her cheeks were reddened, and she crossed her arms. The narrowing of her eyes was his signal that he had said something wrong.

"Well, that's about a chauvinistic thing to say," Mattie muttered as she glared at him. "What do you mean 'for a woman'?"

He bent his head in apology as well as he could in the carriage.

"Perhaps I should have expressed myself better. My experience with women has been that they do not..." He would have removed his top hat and wiped the sweat from his brow if he thought it proper. "That is to say..."

Mattie's eyes warned him to tread carefully. He turned to Sylvie for support. Sylvie watched him with something akin to a smirk.

"Sylvie. Pray, come to my aid. You yourself are not interested in matters of science or mathematics. Is that not true?"

She folded her hands in her lap demurely and stared at him with a perfectly blank expression.

"I cannot help you, William. You have offended Mattie."

He could see he had, although he was not altogether certain her eyes did not twinkle. And was that the faintest twitch of her lips?

"Miss Crockwell, I meant no disrespect." He attempted to bow again. "Please forgive me. It is just that women in this time—"

"Shut up, William," Mattie murmured as she chuckled. "You really should stop talking now. You're just digging yourself in deeper."

Sylvie's eyes widened, and a broad smile spread across her face.

"I beg your pardon," William huffed as he squared his shoulders. "Shut up?" he repeated. "Am I to understand you are telling me to be silent?" He had not been thus addressed since he was a child, and never in those terms.

"Yes, William. That's how we do it in my time." Mattie appeared to be enjoying herself greatly at his expense. "When men start talking about what women can and cannot do..." She shook her head with a sigh. "Well, it's just better that they don't. I know as much as I need to about the sciences to flip a light switch in my time, and Sylvie knows as much as she needs to about the sciences in your time to perch gracefully on the seat of a swaying and jostling carriage without hanging on for dear life."

Sylvie laughed then, and William joined her. Mattie smiled broadly, freed her grasp and raised both hands to show she had conquered her nerves.

They traveled on for another half-hour before the coachman pulled off the path and brought the carriage to a halt beneath a grove of trees at the edge of a small lake. William glanced at his favorite place in the world and turned quickly to see Mattie's expression.

"This is beautiful," Mattie breathed to William's great satisfaction. "What a beautiful lake. Are those deer over there?"

William turned and spotted three does across the lake under another stand of trees.

"Yes," he said as he handed Sylvie down. "They are. The lake is still on our estate."

"Really? But we've come so far." Mattie reached for his upturned hand, and he lifted her out of the carriage. She stepped down and into his arms. He kept Mattie's hand in his a moment more than necessary. Over her head, he saw Sylvie busily directing the footmen in the accompanying carriage as they unloaded supplies.

"William?" Mattie said as she tugged at her hand. Soft sunshine burnished the red curls peeping from under her bonnet.

"Yes, Miss Crockwell?" he replied in a bemused tone. She really had the loveliest hair he had ever seen.

"My hand?" she murmured. William felt the tug in his hand again, and recollected himself and released her hand.

"My apologies, Miss Crockwell." He bowed. "Once again, I am behaving like an oaf."

"An oaf, eh?" she repeated as she smiled. Bright and even white teeth tempted him. Would that he could kiss her lovely smiling lips.

"Miss Crockwell?" he continued absentmindedly. "How is it that your teeth are so straight and white? Your smile is exquisite."

Mattie blushed furiously and raised a gloved hand to her mouth. William cursed himself at his inelegant words. So besotted was he that he was reduced to uttering inanities.

"Years of braces, William. Years of orthodontics and lots and lots of money." Mattie dropped her hand and smiled again self-consciously. "But at the moment, I'm grateful to my parents for giving me a good smile."

"Braces and orthodontics. I do not know what these are, but I am sure you will teach me," William said, his gaze still fixated on her exquisite mouth. "Your parents have indeed given you a pleasing smile."

"Thank you, William," Mattie murmured as she turned away to look toward the lake.

William studied her profile for a moment. What he saw pleased him immensely. Her small upturned nose charmed. He thought he might quite like to kiss the tip of it. Thick, dark lashes blinked as she gazed at the lake. He marveled at their length. Shining red curls caressed her slender white neck, and he longed to run his fingers along the soft-appearing skin.

"Can we walk around the lake?" Mattie asked, with an endearingly wistful tone in her voice. At the moment, William would have deeded her the lake as a gift if it were possible.

"Yes, of course. I would be delighted." William snapped out of his reverie as he held out his arm for her. She looked up at him with one of her engaging, lopsided smiles, and he knew he was lost. Mattie placed her hand on his arm, and he hoped she did not notice the tremor that her touch caused. He inhaled deeply to steady himself as they strolled toward Sylvie and the servants, who were positioning tables under a tree near the lake.

"Thank you, George. That will be all," Sylvie was telling the groomsman as they approached. "What do you think of our lake, Mattie? Is it not lovely?"

"It's breathtaking," Mattie breathed. She pulled her hand from William's arm, and he felt unaccountably bereft. Short of grabbing her hand, though, he had no recourse but to let her go. She moved to the edge of the lake, and Sylvie and William followed.

"Look at all the ducks," Mattie said. "Awwww. Look at the little ducklings. Aren't they cute?"

"Cute?" Sylvie repeated.

Mattie turned with a beaming smile. "Cute. Adorable. Precious. Cute!"

William vowed at that moment to never allow duck to be served in Mattie's presence. He fervently hoped Mrs. White had not provided duck for their repast.

"Yes, they are," murmured William. "Adorable." His eyes lingered on Mattie.

Sylvie laughed. "Oh, goodness, William. You are a changed man. Adorable indeed!" She threw him a pointed look and directed her gaze toward Mattie. William ignored his sister's banter.

Mattie looked from one to the other. What was Sylvie insinuating, exactly?

"Sylvie teases me, I think, Miss Crockwell. Pay her no heed," William directed, although his smile softened his words. He saw Mattie relax as she turned toward the lake again, and he threw a withering look over her head toward his sister, who smirked in response. The sound of horse's hooves startled them, and they turned in unison.

"Hello there," Thomas Ringwood called out as he dismounted from his large bay. George took the horse's reins as Thomas pulled gloves from his hand and approached.

"Thomas! What is he doing here?" Sylvie asked rather ungraciously. Her heightened color betrayed her.

"I asked Thomas to join us, sister. I had hoped you would welcome him as my guest," William said in an even tone as he directed a censorial look at his sister.

Sylvie turned and met William's look squarely.

"You should have told me," she said. "Pray tell me you do not aspire to surpass my mother's matchmaking skills," she hissed as she turned back to face Thomas. She curved her lips into a semblance of a smile.

William looked down to see Mattie's face brightening as she looked toward Thomas. He knew a momentary jealousy and took a step closer to her side.

"Uh oh! Looks like trouble in River City," Mattie whispered as Thomas approached.

"River City?" William asked.

"An old expression," Mattie said with a quick shake of her head.

"Good morning!" Thomas stopped before them and executed a brief bow. "Sylvie. William. Miss Crockwell."

"Mattie, please," she said.

"Good morning, Thomas," Sylvie responded. She half turned to ostensibly gaze at the lake, although William knew her well enough to see the tension in her spine.

He sighed inwardly. When would the two cease and desist with their quarrel? Sylvie was right. He had set himself to matchmaking. Sylvie and Thomas would marry. Louisa and Stephen appeared to suit each other very well. And as for him...

He looked down at Mattie's profile under the fetching bonnet as she greeted Thomas with her charming smile. Who knew what the future would hold for him? Would his future end in twenty-eight days, or was it just beginning? He fervently hoped it was not the first.

CHAPTER ELEVEN

"Hello, Thomas. How are you?" Mattie offered her gloved hand for a shake. To her surprise—and embarrassment—Thomas bent over it and dropped a light kiss on the back.

"Oh, I only meant to shake—" Mattie bit her lip. There was no point in trying to explain that she wasn't fishing for a kiss. This hand-kissing thing seemed to be quite common around here, and she suspected she had better get used to it. It wouldn't be that hard, she mused as she looked down at her hand.

"I am well, Mattie. Thank you. You look well rested after the evening's festivities," he said with a warm smile. He threw an inquiring look in Sylvie's direction, but Sylvie continued to ignore him...partially. Although her face was turned toward the lake, she appeared to be listening intently to the nearby conversation.

"Welcome, Thomas. Miss Crockwell, Sylvie and I were just about to stroll around the lake. You must join us," William said as he extended his arm for Mattie.

Mattie threw him a suspicious look and put her hand on his arm. Was he matchmaking, as Sylvie had accused?

"Shall we?" William asked with a disarming grin. Her knees weakened suddenly at the sight of his handsome face, and she clutched his arm a little tighter, wishing she could just tuck her hand up under his strong arm and hang on for all she was worth. She suspected, however, that such familiarity would wipe the smile right off his face. It probably wasn't done. Although Sylvie was adept at countering William's occasional disapproving looks, Mattie thought she might just burst into tears if William directed one of those disdainful expressions her way.

"Sure," Mattie murmured. She looked over her shoulder to see

Thomas offer Sylvie his arm. Sylvie lifted her chin and laced her hands behind her back as she began to walk. Short of quirking an exasperated eyebrow, Thomas could do nothing but fall into step beside her.

"If you're matchmaking as Sylvie said, William, it's not working," Mattie said in a low voice. "So, are they a couple? I know you said they had an understanding, but I don't see it."

"If by 'are they a couple,' you mean do they have an understanding, I would say yes," William said. He glanced behind for an instant and turned back with a wry expression. "However, at the moment, I would say the understanding is quite misunderstood."

Mattie grinned.

"Are they angry with each other?" she asked.

"I believe Sylvie is much more put out than Thomas. She disapproves of his constant travels, feels he is away far too much."

Mattie cast a quick glance over her shoulder. Sylvie marched more than she actually strolled, turning her face away from Thomas, who was forced to look at her profile. He too clasped his hands behind his back. Mattie turned back to peer up at William.

"And Thomas?"

"I think he would marry Sylvie at once if she would agree to travel with him. He is quite the gypsy."

"That sounds wonderful!" Mattie breathed with another quick look over her shoulder. "Why doesn't Sylvie marry him?"

"She does not wish to leave England," William said quietly. "She fears the unknown. As do many of us, I suppose."

Mattie's ears pricked. She looked up at William. His eyes were narrowed, a deep crease between them on his forehead as he stared straight ahead at some unknown spot.

"Do you?"

He looked down at her for a moment before giving a short nod and returning his gaze to the path as they rounded the lake.

"I do not fear traveling to the continent as Sylvie does. I have done so in the past. Nor do I fear traveling to America, although I have not yet been." He paused. "However, at the moment, I cannot deny that I fear the unknown."

"What do you mean?" Mattie thought she felt a tremor in William's arm. His expression gave away little, save for a tightening of his jaw.

William didn't respond for a moment, and Mattie wondered if he'd heard her question. He seemed lost in thought. She wondered what his "unknown" was. Was it Louisa? Marriage? Something she didn't know about? Surely, there were many aspects of his life she hadn't yet discovered. William spoke at last.

"I spoke without thinking," he said. "Pay no heed to my foolish mutterings."

Mattie looked up to see William's jaw relax with a wide smile. The smile seemed forced, and she realized with a pang that he wasn't going to confide in her. Why should he? She was just a stranger, a temporary visitor who would soon be gone. An unknown entity.

"I am famished," he said in a louder voice as he turned to see Sylvie and Thomas trailing behind them. "Shall we dine?"

"As am I," Thomas said. "I hope Mrs. White set aside a bit of the pie from last night's supper for your picnic basket."

"I should think most likely not. *I* did not know you were joining us today, and so how could Mrs. White have known?" she said with an unladylike shrug as she turned on her heels and returned the way they had come.

Mattie watched Thomas sigh deeply before he followed Sylvie.

They returned to where the footmen had rolled out several carpets and set out hampers of food on several linen-covered tables, in what appeared to Mattie to be a delightful buffet.

Mattie accepted William's help to lower herself to the ground, and taking a cue from Sylvie, she positioned herself on her hip, tucked her legs beside her and spread out her skirts.

"Whatever are you searching for, William?" Sylvie asked as William could be seen lifting cloth-covered platters to peer beneath. Mrs. White's young assistant, who had been removing the cloths, seemed taken aback and waited silently with her hands clasped in front while William examined the food. He turned to speak to her in a low voice, and with a flaming face, the young woman answered with a shake of her head.

"William, for goodness' sake, please show some decorum," Sylvie said. "Mattie will think this is acceptable behavior." Her eyes shot to Thomas who gave her a curious look. "That is…Mattie will think our English manners quite crude." She flashed a quick smile in Mattie's direction.

Mattie blithely ignored Thomas's inquisitive gaze.

William nodded an assent to the footman, presumably to begin serving, and he returned to the group to seat himself beside Mattie.

"I was just examining the food to see what Mrs. White prepared for us," William said nonchalantly. He flashed an uncharacteristically crooked grin in Mattie's direction, and she responded with an awkward smile.

"Whatever it is, I am sure it will be delicious," Thomas said. "She is an exquisite cook."

As a footman set plates and cutlery before them, Mattie noted Sylvie continued to eye William suspiciously.

"Yes, of course," Sylvie said. "Mrs. White would not send us on a picnic with any food which she knew we expressly did not like."

"No, of course not," William acknowledged promptly, his attention seemingly more on the footman approaching with a platter of food than on the conversation.

A sudden splash in the nearby water and the sound of the ducks quacking caught Mattie's attention as the footman bent toward her with what looked like a small roasted chicken, his serving fork poised to deliver a slice onto her plate.

Water rippled as several new arrivals skimmed along the surface of the lake, albeit at a distance from the young family of ducks. Mattie turned back to eye the bird on the plate, and thrust up a hand to ward the footman off.

"That's not..." she squeaked, unable to say the word. She glanced toward the lake once again with rounded eyes before turning back.

"No, no, Miss Crockwell," assured William without hesitation. "I can assure you it most certainly is not—"

"Duck!" Sylvie interrupted with a crow. "Is that what you were searching for, William? Duck? Did you wish to see if Mrs. White had sent along some duck for our meal?"

William's face colored, and he waved off the footman as well.

"I am assured it is quail, Miss Crockwell," William said soberly as he scanned Mattie's face.

"Quail?" she asked on a mournful note as she watched Thomas accepting some slices on his plate. Those adorable little birds that scurried around with the jaunty feathers perched above their heads?

"Do you have some objection to eating duck, Miss Crockwell?" Thomas asked. "Or quail?"

"Do you not eat poultry in America, Mattie?" Sylvie asked as she too accepted a serving of quail.

"I...I..." She didn't know how to respond, and wished she hadn't made a fuss about the food but simply waved the serving off in an inconspicuous way.

"Perhaps Miss Crockwell simply does not wish to eat the waterfowl which she has just admired," William stated flatly. He gestured to another footman, who hurried over. "Please bring Miss Crockwell another course."

"Just fruit and some cheese, please?" Mattie said. The footman nodded and moved away toward the table.

"Is that all you are going to eat, Mattie?" Sylvie asked with a concerned face.

Mattie nodded.

"Some venison, perhaps? Would that be more to your liking?" Sylvie asked.

"Oh, no. No, thank you," Mattie said with a vehement shake of her head. The menu was only getting worse. Deer? Gosh, no!

"Sylvie, we must allow Miss Crockwell to eat as she sees fit," William said. He leaned back and looked toward the lake as he chewed thoughtfully on a piece of bread. Mattie noted he hadn't taken any other food.

"Yes, of course, William," Sylvie said instantly with a contrite smile. "Forgive me, Mattie."

"No problem. I just don't eat..." She saw Thomas' odd look and thought better of that line of thought. "I just... I'm not very hungry," she finished briefly.

The footman arrived with a tray of fruit including grapes, peaches, plums and various cheeses, which looked nothing like what Mattie had seen in a grocery store before. She took a sampling of several slices of cheese and a few pieces of fruit. She was actually starving, but now that she'd said she wasn't hungry, she couldn't very well load up her plate.

William also took cheese and some fruit, she noticed. Why wasn't he eating? She hoped it wasn't some sort of sympathetic courtesy to a guest. That seemed a bit exaggerated, even for an era so defined by good manners as the Georgian period.

As she chewed on the rather delicious white cheese, she imagined a scene in which William jumped up, dramatically thrust out his arm in a motion of rejection and said, "I too shall not eat duck, quail or venison while my guest does not."

She grinned and looked up to see William watching her.

"The food is to your liking, Miss Crockwell?"

"Yes, it is. The cheese is wonderful." She arched an eyebrow. "I notice you are not eating very much yourself." If he was going to jump up, thrust out his hand, and announce he could not eat what Mattie could not, this was his chance. Her grin broadened.

"Yes, William, I also observed that you are eating very little," Sylvie chimed in. "Mrs. White has gone to great lengths to prepare a wonderful picnic for us. She will not thank us for bringing most of it back. Are you well?"

"Quite well, Sylvie, thank you. I do hope Mrs. White forgives us." William turned toward Mattie. "You seem amused, Miss Crockwell. May I ask why?"

Mattie attempted to school her expression into a more serious one.

"Umm. Did I? I don't know why," Mattie demurred. "Maybe I'm so happy because the cheese is so delicious."

"Yes, I agree, it is," William responded, with a skeptical expression. Mattie could see he wasn't convinced by her answer, but he let it go. For now.

The conversation turned to other matters involving nearby neighbors, and Mattie took the opportunity to stuff as much food as she could into her mouth from the tray the footman had kindly left in front of her. She nonchalantly snagged a couple of pieces of bread and munched on those while she listened to the ongoing conversation.

"But we are being rude to Mattie, who does not know of whom we speak," Sylvie said as she dabbed a linen napkin delicately in the general area of her mouth. "Shall we resume our walk?" she said brightly.

Sylvie made as if to rise, but Thomas jumped to his feet and offered his hand. She placed her hand in his with some reluctance, and pulled it away as soon as she'd risen.

William helped Mattie rise, thankfully, because she wasn't quite sure she could disentangle her legs from her long skirt without squatting unbecomingly or falling flat on her face.

He seemed to hold her hand longer than he needed to. Mattie looked at their joined hands and raised her eyes to his face. She caught her breath at his searching look. Startled, she tugged at her hand, but not truly because she wanted to be free of him.

"Forgive me," he said as he released her hand with a quick bow.

Mattie instantly regretted her kneejerk reaction. Of course, she would have loved to stroll about with her hand in his. *Yes, yes, yes!*

Sylvie and Thomas walked ahead toward the lake, an awkwardly unnatural distance between them, which spoke volumes. William and Mattie followed.

"Miss Crockwell," William began, "now that you are no longer the center of unwanted attention, would it be possible for me to inquire about your eating habits?" He paused to look at her, and Mattie stilled as well.

"My eating habits..." Mattie drew the words out as she wondered what to say. Out of the corner of her eye, she saw Sylvie pause to turn around to look at them. She seemed to be waiting, so Mattie moved on. William walked beside her.

"Yes, I have noticed ever since you...ah...arrived, that you do not eat meat. At least, not that I have seen."

Mattie, her eyes on her feet as she walked, peeped up at William from under her bonnet with a half-smile. She shook her head.

"Nope, I don't," she stated, her vernacular reverting to the more modern American standard. "I'm a vegetarian."

Sylvie resumed walking, with Thomas at her side.

"A vegetarian? What, pray tell, is a vegetarian?" William asked with a puzzled frown.

"Someone who doesn't eat meat," she said. "Where I come from, there are lots of different kinds of vegetarians—some who eat eggs, vegetables and fruit, but no dairy foods. Some who eat dairy, vegetables and fruit, but no eggs. Or some who eat both eggs and dairy as well as vegetables and fruit. That would be me," she said.

"Vegetarian," he repeated slowly. "And what would be the purpose of this particular diet?"

Mattie couldn't help but chuckle. "Well, I just love the little animals," she said. "Big ones too. And I don't want to eat them."

William paused to look at her with curiosity. "But can man—or woman—subsist on nothing but vegetables?" He clasped his hands behind his back. "It would seem a very unhealthy way to live."

Mattie smiled. "Not really. And it's not *just* vegetables, as you well know. I eat cheese and bread, and they have plenty of protein."

"Protein? Is this another food?" William asked.

Mattie sighed inwardly. She couldn't possibly explain almost two hundred years of nutritional science and discovery.

"Something we all need to eat to survive. There is protein in meat, poultry, fish, dairy, beans and some vegetables."

"Interesting," William said. "So you derive your...*protein*...from dairy, beans and some vegetables."

"Yes."

"I am not sure what Mrs. White will do with you, Miss Crockwell," William said with a smile. "Nor how we will hide the fact that you do not eat like the rest of us."

"We could say I have allergies," Mattie said with a laugh.

"Allergies?" William said with a frown. "And what, pray tell, are allergies?"

"Oh, William," Mattie sighed. "I'm out of my depth here. But I'll try to explain."

For the next half-hour, she explained what little she knew of food allergies, and answered his questions as best she could. And he had a lot of questions. When they had circled the lake, they joined Sylvie and Thomas by the carriage, Sylvie looking more peeved than ever with Thomas, who stood rigid, his hands locked behind his back, his face the epitome of frustration.

Mattie suspected they'd had another misunderstanding, or a continuation of the original.

"Please accept my gratitude for allowing me to accompany you on your outing today," Thomas said to the group in general with a bow.

"Miss Crockwell, Sylvie, William," he said with a nod of his head.

"Bye—" Mattie was starting to say, but Thomas had hopped on his horse and spurred it away, seemingly in one movement.

Sylvie's lower lip quivered for a moment, but she bit it, straightened her shoulders, favored William and Mattie with a forced smile and turned toward the carriage.

William, watching his friend's departure with a frown between his eyes, sprung forward to hand his sister up without a word.

Mattie grabbed her skirts, took his hand, and climbed into the carriage. She slid into the seat next to Sylvie and reached for Sylvie's hand. Sylvie attempted a gracious smile, which fell short, but she clung to Mattie's hand. William took the seat across from them, averting his eyes from Sylvie's unhappiness.

They had just returned to the house when Mr. Carver arrived punctually at two o'clock. Sylvie pled a headache and retreated to her room.

Mattie tried to sneak up the stairs but John, the footman, advised her that Mrs. Sinclair desired her presence in the drawing room, as well as that of Mr. Sinclair.

As John moved away to open the drawing room door, Mattie threw William a pleading look, and he gave her a silent nod of encouragement.

"There you are, Miss Crockwell," Mrs. Sinclair said upon seeing them enter. "And William. I trust your outing was invigorating. Where is Sylvie?" She looked beyond them to the door.

"She feels unwell, Mother. Carver, how do you do?" William said.

Stephen Carver jumped up from his seat across from Mrs. Sinclair.

"I am well, thank you, Sinclair." He bowed in Mattie's direction. "And how did you find the countryside, Miss Crockwell? Mrs. Sinclair tells me that you went out for a ride this morning."

"It was great—wonderful, Mr. Carver. Thank you."

Mattie cringed. She just didn't think she could fool this man for some reason. She was tempted to just confess all and be done with the anticipation of discovery.

"At the risk of boring Mrs. Sinclair and Mr. Sinclair, I had hoped to speak to you more of home—America," he said with a winsome smile in their direction. "Since we are countrymen."

Mrs. Sinclair's mouth tightened. William adopted the same forbidding look.

"I understand that you are eager to reminisce about your common heritage, Mr. Carver, but perhaps Miss Crockwell might wish to refresh herself with a cup of tea after her outing this morning," Mrs. Sinclair said. "Will you ring for tea, William?"

Mattie wondered if Mrs. Sinclair had seen the panic in Mattie's eyes. Although Mrs. Sinclair wanted her to be gone, she clearly didn't want Mattie's secret discovered either, and perhaps she shared Mattie's concerns regarding Stephen Carver.

"Certainly, Mrs. Sinclair," Stephen said. "How inconsiderate I am. I should like some tea as well. I drink coffee when I am at home, but I do so enjoy English tea when I am here. Do you drink coffee at home, Miss Crockwell, or do you prefer tea?"

After pulling the servant's bell, William moved over to the fireplace and leaned one arm on the mantle. At Stephen's question, he coughed slightly.

"Miss Crockwell informed me that she also drinks tea in America, did you not, Miss Crockwell?" William said.

Mattie looked up at him and nodded. Of course, they hadn't had such a conversation because she actually did like coffee, but no doubt Stephen would want to compare coffees.

Just then, the door opened, and John announced a Mrs. Covington and Miss Louisa Covington.

Mrs. Covington, a slender woman of about Mrs. Sinclair's age, sailed in. Louisa followed more sedately. Mrs. Sinclair rose to greet them, as did Stephen. Unable to remember what folks did during calls in her books, Mattie stood as well.

"Sally, my dear," Mrs. Sinclair said as she leaned forward to kiss Mrs. Covington and Louisa on the cheek. "How kind of you to call. Please sit here," she said, indicating the sofa.

Mattie noticed that Stephen's eyes were riveted on Louisa. Louisa moved to sit on the sofa between her mother and Mrs. Sinclair with a bright smile in William's direction. She seemed not to see Stephen for a moment.

"Mother, this is Miss Matilda Crockwell from America. She is a distant cousin of the Sinclairs."

Mrs. Covington, an older replica of Louisa, eyed her with interest.

"Yes, I had heard of Miss Crockwell's origins." She turned to Stephen. "A countrywoman of yours, Stephen. You must have so much to talk about," she said innocently.

Mattie cringed.

"I had hoped to share our mutual experiences, Mrs. Covington, but Miss Crockwell and I have not had an opportunity as of yet to do so. I remain hopeful," he said with a bright smile in Mattie's direction.

Mr. Smythe and John arrived with the tea just in time, in Mattie's opinion, distracting everyone from their attention on her. She glanced at William out of the corner of her eye, and he gave her a nod of encouragement. She wondered how far he was prepared to intercede on her behalf. Sometimes he did, and sometimes he let her fend for herself. She hoped he wasn't in his fending-for-herself mode.

Another footman opened the door to announce that Lord Hamilton, Lord Reginald Hamilton and the Honorable Samuel Hamilton had arrived.

Mrs. Sinclair rose hastily from her chair, scanning the room, Mattie guessed, for empty seats.

"Mrs. Sinclair." Lord Hamilton bowed on entering. His sons mimicked his bow. Lord Hamilton scanned the room in some surprise.

"But we are interrupting," he said. "We have come at an awkward time."

"No, Lord Hamilton, you and your sons are very welcome," Mrs. Sinclair said as she signaled to the footman to bring more chairs. "You know Mrs. Covington, of course, and her daughter, Miss Louisa Covington. And Mr. Carver is not, I think, a stranger to you."

Lord Hamilton bowed before them. He turned to Mattie, much to her dismay. She hadn't missed that his sons were ogling her with reddened cheeks.

"May I present Miss Matilda Crockwell, Lord Hamilton?" Mrs. Sinclair said. "I do not believe you were introduced last night, although Reginald and Samuel made her acquaintance."

"Ah, yes, the young lady whose praises my sons have not stopped singing. So much so that I needed to come meet her for myself," he said with an amused smile. He bent over Mattie's hand, with Reggie and Samuel following suit.

Mattie tried to smile graciously, but her dry lips stuck to her teeth. As the boys came to stand on either side of her chair, she panicked and threw William a glance of desperation. To her surprise, his lips twitched as he surveyed the room. A lot of help he was, she thought. It would serve him right if she were to "plead a headache" and run to her room. Better yet, if she were to just jump up, disclose all and relieve the anxious tension which threatened to explode.

"Well, what a merry party we are," Mrs. Covington said dryly. "Come, Lord Hamilton, come sit by me. You are safe with me. I am a married woman. The same could not be said for anyone else in this room, though."

Mrs. Sinclair's pale cheeks colored. Lord Hamilton coughed and did as he was bade.

"You say that Reginald and Samuel have talked of little else other than Miss Crockwell, Lord Hamilton?" Mrs. Covington asked. "This is a most fortunate occurrence, Miss Crockwell, to have incurred the favor of two young men of such favorable circumstances."

"Mother!" Louisa protested, her cheeks bright. Lord Hamilton coughed behind his hand once again, while his sons seemed to fail to catch Mrs. Covington's meaning.

"I-I..." Mattie couldn't begin to think how to respond. She didn't know the rules. What could she say? A quick look toward William, her protector, showed her that he was directing a piercing gaze at his mother, who caught his look.

"I do not know that Miss Crockwell is at present engaged in seeking to form an alliance, Sally," Mrs. Sinclair said with a gracious smile. "But I am sure that she is most flattered by the esteem in which Reginald and Samuel hold her."

"Let the girl speak for herself, Lucy," Mrs. Covington pursued with a sharp look in Mattie's direction. "Is she shy?"

"No, I don't believe she is shy, Mother." Louisa rose swiftly. "Perhaps just well mannered." She came to Mattie's side to offer her a hand. Mattie, unclear what Louisa wanted, put her cold, clammy hand in Louisa's cool and dry one.

"Could we walk in the garden, Miss Crockwell? It seems such a lovely afternoon."

"Oh, sure," Mattie said as she rose unsteadily on rubbery knees. So many people in the room, with their eyes focused directly on her.

"I would like to accompany you, if I may," William said quickly.

"Let us make a walking party of it," Stephen said. He rose and bowed to Mrs. Sinclair. "With your permission, madam."

"Yes, let's," Reggie said. "I hope you will not object if Samuel and I accompany you. Fresh air will do us both good." Mattie, wondering if she was really getting away from anyone at this point, eyed Reggie wildly. His face flamed with the boldness of asserting himself, and she was touched by his flattering admiration.

"Let us go, then," William said shortly. He directed a narrowed gaze toward the younger men who seemed oblivious.

He led the way out into the garden behind the house. Mattie looked back to see that the floor-to-ceiling windows of the drawing room appeared to overlook the garden. The exterior of the house—the mansion, Mattie corrected herself—gleamed, its sandstone seemingly absorbing the golden rays of the afternoon sun. She turned to look at the garden, which sported a water fountain, well-manicured shrubs and flowers, and paths dotted with iron benches.

Louisa tucked Mattie's arm in hers as they walked ahead of the men.

"I apologize for my mother's comments, Miss Crockwell. I know it is not my place to do so, but there are times when her tongue runs away with her. I believe she thinks she is being droll."

"Oh, no," Mattie murmured. "That's okay. You're right. I think she was just trying to be funny." She felt eight eyes on her back as they walked and looked over her shoulder. Reggie and Samuel followed directly behind, while William and Stephen brought up the rear. They appeared to be in conversation.

"Besides," Mattie said, "I *am* supposed to be looking for a husband at my age, aren't I?"

"Miss Crockwell!" Louisa laughed lightly, appearing to pretend shock. "Well, yes," she conceded. "We are expected to pursue advantageous marriages. Is this not the case where you are from?"

"I imagine so," Mattie answered.

"Imagine?" Louisa asked with curiosity. "Perhaps your parents have not pursued the matter?"

"My parents passed away," Mattie replied. "So, I'm on my own." As soon as she said the words, she regretted them, as she had to engage in the same conversation with Louisa that she'd had with William regarding the lack of a companion, that she was independent, etc.

"How very interesting," Louisa answered. "You do not intend to marry, then?"

"No, I'd like to get married," Mattie murmured. "I'm just not sure when."

"I must marry soon," Louisa said matter-of-factly. "Mother fears I will become a spinster, as I am already five and twenty."

Mattie threw a speculative look over her shoulder. William caught her eyes and smiled, and a delightful shiver ran up her spine. Stephen smiled as well.

"Do you have anyone in mind?"

To Mattie's dismay, Louisa also looked over her shoulder. Mattie dreaded her response. Not William, she prayed. Please don't say William!

"I have known William for many years," she said softly.

Mattie bit her lip. She pulled her arm from Louisa's as casually as she could and clasped it behind her back, locking her fingers so tightly she thought they might break. Of course, she had seen it in Louisa's eyes when she looked at William. Why wouldn't she want to marry the most handsome, most endearing and most charming man around? That he was incredibly wealthy probably didn't hurt.

Mattie resisted throwing another look over her shoulder, as if to beg William to pick her, to choose her over Louisa.

If her theory held true, she would be gone soon, and William would go on with the life he was intended to have in the nineteenth century, probably with Louisa. She gritted her teeth.

"And you, Miss Crockwell?" Louisa asked with a friendly smile. "Is there someone special for you?"

Mattie shook her head. "No," she answered shortly. She couldn't even imagine what her life would be like when she got back home. She didn't think she was ever going to be able to read her book again without seeing William Sinclair's face. It would be like losing him over and over.

"No one at home?" Louisa prompted.

"No, no one," Mattie said. She smiled faintly before dropping her eyes to the ground.

"Oh, Miss Crockwell, please forgive me!" Louisa said quickly with a contrite expression. "I can see that I have distressed you. How ill-mannered of me to press you on such a personal matter."

"No, that's okay," Mattie said. Louisa did sound genuinely apologetic.

"We will say no more," Louisa said.

Mattie gave in to temptation and looked over her shoulder. Reggie and Samuel had slowed to speak to William. Stephen's eyes were riveted on Louisa's back. When he saw Mattie watching him, he shrugged slightly and gave her a self-deprecating smile.

Mattie returned the smile and faced forward, with a sideways glance in Louisa's direction.

Should she say something to Louisa? About Stephen? Or would it look like she was trying to steer Louisa away from William. Mattie sighed inwardly. What did it all matter anyway? She didn't belong here. This wasn't her life. William needed to marry, Louisa needed to marry and Stephen would probably marry. It was up to them to sort themselves out. She was just passing through.

CHAPTER TWELVE

"You can't go away!" Mattie almost shrieked the next morning. "You can't leave me here alone!"

"I am so sorry, Miss Crockwell," William said. He clasped his hands tightly behind his back as he fought against the urge to take her into his arms and reassure her. The distress on her face tugged at his heart.

"My solicitor needs to see me regarding matters of estate, and I must go to town," he said. "I will be away for no more than three days."

"Three days?" she gasped. She jumped up from the bench in the garden where he had seated her. William rose. He had thought it best to discuss the matter with her out of hearing of the servants, suspecting she would protest his impending departure.

"Oh, William, I don't think I can do without you for three days," she murmured as she paced back and forth.

Unused to such candor from a woman, William's heart rolled over as she spoke. That she saw him as some sort of protector touched him deeply. Suspecting her to be quite accomplished in her time, he had already deduced that she was not some sort of miss-ish girl without strength of character. But she was the perennial fish out of water in his time, and it lent her an air of vulnerability, which prompted his protective instincts. He loved his mother and his sister and considered himself their guardian in the absence of husbands, and almost before he'd understood what was happening, Miss Crockwell had joined their ranks—that of a beloved female family member who depended upon him. He wondered what it would be like to be loved by her, as a woman loves a man.

"I would not go at this time, Miss Crockwell, if I could possibly avoid it. Please do not fret. All will be well. You are very resourceful, I have noted."

She stopped her pacing to face him, her lovely lower lip caught between her teeth.

"Can't I go with you?"

William stiffened and coughed. His heart's desire. To be with her always.

"I am afraid that is not possible, Miss Crockwell. I would take you with me if I could, but no female is traveling with me, and you are not such a close 'relative' that there would not be cause for gossip were you to accompany me to London."

"What about Sylvie? Wouldn't she like a trip to London?" Her green and gold eyes sparkled.

"There is no one in town at this time of year, Miss Crockwell. I could ask Sylvie if she wishes to go, but she has engagements here in the country."

Mattie clamped her hands over her mouth.

"No, you're right, of course," she said through muffled fingers. "I can't believe I suggested such a thing."

"I understand your concerns, Miss Crockwell. I do," William reassured her. "If Sylvie's presence makes you comfortable, then you will have no concerns. She will stay by your side while I am away."

"I know she will," Mattie murmured as she resumed pacing. "She'll keep me out of trouble."

"And yet you still seem distressed, Miss Crockwell," William said as he watched her alternately wring her hands and clasp them behind her back. "What troubles you?"

She paused, and he held his breath. Her eyes, when she turned, gave him the sensation of being swallowed whole—a not unpleasant experience, he thought.

He thought he heard her to say "I'll miss you," but he wasn't quite certain.

"Here you are," Mrs. Sinclair said as she rounded a corner of the garden, clearly seeking them out. "I presume from your downcast face, Miss Crockwell, that William has informed you he must go to London for several days."

"Yes, I have just told her, Mother," William said, "and assured her that Sylvie would stand in my stead to assist her as needed."

"Of course, we are all available to assist Miss Crockwell, William."

William failed to understand his mother's resistance to Mattie, for resistant she was. She had yet to show Mattie the warmth he knew her to be capable of, offering instead a cool demeanor, which never failed to chill him when he witnessed it. He could not imagine how Mattie contended with it, and suspected she wished herself home and well away from the lot of them.

"Thank you," Mattie murmured. "I think I'll just..." She paused and looked toward the house. "I'll just return to the house. I have a headache." She turned as if to leave, but paused. "When are you leaving?" she asked William. She kept her eyes averted from his mother's gaze.

"Within the hour," he said. Her face drooped, but she nodded and hurried away. This was not how he had intended to say goodbye, he thought with anger. What if their moon theory proved wrong? What if he returned and she were gone?

He turned to his mother, who followed his eyes as he watched Mattie stride away quickly, her skirts caught up in an unladylike fashion.

"Please explain to me, Mother, why you must continue to treat Miss Crockwell as an unwanted guest."

"I beg your pardon?" his mother said indignantly. "I do not think I have been unkind or cruel to Miss Crockwell."

"No, Mother, not unkind or cruel, but you have been as cold as a fish to her. That is not like you," William said with an anger he rarely felt toward her. "It is not Miss Crockwell's fault that she arrived on our doorstep. She was unconscious. I am sure she did not simply prance over to our garden and decide to faint there. You must see how frightened she is," he said.

"I do not know where Miss Crockwell comes from, William, and I continue to feel what I believe is a very natural reserve regarding the entire matter," she said in a frosty voice. "I do not know that she has not foisted herself upon you with this story of time travel via moonbeam in order to gain your sympathy, perhaps with an eye toward acquiring your fortune through marriage."

William turned an incredulous eye upon his mother.

"Madam, I understand that you have had a difficult time believing in Miss Crockwell's origins, but I assure you, she does not have designs upon me or upon my fortune. I would be honored if she did." William could have bit his tongue, to so declare himself in front of his mother in such a premature fashion.

"William! Do not tell me that you have become enamored of this...this chit," his mother remonstrated with a shocked face. "You hardly know her." She nodded in the direction of the house. "However, it does not signify. You have agreed that she will return to wherever she hails from in less than one month's time."

"It is true, Mother. To my surprise, I have become inordinately fond of her, and yes, she will return to wherever she comes from in one month's time," William said with a hint of bitterness. "In the meantime, please try to find it in your heart to warm to her. I remind you again that she is very frightened, has no idea what transpired to bring her here and desires nothing more than to return to her own time."

"Although I detect more than a hint of reproach in your voice, William, which I do not welcome, I will attempt to 'warm' to Miss Crockwell as you ask. But you must assure me that you have no intention of offering her a proposal of marriage."

William looked down at his mother, her chin set, her eyes harder than he was used to seeing. Why did she dislike Miss Crockwell so much?

He shook his head. "I can make you no such promise, Mother, and I am sorry that you must ask it of me. Please be assured that I have no current intention of asking Miss Crockwell to marry me, but that may only be because I fear she will leave, or that she may have no choice and may be forced to leave." He sighed heavily as he gazed at the house, Mattie no longer in sight. "But I will make you no such promise."

Mrs. Sinclair echoed his sigh. "You are such a foolish romantic, William."

"So you have told me before, Mother." He bent to kiss her cheek. "I must go if I am to arrive before nightfall. Please be kind to Miss Crockwell. I am still unclear as to the source of your concerns regarding her, but do it for my sake."

"I will try, my son," she said.

A short while later, William poked his head into the library in search of Mattie, having had no luck locating her in her room, the sitting room or with Sylvie in her bedchamber.

He spied her seated in an armchair, a book in her lap. She had apparently been gazing out the window onto the lawn, but jumped up as he entered the room.

"Please sit, Miss Crockwell. Do not let me disturb you."

She retook her seat.

"And what book do you have there in your hands, Miss Crockwell?"

"*Sense and Sensibility*," she said. "Although I'm having trouble deciphering some of the text," she murmured. "The print is a bit different from ours."

William seated himself at the edge of the chair facing her.

"I am pleased to see you utilizing the library, Miss Crockwell, and urge you to read as many books as you like." He hesitated for a moment as he regarded her. Her eyes looked suspiciously wet.

"Miss Crockwell." He paused, searching for words. "Please do not allow my mother to distress you. I understand that I leave you in her care and that of my sister, but my mother is possessed of a generous heart. I acknowledge that she is withholding that from you, and I am unclear as to her motives."

Her drawn face relaxed as he spoke, and he hoped he had eased her worries, if only in small measure.

"I'm sure she's just worried about you, William," Mattie said with a faint smile. "Mothers…you know. I'm just a strange woman who showed up on your doorstep. I'm sure she's worried that I might have 'designs' on you."

William's cheeks bronzed at her astute observation.

"I will not deny I have heard something of that nature," he conceded with a resigned smile.

"But she doesn't need to worry, does she?" Mattie stated flatly. "I'll be gone soon."

William swallowed hard.

"Not so soon, Miss Crockwell. We still have some weeks."

"Yes," she murmured.

He studied her face, but suspected she masked the emotions normally expressed on her countenance.

"I must go, Miss Crockwell," he said, rising from the chair. She rose as well. "I only wished to bid you farewell."

"Thank you," she said with her head downcast.

He reached to raise her chin.

"I am not certain that I can do without you as well, Miss Crockwell, albeit for different reasons than you, I suspect." With a heavy heart, he dropped his hand, bowed, and left the room without a backward glance, fearing he might take her into his arms in a most ungentlemanly manner.

****

"I am of a mind to walk in the garden this beautiful morning. Would you care to accompany me, Miss Crockwell?"

Mattie froze in the act of buttering her toast as Mrs. Sinclair spoke to her. Sylvie's eyebrows lifted as she regarded her mother.

"Um…okay, sure," Mattie stuttered. Oh, boy. What was coming? There was no hint in Mrs. Sinclair's studied expression of pleasantry of what she would say. Mattie looked toward Sylvie, who shrugged her shoulders and favored her with a sympathetic smile. It seemed Sylvie would not be included in the walk.

"Sylvie," Mrs. Sinclair began, "would you be a dear and attend to our correspondence? I am afraid I am sadly behind in responding to invitations."

It was confirmed. Sylvie would not be joining them. Mattie wondered if Mrs. Sinclair was going to send her "packing," not that she had anything to take with her except the pink robe and slippers currently residing in the large mahogany cupboard in her room.

Breakfast finished all too quickly in Mattie's opinion, and she found herself out on the lawn with Mrs. Sinclair as they strolled toward the gardens. Well, Mrs. Sinclair strolled. Mattie felt like she waddled on rubbery legs, which threatened to give way at any moment.

"Miss Crockwell," Mrs. Sinclair began. Mattie cringed.

"I apologize for my behavior these past few days. My son has made it very clear to me that I have been...*cold* to you. Those are his words. And he is correct. I have been unusually reserved in my treatment of you, withholding warmth or kindness."

"Oh, no, Mrs. Sinclair" Mattie said hastily. "In all fairness, you have been very kind and generous in allowing me into your house, feeding me and clothing me."

Mrs. Sinclair nodded graciously. "Thank you, Miss Crockwell. I hoped I had been polite, if nothing else." She sighed. "But William is disappointed in me, and I hate to disappoint my children. He feels I could be warmer toward you. He states you are frightened by your circumstances, and that I have inadvertently added to your worries by my behavior."

Mattie held her tongue. She couldn't argue this point. Her heart beat happily with the thought that William had spoken to his mother about her, and that he actually understood some of what she felt. She was scared, that was true—of not being able to return to her time, and of returning and never seeing William again.

"Please be assured, Miss Crockwell, that I will continue to endeavor to protect you from discovery, and I will guide you in our ways as necessary. I vow to be more...tolerant of your ignorance of our customs. I admit that I have judged you unnecessarily in this regard, and for that, I beg your forgiveness." She paused. "I have been skeptical regarding the circumstances of your arrival, and am only now coming to believe that something untoward has occurred, and that you are not of our time."

"Thank you, Mrs. Sinclair," Mattie responded. "It *is* true." She offered nothing more, still herself skeptical about the other woman's motives.

"Shall we sit?" Mrs. Sinclair asked as they neared the bench where William and Mattie sat the day before.

Upon sitting, Mattie held her tongue and waited to see what else Mrs. Sinclair had to say. She really doubted that she and Mrs. Sinclair had suddenly become the best of buds.

"Your eyes reflect your distrust, Miss Crockwell," Mrs. Sinclair said after a quick survey of Mattie's wary face. "I am to blame for that, I fear."

Mattie waited. What could she say? She really was at the woman's mercy, and had no inclination to go wandering off the property in search of another place to stay.

"Let me speak frankly," Mrs. Sinclair said as she shifted her body to face Mattie. "If, in fact, you have come from the future, you and William believe it is likely you will return on the next full moon. My concern, Miss Crockwell, is that my son will have become so infatuated with you, that he will seek to accompany you to your future and that I shall never see him again."

Mattie stiffened. Mrs. Sinclair voiced the hope that Mattie hadn't wanted to put to words—the dream that William would somehow come back with her. But the stark look of fear that passed across Mrs. Sinclair's face for a brief moment gave her pause. Mattie's foolish fantasies of life with William lost their appeal at the unexpectedly bleak look on the older woman's face as she contemplated the loss of her son.

Mattie chose her words carefully.

"Mrs. Sinclair. Please don't worry about that. William doesn't think of me that way. He's just being kind to a stranger, and trying to protect me because I'm a bit lost. When and if I go, he's not going with me. I don't think that's possible, and I am absolutely sure he would never leave his home and his family." She had no trouble sounding firmly convinced. She said nothing that she didn't truly believe.

Mrs. Sinclair's face relaxed…slightly.

"I do not think you can be fully aware of how fond William has become of you over these past few days, Miss Crockwell, in addition to establishing himself as your knight in shining armor." She paused and smiled kindly, the first such smile that Mattie had seen from her. Suddenly, Mattie saw the woman that William said his mother was capable of being.

"But I think you are right," Mrs. Sinclair continued. "Even were it possible for William to accompany you to your time, he would not leave his estates, or his family. We women are destined to depend upon men for our food and shelter. And as I am a widow, and Sylvie seems determined to become a spinster, we are dependent upon William to provide for us. If William were to"—she seemed to struggle for words—"disappear, the estate would pass to a distant cousin of my husband's, and Sylvie and I would have to find a home elsewhere."

Mattie couldn't bear the image of Mrs. Sinclair and Sylvie holed up in some rat trap somewhere in the slums of London.

"That's not going to happen, Mrs. Sinclair," Mattie said firmly.

Mrs. Sinclair nodded and eyed her pensively.

"And what if you cannot return to your time, Miss Crockwell?"

"Me?" Mattie said as she stalled for time. What of her? She had no earthly idea.

"You don't need to worry about me, Mrs. Sinclair. If that happens, and I hope it doesn't, but if it does, then I'll probably try to find a job as a bookkeeper or maybe a teacher."

"A bookkeeper? A teacher?" Mrs. Sinclair echoed. "I am not aware of any women in these professions. Did you mean a governess?"

Visions of *Jane Eyre* ran through Mattie's mind. "Oh, gosh, no," she said. "Not a governess."

"It is not always an enviable position, I admit," Mrs. Sinclair said sympathetically. "And yet a profession Sylvie might need to pursue one day if she does not marry and William were to abandon his estates. Perhaps even myself. William must marry and produce an heir."

Mattie searched her face to see if she was smiling, but she was not. She was serious. Mattie really couldn't bear the thought of the two women working as governesses. It seemed ludicrous. As for herself, was it too early in the nineteenth century for women teachers? Surely, they had female teachers in the United States in 1825, didn't they? One-room schools?

"I would not wish that on either of you, Mrs. Sinclair," Mattie said. "I am sure William will marry and produce an heir."

"That has been my dearest hope," Mrs. Sinclair sighed. She rose. "Let us return to join Sylvie. She will have grown tired of attending to my correspondence. Perhaps you and she could pay a call on dear Louisa Covington. She is such a lovely young woman."

Mattie clasped her hands behind her back and squeezed her fingers so hard that they hurt. *Dear Louisa Covington.*

She didn't think Mrs. Sinclair had raised Louisa's name deliberately to distress her. The vision of lovely Sylvie acting as a governess prompted Mattie to ask the question.

"Do you intend for William to marry Louisa Covington?"

Mrs. Sinclair hesitated before resuming her step. She directed a sharp eye toward Mattie, who gave the older woman her best blank stare.

"Would that upset you, Miss Crockwell?"

"Me? Oh, no! I'm sure they would get along just fine," Mattie said through her teeth.

"I think they would suit as well, but I am not certain that William sees her as a potential wife."

"At the risk of sounding nosey, have you suggested it to him?"

"I have not." Mrs. Sinclair gave a short laugh. "William is headstrong. He will resist any suggestions I might make in the selection of a wife, and in fact, has already."

"Do you think Louisa wants to marry him?" Mattie seemed almost to relish the painful discussion in some sort of masochistic way.

"I am not sure," Mrs. Sinclair replied. "I thought so at one time, but since the arrival of Mr. Stephen Carver, I am not at all certain she would choose William."

Mattie relished Mrs. Sinclair's response. Yes! Stephen! Mrs. Sinclair's next words caught her off guard.

"I fear the subject of a potential wife for William must be distressing for you, Miss Crockwell."

A hot tear spilled from Mattie's right eye, and she wiped it away hastily.

"No, no. As I told you, William and I don't..." She tried again. "That is, there's nothing..."

"For your sake, Miss Crockwell, if and when you return to the future, I hope there is not."

Mattie fought against further tears as they returned to the house to find Lord Hamilton awaiting Mrs. Sinclair. His sons were engaged elsewhere, he mentioned, otherwise they would have accompanied him to visit Miss Sinclair and Miss Crockwell.

Mattie pled another handy Georgian headache and retreated to the library to hold vigil until William returned. She knew she couldn't exactly hang out in the room that reminded her of William for the next forty-eight hours until his return, but she determined to give it a good try. Sylvie went to pay a call on Louisa, unaccompanied by headachy Mattie.

****

William found her there two days later eagerly anticipating his return. She'd heard the sound of a carriage, not an unusual sound in the busy lives of the social Mrs. and Miss Sinclair, and she hoped it was William.

She smoothed her borrowed rose-colored muslin dress and listened to the sound of his voice greeting servants as he entered the house. Given the need to greet his mother and sister, she doubted he would come to the library any time soon, but she hoped he would make his way there eventually. If he didn't come, she would have to peep out into the hall and appear to nonchalantly pass by when she heard his voice.

The door burst open, startling her.

"Miss Crockwell," William exclaimed. "You are here, just as I imagined you."

Mattie, unsure of what he meant, jumped up.

"William! It's so good to see you." She choked down the rush of emotion in her voice.

He moved to her side to take her hands in his. Mattie hated the cold, clammy feel of her hands, but he didn't grimace.

"It is good to see you as well, Miss Crockwell," William said. He continued holding her hands beyond what even she knew to be appropriate for the era. Maybe he really did have feelings for her, she thought. It hardly seemed likely, though. She was not one of the polished and elegant Georgian women he was used to.

"How was your trip?" she asked.

"Too long," he answered. He ran his thumbs across the back of her hands before releasing her. Unsupported by legs suddenly gone weak, she sank down onto the edge of her chair.

"Have you been well?" he asked as he moved to the side table to pour himself a drink. He offered her one, but she declined, remembering what the strong alcohol had done to her last time.

"Yes. I've been reading a lot, spending a lot of time in your library. I hope you don't mind," Mattie said.

"Not at all," he said as he took a seat across from her. "I am happy to see you using it."

"Oh, good," she murmured. She dropped her eyes from his searching gaze. What was he looking for in her expression? What was she showing? She pressed her lips together and lifted her head.

"You just arrived. Have you seen your mother and Sylvie? I think they're around."

"Are they?" he asked vaguely. He settled back into his chair and regarded her steadily. She squirmed under his gaze. "I came first to the library to see if you were here."

"Oh!" she said. Her breathing felt shallow, and she tried to take a deep breath to steady her nerves without seeming to do so.

Abruptly, William leaned forward again.

"I am so pleased to see that you are still here, Miss Crockwell," he said. "I feared the worst."

Mattie thought she'd die with joy at his words.

"The worst?"

"That you would be gone, back to your time. That we did not have the thirty days we—*I*—hoped for."

Mattie stared at him open mouthed. The man was saying whatever came to his mind, she thought, without the usual reticence of his society.

"William," she began, "I-I don't know what to say. Your mother—"

William set his drink down with a clatter, rose swiftly and pulled her up. She thought he was going to pull her into his arms, but he stopped short and held her hands.

"Miss Crockwell! I have missed you. I hoped I could hold my tongue when I arrived, but I find myself groveling before you like some besotted youth."

"Oh, William," Mattie breathed. "I really, really missed you too. And I promised myself I'd keep my mouth shut as well."

He kissed the back of her hands, and she thought she finally understood the full sense of the word "swoon," as she was just about to do. For a Georgian man probably long gone in her time, his lips were remarkably warm. She wondered briefly if she were still dreaming. This couldn't really be happening to her, could it?

He raised his head and smiled warmly.

"And what did my mother say?" he asked. "I trust she was gracious to you as I asked."

"She was, William," Mattie reassured him. "She is. But she's worried about you. About us."

He nodded.

"She is correct to be worried. I am completely enamored of you."

"What?" Did he mean love? This fast? Mattie seriously doubted that. She knew *she* was in love, but she'd been in love with him for months—in a book.

"William," she said, attempting to reason with him, "Your mother thinks that if I manage to leave on the next full moon, you will try to leave with me." She ignored the pounding in her ears. What possessed her to actually say that? Of course, he wasn't coming with her. This wasn't some fairy tale romance. This was real life! And her hero had a life here in the nineteenth century. She almost laughed at the words "real life."

"But you cannot leave, Mattie," he said as he pulled her hands against his chest. "I will do everything in my power to ensure that you do not leave me."

Mattie's already weakened legs gave way, and she started to sag. William, his face showing alarm, pulled her into his arms.

"Oh, gosh, I'm sorry," Mattie said in a muffled voice, her face pressed against his chest. "My legs are wobbly."

"I think mine are as well." He chuckled as he rested his chin on the top of her head.

Mattie resisted the urge to raise her face to his. If she did, she knew she would be lost. She feared she wouldn't have the willpower to try to get back to her own time. She had no idea what William wanted from her. Surely he wasn't suggesting marriage, was he? After only a few days? She wondered if he wasn't just in love with the idea of being in love with a strange phenomenon—a woman from the future.

"Mattie," he whispered against her hair.

"Yes?"

147

"Will you look at me?"

"Why?" she stalled. Her heart pounded. Surely, he could hear it, feel it against his chest.

"Mattie," he repeated. "Look at me."

Mattie raised her face. He cupped her face in an exquisitely gentle caress, and she closed her eyes against the intimate sincerity in his brown eyes.

Warm lips touched her lips in a gentle kiss. She remembered the feel of his lips, and she thought she might drown in the sensation. His kiss was tender, with an undercurrent of passion that resonated in his body. A tremor ran between them, and William raised his head.

"Mattie, Mattie," he whispered. "What shall we do? What will the future hold for us?"

She buried her face against his chest again.

"I don't know. I don't know," she said.

"If you could, if you can, will you stay with me?"

Vague images of the plague, inadequate medical care, infant mortality and a lifetime without running water bounced around in her mind.

"I can't—" she began when the door flew open.

"William!" Sylvie almost shrieked. "Our mother follows!"

William dropped his arms and took a step back from Mattie. She caught his look of pain and confusion before she turned to look toward the door.

Sylvie entered the room, a shocked expression on her face, albeit with a slight lift of her lips. Mrs. Sinclair followed. Sylvie approached her brother and embraced him, and Mrs. Sinclair, her eyes darting between Mattie and William, offered her cheek for a kiss.

"I wonder that you did not seek us out on your return, William," Mrs. Sinclair said. "Sylvie and I awaited you in the drawing room."

"Forgive me, Mother," William said in a quiet voice. He gave Mattie one last puzzled look before he addressed his mother. His smile was forced. "I stepped into the library on arrival and found Miss Crockwell here." He offered no further excuse.

Mrs. Sinclair took a seat on a nearby chair, as did Sylvie. Mattie, wanting nothing more than to head for the hills, slid back down to her seat. She didn't miss Mrs. Sinclair's assessing look.

"Sylvie, could you ring for tea, please?" Mrs. Sinclair said. Sylvie moved to pull the rope by the door and returned to her seat, a look of curiosity on her face as she looked from Mattie to William. Mattie smiled weakly, and Sylvie returned the smile. William moved to stand by the fireplace, one arm on the mantle in true Georgian fashion.

"I hope your journey went well," Mrs. Sinclair said. "You have arrived just in time for tonight's festivities. Mrs. Covington desires to have a ball in honor of Louisa's birthday, and she most expressly desired you to attend."

William allowed a sigh to escape his lips.

"Another ball," he murmured. "I suppose I must attend, if only for Louisa's sake."

Mattie chewed on her lip. *If only for Louisa's sake.* She kept her eyes lowered, focusing on his well-shined boots, avoiding his gaze. She couldn't stay. Louisa and William belonged in this world. Not her. They would marry, have children, live to be...forty? Forty-five? Mattie swallowed hard. So young! William was already thirty, fairly old for a bachelor in his era. Would he be long lived? She fervently hoped so.

Mattie tried to hold on, to stick it out, but she couldn't. She rose, keeping her eyes on Mrs. Sinclair and Sylvie.

"I'm so sorry. I have a headache. I hope you don't mind if I don't stay for tea."

"Of course, my dear," Mrs. Sinclair said. "Shall I send Jane to you? Perhaps a cold compress?"

"Miss Crockwell, this is your third headache in as many days! Should we send for a physician, Mother?" Sylvie asked. Her look of concern almost made Mattie blurt out *I don't have a headache. I just need to get away. I've been hiding in the library, but now you're all here!* But she held her tongue and shook her head.

"What is this about headaches? Have you been unwell, Miss Crockwell?" William asked, his voice unexpectedly gruff.

"No, no," she muttered as she dipped an awkward curtsy and hurried to the door. "I'm fine. Just a headache." She escaped from the library, and instead of hurrying up the stairs to her room, took the back stairs down to the kitchen with the intention of making her way out to the garden, maybe even farther.

She ran full tilt into Mrs. White, who steadied her. To her dismay, she broke down into tears and threw herself into the cook's arms.

"There, there now, miss. What's this about?" the plump woman asked as she peered at Mattie's face. "Tears? What are they doing to you upstairs? Come sit by the fire and have a cup of tea, miss. You'll feel better." She led Mattie to the chair by the fire, and bustled over to the stove to pour hot water from the kettle.

Mattie held her cold hands out to the fire. Although it was only September, she felt cold, and the fire helped dispel some of her gloom. That, and the healthy dollop of sugar Mrs. White put in her tea. Certain she had hit an instant sugar high, she downed the cup. Mrs. White, who looked as if she were ready to sit and chat, rose to refill Mattie's cup.

"Thank you, Mrs. White. That tastes soooo good."

"A couple healthy teaspoons of sugar are certain to make everything right, miss. Now, tell me what's brought you to such tears. Surely not Master William! I know that boy would never wish to bring a female to tears. Why, when his sister cried on the rare occasion that she scraped her knee or elbow in play, he was the first to administer to her wound and to dry her tears."

Mattie shook her head, the image of young William tending to his sister's injuries warming her heart as the fire warmed her hands.

"No, Mrs. White. He's been very good to me."

"Is it the mistress? I cannot speak against her, mind. She may seem stern on occasion, but she is a kind woman."

Mattie shook her head again and cradled her hot cup. "No, not Mrs. Sinclair. Everyone has been just wonderful to me, Mrs. White."

"My poor girl. What brought on your tears then, your attempt to escape the house through the kitchen?"

"So, you didn't miss that, eh?" Mattie gave her a watery grin.

"No, miss. Few people from upstairs come down to the kitchen for a chat and some tea. Master William is the only one."

"It's complicated, Mrs. White. I don't belong here. You knew I didn't belong here the first night William found me. Nothing has changed." Mattie looked toward the fire. "And I have to wait for the next full moon to go home."

"The next full moon. What nonsense is that?" the older woman asked.

"Miss Crockwell refers to the tides, Mrs. White. The next full moon is when the tides will be advantageous and she can set sail back to America. As you heard, she is most anxious to return." William had entered the kitchen quietly. Both Mattie and Mrs. White jumped at his voice.

Mattie looked up, stricken by the distant look on his face.

Mrs. White rose hastily. "Master William, you frightened us, sneaking in like that. Would you like some tea?"

"No, thank you, Mrs. White. If you do not mind, I shall take Miss Crockwell out to the garden for a spell. Miss Crockwell, if you please?" He bowed and held out an arm toward the door, leaving her in no doubt as to where she would be in the next few minutes.

"Thank you for the tea, Mrs. White," she said softly as she preceded William out the kitchen door.

"I thought you had a headache," he said quietly as he closed the door behind him. Mattie stood uncertainly.

"Not really. I just had to get away."

"From me?" His voice was husky, and Mattie fought the urge to throw herself in his arms. She looked up toward the house, with its seemingly thousands of windows gazing down on them. William followed her eyes.

"Come." He tucked her hand in his and led her around the side of the house and toward a treed area she'd seen previously. Once they entered the protection of the trees, they slowed, and Mattie withdrew her hand.

William stopped to face her.

"Tell me your thoughts, Mattie. Please do not dissemble with me. I value your candor above all."

Mattie looked up at William's beloved face. How could she leave him? How could she stay? She shook her head and dropped her eyes to pace.

"William, I feel the same way about you as you say you do about me—"

"Love?" he interrupted. He stood as still as a statue and watched her.

She paused to look at him. "I think so. It's so hard to think in those terms. We've only known each other a short while. But I've loved you for a long time."

William drew his brows together in confusion and opened his mouth to speak, but Mattie rushed in.

"I know that doesn't make sense. You see, I used to read romance novels. Still do," she said with an embarrassed smile. She avoided looking at him. "And you were in them, William, only your name was Lord Ashton of Sinclair House, not Mr. Sinclair of Ashton House."

"Is this about a title, an earldom?" William's voice took on a haughty note.

"No, no, William, it's not about that at all. The point is, you were in my story, no matter what the title, and I read the book every chance I could get for months, falling in love with you more and more every day. And then for some reason, I was transported here through time…to you." She stopped pacing and looked at him. His face registered confusion. "I don't know what it means, and I'm so grateful I got to meet you in person. So grateful." She took a deep breath as he took a step toward her, and she thrust out a hand to stop him. "But I can't stay here. I can't!" Tears choked her voice. "This is almost two hundred years ago. So much has changed. I don't even know if I can survive here."

Mattie cursed herself for sounding selfish and self-serving, but it was hard to describe the deprivation she would knowingly face in his time. What about children? Their health?

William froze and locked his arms behind his back. She recognized his distant look. He was withdrawing from her, and rightly so. If she were to leave, she would rather leave him with distaste in his mouth than yearning and longing.

"I see," he said quietly. "So, it is your wish to return as soon as possible."

Mattie pressed her lips against a scream. "Yes."

"Then I shall trouble you with my addresses no longer, Miss Crockwell. Forgive me for taking advantage of your vulnerability. Following the ball tonight, I will remove to town once again and shall return the night before the next full moon. I feel certain my presence will be required to counteract this spell you and I have conjured between us—mistakenly, it would appear. You have nothing to fear from me."

He held out his arm without looking at her. "May I escort you back to the house?"

"No," she mumbled against trembling lips. "I'll stay here awhile."

"But madam—" he protested with a look in her direction.

"Just leave me here, William!" she snapped, unable to hold the tears back much longer.

William stiffened, dropped his arm and strode toward the house, his back ramrod straight. Even as he walked away from her in anger, Mattie realized she had it within her power to run after him, tell him she loved him and would stay, and he would forgive her and tell her he loved her.

But she stood her ground, tears pouring down her face.

CHAPTER THIRTEEN

An hour later, finally composed, Mattie slipped back in to the house through the kitchen. Mrs. White turned to see her enter, but Mattie gave her a wan smile and hurried through the kitchen without a word. She managed to get to her room without meeting anyone and threw herself onto the bed to contemplate the coming weeks.

She couldn't imagine staying in the house with William gone, and yet if he stayed, she couldn't imagine seeing him daily while he treated her like a stranger. To see her staunchest ally and the closest person she had to a friend in this century turn from her would be devastating. She wanted nothing so much as to run away, but she had no choices, no money, nowhere to go.

A soft tap on her door startled her, and she held her breath. William? She sat upright but remained silent.

"Miss Crockwell?" Jane opened the door and peeked in. "Oh, you are awake!" She stepped inside the room and closed the door behind her. "Mr. Sinclair said he had seen you come in and that you appeared to go up to your room. Are you well, miss? You look so unhappy." Her sympathetic gaze threatened to send Mattie over the edge again.

Mattie rubbed her temples. "No, I'm fine, Jane, just some lovelorn stuff." She gave the maid a quick grimace. "What's going on downstairs?"

"Dinner is being served. Mr. Sinclair wondered if you wished to join the family or whether you wished to have a tray sent to your room."

Mattie had already figured out in the past few days that "dinner" was a late lunch.

"Oh gosh, Jane, I wish I could stay in here for the next three weeks or so. Do you think I could?" Mattie eyed the young maid with a wan grin.

Jane bit her lips and wrung her hands, and Mattie took pity on her.

"I'm sort of kidding, Jane. Kind of. Should I go downstairs?"

"No, miss, not if you do not want to. It is quite appropriate to take a meal in your room. I'll bring you a tray." Jane turned to leave but paused at the door. "Miss Sylvie asked after you, and expressed her fervent desire that you attend the ball tonight, Miss Crockwell. Shall I bring some clothing by later?"

Mattie dropped back down on her bed. "You've got to be kidding! Do I have to go, Jane?"

"I think you must, miss."

Mattie lifted her head and eyed the maid with sympathy for having such a temperamental charge. "Thank you, Jane. I'll see you when you return."

"Yes, miss." Jane curtsied and left quietly. She returned in twenty minutes with a tray of bread, cheese, fruit and some tea, which she left on the table.

Mattie rose after she left and shuffled over to the settee to pour herself a cup of tea. She sipped a cup of refreshing hot liquid and contemplated the room. Maybe life in the early 1800s wouldn't be so bad if one were wealthy. Jane did most of the work—brought her food, prepared her bath, emptied the disgusting chamber pot, even dressed her. Maybe she could learn to live this way, if William ever consented to forgive her.

As much as she'd loved her historical romance novels, nothing in them had prepared her for the realities of actually living in the nineteenth century. All well and fine for a gal born in the Georgian era, but how did a twenty-first-century woman give up the security of hospitals, over-the-counter female products, neonatal care, cell phones, the internet, anesthesia, a car, the right to vote, movie theaters, antibiotics, popcorn, pain relievers, chlorinated water, flushing toilets, e-mails, ATMs and lattes?

A soft tap on the door caught her attention, and she called "Enter," assuming it was Jane again.

Sylvie slipped in and closed the door quietly. She eyed Mattie with a worried expression.

"Mattie? Are you unwell again? I am concerned about you." She laid a soft hand against Mattie's forehead in a motherly gesture.

Mattie patted her hand and smiled.

"No, Sylvie, I feel fine. I'm so sorry to be such a cause of concern. I hoped that by hiding out in here, no one would notice me or worry about me."

"I have been so busy with my own concerns and appointments that I have not been able to speak with you as I wished, and you have been ill with your headaches. Was my mother severe with you the other day? I do apologize if she was."

"No, no, not at all. She's just worried about William." Mattie clamped her mouth shut. The less she said about that, the better. She didn't want to add to Sylvie's concerns, especially with a suggestion of William abandoning Sylvie, her mother and his estates. Of course, he couldn't do that.

"As we all are," Sylvie said with a frown. "He is not himself. He has always been a bit of a dreamer, but he has seemed much more distracted than usual since your arrival." She blushed. "You know he believes himself in love with you, do you not?"

Mattie bit her lip but didn't answer.

"Well, of course he would, how could he not? You seem a very fine person, interesting, kind and perhaps a bit mysterious. I know my brother, Mattie. Once he sets his sights on something, he will not let go. He is the most determined man." She took Mattie's hand in hers. "Has he declared himself to you?"

Mattie's eyes shifted away from Sylvie's perceptive blue ones. "I'm not quite sure what you mean, Sylvie."

"Do you not?" Sylvie asked with a mischievous smile. "I think you must. Your face reveals all. Did you turn my poor brother down?" Sylvie shook her head. "I suppose that explains why he says he is away to town again for several weeks though he just returned. I suspected as much."

"Well, I don't know if I turned him down exactly. I don't think he asked me a question, but I did tell him that..." Mattie hesitated. Surely she could leave without disparaging their lifestyle any further.

"Yes?"

"I told him I had to return home."

Sylvie's smile drooped. "Oh, dear. Poor William. I cannot imagine. I believe he is quite enamored of you."

Mattie set her teacup down with a clatter, jumped up and began to pace.

"Sylvie, that's just impossible. There are so many other eligible women around here. He doesn't even know me."

"He must feel he does, Mattie, else he would never have committed himself to you."

"He can't *commit* to me!" Mattie paused and stared. "He can't. I have to go."

Sylvie rose and took Mattie's agitated hands in hers. "Please calm yourself, Mattie. I understand, and I apologize if I have added to your concerns. I wish only for William's happiness, and for yours. Is there no chance they can be achieved by the same means? There must be a reason you came to us when you did. It cannot simply be a random happenstance."

Mattie slumped back down onto the settee. "I know, Sylvie. I keep thinking the same thing. It's not that I don't think I wasn't meant to meet William, but..." Again Mattie hesitated. It had seemed much easier to screech at William that she couldn't live in his time than it was to say to tenderhearted Sylvie.

"But?" Sylvie sat down beside her.

"All I can say is that I have to go home, Sylvie. I can't stay. I wish I could explain, but I can't."

Sylvie patted her hand again. "Of course, you must be homesick. I understand, and I am sure that William does as well. He would not ask you to leave the only life you have ever known."

Mattie shook her head but remained silent.

Sylvie turned to eye the clock on the mantle. "You would do well to rest this afternoon. You are coming to the ball this evening, are you not? Please say you will, Mattie!"

Mattie, feeling exhausted by the onslaught of emotions, nodded.

"Good! I shall leave you now. Jane will bring you something of mine to wear."

Sylvie kissed her on the cheek and left the room quietly.

Mattie thought she would scream if she heard one more knock on the door, and yet, she longed to hear William's tap, knowing it would never come.

****

How Mattie got through the ball that night, she would never know. Jane had delivered a beautiful white silk gown with a lace overlay and royal blue ribbons, which Mattie thought probably suited the younger Sylvie better. The carriage ride to the Covington's home with a silent and distant William had been excruciating. He had been unfailingly polite, but avoided her eyes like a stranger on a bus. Mattie mourned the loss of her best friend in this century, and she wondered what her life would be like when she returned to her own century. One thing was certain: she wouldn't be able to return to her dreams of Lord Ashton of Sinclair House anymore. That romantic nonsense was now lost to her, and she was faced with stark reality of the historic details of daily living that the novel conveniently glossed over.

She had never even been to another house before. Where did one go to the bathroom? Did they have a guest privy? Guest chamber pots? She didn't want to know, and determined to avoid the matter until she returned to Ashton House.

From under her lashes, Mattie studied William, sitting across the coach. Dashing in a top hat, black cutaway coat, silver vest and black knee breeches, she thought she could happily stay with him—if only they at least had running water and electricity. Her needs and can't-do-withouts seemed to diminish the closer he came to leaving.

Mattie hadn't been inside the ballroom of the Covington's home for more than a few moments before she started thinking about pleading a headache, but she couldn't very well do that to the family again. The logistics of sending her home in a carriage and then returning for the family seemed unfair to the Sinclairs. She didn't want to dance, didn't know how to dance and felt generally tired of trying to pretend to be someone she wasn't.

With a glass of punch in her hand, she stood by Mrs. Sinclair and watched Sylvie dancing. William had disappeared from sight. Mrs. Sinclair's attention was claimed by Lord Hamilton on her right.

"You look to be under the weather, Miss Crockwell. Are you feeling quite well?" She looked up, startled to see Stephen Carver at her side. She could have rolled her eyes. Stephen was the one person she probably had to be the most diligent at fooling.

"Just tired, Mr. Carver."

"I cannot place your accent, Miss Crockwell. It does not remind me of New York. Did you grow up there?"

Mattie sighed. Why couldn't anyone just leave her alone? At least in her time, she could just wander away casually from an unwanted conversation and hide in the bathroom if necessary. That wasn't going to happen!

"No, I didn't." She realized she'd slipped on a contraction but hardly cared.

"If I may be so bold, Miss Crockwell, I think there is something quite unusual about you, even for an American. At the risk of sounding enigmatic, let me say that if you need a countryman to confide in, please allow me to be at your service." Stephen had leaned in and lowered his voice. At that moment, William came into sight and saw Stephen leaning toward her. He stilled, with narrowed, glittering eyes before turning away abruptly and disappearing into the crowd again.

Mattie could have cried, but she bit down hard on her lip to the point where she tasted blood.

"Miss Crockwell! You are bleeding. Here!" Stephen handed her his handkerchief, and Mattie grabbed it and dabbed at her lip.

"Thank you, Stephen." She turned to look at Mrs. Sinclair, still involved in conversation with Lord Hamilton. She lowered her voice. "Look, you're right. I don't have a New York accent. I'm from the west.

It's complicated, and I can't explain it, but trust me, I *am* American. And I actually *do* need someone to confide in."

Stephen threw a glance in Mrs. Sinclair's direction and bowed. "What can I do?" he asked simply.

"Is there a way we can talk privately? The thing is, I need to leave Ashton House. I'm not due to return to the States—America—for three weeks, but I just don't think I can stay there."

She watched a myriad of expressions cross Stephen's face, from confusion to wariness to suspicion to sympathy.

"Has William offended you in some way, Miss Crockwell?"

"No, it's nothing like that. He's great!" She smiled crookedly in the general direction of the ballroom, unsure of William's exact location. "I just need to talk to someone whom I can trust and who doesn't have a vested interest in what I do. That would be you, I think."

Stephen tilted his head and regarded her but nodded. "I am honored you consider me so. I fear it is difficult to think of somewhere we might speak in private, Miss Crockwell. English customs are much more strict than ours in America, as you know. Do you have a trusted maid who might accompany us on a walk in the garden if I call upon you tomorrow?"

Mattie thought of Jane. "Yes, but won't Mrs. Sinclair and Sylvie insist on walking with us, from what I've seen?"

"Fortunately, my aunt is due to visit Mrs. Sinclair tomorrow. Meet me in the garden at noon with your maid. It seems somewhat clandestine, but I think we will manage to avoid scandal if we are discovered. Surely, they must understand you and I wish to exchange some talk of our mutual homeland. I certainly have mentioned it before."

"Noon," Mattie said in a quiet voice. Stephen bowed and moved away. By noon, William would probably be gone. Would she feel like talking to anyone about anything? And what had she hoped for when she spontaneously asked to talk to Stephen in private? He couldn't buy her a ticket home. Even if he did, it would be to the wrong century!

The rest of the night stretched endlessly. Mattie turned down offers to dance, and hovered near Mrs. Sinclair. Sylvie popped by occasionally to urge her to dance, but Mattie declined. Lord Hamilton's sons attempted to fetch her drinks, but she turned down their offers and coughed as if she had a cold. William did not approach her, not once. She saw him occasionally on the other side of the room. He danced with Louisa Covington only once, she noticed, and appeared to keep to himself for the rest of the evening. She felt as if she were making his life miserable, and she missed the smile on his face.

William continued to keep his eyes averted from her even on the way home. He said nothing as they descended the carriage, only bowing before turning away. Mattie thought at the moment that she could have done without electricity to bring a smile back to his face. But the prospect of chamber pots for the rest of her life brought her up short from her fantasy of begging William to take her back, if indeed he had ever taken her in the beginning.

CHAPTER FOURTEEN

Mattie rose early to the sound of horse's hooves on the ground below. She ran to the window just in time to see William mount his horse and ride away, disappearing in the morning mist down the drive.

She'd suspected he would leave without saying goodbye, but the awful reality of it almost took her breath away, so painful was the feeling. In tears, she slumped to her knees at the foot of the window, hugging herself and rocking back and forth. Vague images of the memory of his cold eyes and flat expression from the night before tore at her heart.

Now, more then ever, she felt she had to leave the house, but the idea terrified her. To be out amongst the general populace of 1825 without a protector—a woman alone in the early nineteenth century? The idea that William would no longer be around to protect her terrified her just as badly.

She allowed Jane to serve her toast and tea in her bedroom, and then dressed with Jane's help in a lovely pale yellow dress of Sylvie's just before noon.

"Jane, I need your help."

"What can I do, Miss Crockwell?" Jane asked as she finished dressing Mattie's hair.

"I need you to come with me to the garden. I have to take a walk, and I need a chaperone."

"Of course, miss, I can accompany you. But a chaperone?" Jane gave her a worried look.

"Well, you'll find out anyway, but I'm going to meet Mr. Stephen Carver."

Jane's eyes rounded, and her hand stilled as she set a pin in Mattie's hair.

"Miss, are you sure? That doesn't sound quite—"

"Proper, I know. Well, it's okay. We're just going to talk about America, and we can speak to each other without the more formal restrictions of Georgian society there. I hope you don't mind. You won't get in trouble, will you?"

Jane shook her head. "No, miss. I do not think so. Mrs. Bailey said I should attend you."

"Good! Are we ready?"

"Yes, miss."

Mattie made it down to the garden only moments before noon, when Mrs. Brookfield and Stephen were expected to arrive. She hoped Mrs. Sinclair or Sylvie wouldn't come looking for her to attend a house call.

She wasn't sure where in the garden Stephen might think to find her, so she headed over to the formal gardens on the side of the house facing away from the drawing room, and she sent Jane over to the front of the house as a lookout so the maid could let Stephen know where she was.

Tippy-toeing around such a massive estate was presenting itself as a complex task, and she wasn't sure she had the imaginative creativity to handle it. What she would give to be able to text Stephen on her cell phone at the moment, or even William for that matter, just to let him know she thought of him and to ask him to understand and forgive her.

She wandered through the gardens, nervous about being in full view of anyone in the house except those on the front side such as the drawing room. Jane hurried back within ten minutes.

"I am certain that Mr. Carver saw me as he descended the carriage," she said. "I gestured in this direction, and I believe he understood the message. He nodded before he handed Lady Brookfield down."

"Thank you, Jane!" Mattie said. "Let's sit for a moment." She seated herself on a bench. "What I have to say to Mr. Carver is private, though, so…" Mattie looked at the maid with a cheesy smile.

"I shall stay out of hearing but within view, miss," Jane said.

"You're a pal, Jane, you really are."

Jane scrunched her forehead inquiringly, but at that moment, Stephen came into view. He strode confidently across the lawn, not appearing in the least concerned whether he was discovered. With a nod to Jane, he tipped his hat to Mattie as he approached her and took a seat. Jane moved away to wander the paths.

"Alone at last," Stephen said with a pleasant smile.

"Please don't get the wrong idea, Stephen," Mattie warned.

"Not at all, Miss Crockwell. At any rate, my interests are fixed, as I think are yours."

Mattie thought she understood what he meant.

"You mean Louisa Covington?"

Stephen jerked his head in her direction and nodded sheepishly.

"Am I so transparent?"

"Yes, you are, actually," Mattie smiled. "How does she feel about you?"

He looked down as if to study the ground. "I am not certain. Marriage to me would involve a very long journey. I enjoy England, but America is my home and where I wish to live. That I have fallen in love with an Englishwoman is ironic." He looked at her quickly and straightened. "But we are not here to discuss my affairs. How may I assist you, Miss Crockwell?"

Now that the moment was here, Mattie was reluctant to tell Stephen about the time traveling. There was always a danger that someone would haul her away.

She looked down at her hands, lacing and unlacing her fingers together.

"I need to leave this house, to find somewhere to live for the next three weeks, but I can't tell you why." She looked up at him with a hopeful expression. "I wondered if you had any ideas. I'm absolutely penniless—in fact, the clothes on my back were loaned to me by Sylvie."

Stephen reared his head back with a startled look. "Penniless? And no clothes of your own? Goodness, Miss Crockwell, what has befallen you?"

"Would you believe I stowed away aboard a ship? That I'm actually from the working class in the United States?" Mattie thought the stowing-away part was very clever.

"A stowaway? I cannot imagine how arduous that must have been. And why would you wish to stowaway aboard a vessel to come to England?"

"Oh, I don't know," she shrugged. "A silly idea."

Stephen regarded her with a puzzled face. "I must confess, Miss Crockwell, that your tale lacks a certain…conviction. And you tell me that you must leave the house, but cannot say why, for three weeks."

Mattie's cheeks burned. It was difficult being called a liar, especially when she was one.

"I know, I'm sorry, but I really can't tell you much of the truth. What I can tell you is that I have fallen in love with William, and I really can't, so I have to leave."

"That is certainly frank, Miss Crockwell. From what I have seen, I think William may share your affections. Why must you leave? I was under the impression from your conversation last night that he had done nothing to offend you. Has the family discovered your situation, your status, and asked you to leave?"

"No, they actually know about me and have taken care of me. And they know I have to leave in three weeks. Oh, gosh, listen to me. They sound perfect! How could I walk out on them without so much as a thanks?"

"I am certain you would thank them, Miss Crockwell, but I must admit I still do not understand the dilemma. However, if you feel you must leave, I can loan you the necessary funds to travel to and secure quarters in Southampton until the sailing of your ship. I do so with misgiving, Miss Crockwell, as it is not at all proper, nor safe for you to travel alone either to Southampton or back to America. Is there no other recourse?"

Mattie colored at his offer of money, but frankly, that was probably just what she needed most. Money and courage. The idea of hanging out in Southampton, wherever that might be, didn't appeal to her. She felt she was only digging herself deeper in a time-traveling hole.

"Oh, gosh, Stephen. What a generous offer, but the thing is, I'm not going to Southampton. Please don't ask me to explain. I can't." Mattie winced under his look of confusion. What was she thinking? She didn't even know what she wanted from the man.

"You know what? This was a mistake." Mattie rose hastily. "I shouldn't have pulled you into this. That was silly of me. I'll be fine here."

Stephen jumped up to join her, and took her hands in his. "Please forgive me if I have failed you in any way, Miss Crockwell. It is my desire to assist you, but you have not told me what I could do to help."

"I know. You've been great." Mattie almost hugged him but remembered where she was and pulled back. She gently withdrew her hands. "Because I can't explain, it makes everything more difficult. I'm just a foolish girl in love with the wrong man at the wrong *time*, and I'm trying to run from it, instead of just survive it. That's probably the crux of the matter. I need to just buck up and deal with it. This won't last forever." She sighed and looked toward the house.

"If there is anything you think I can do to help you, Miss Crockwell, please let me know. Short of inviting you to stay with my aunt, which would be thought unusual and would elicit comment, I do not know how else I could remove you from the house. I understand the pain of unrequited love, Miss Crockwell, though as I mentioned I did not think that was the case between you and William."

"Have you ever told Louisa how you felt? Asked her if she would consider moving to America with you?"

"No, I have not." Stephen grimaced as he looked down at the ground. "I did not wish to ask that which might make her unhappy."

"You'll never know unless you ask, Stephen," Mattie said. "I could find out how she feels. I don't want to worry you, but I think some folks plan for her to marry William."

Stephen's head shot up. "Ah! So you have heard. I did not wish to mention it to you and thought perhaps that might be the reason you wished to leave." He frowned. "I am not at all certain William shares that hope. How could he if he is enamored of you?"

Mattie smiled. "Hmmm. Well, I know she has thought of marrying William, but she didn't sound too enthusiastic about it either. She seems to be just kind of accepting of the idea. Maybe she's not in love with him." Over his shoulder, Mattie saw Jane check the watch pinned to her dress.

"I think Jane is telling me we have to go," Mattie said. "I appreciate your offer of help, Stephen, but I think the only thing I can do is stick it out for the next three weeks until I leave." She held up a hand to his inquiring face. "Don't ask! But in the meantime, you and I could figure out how Louisa feels about you, and if she'd be willing to go with you. This isn't about separating her from William, because I don't think she's that invested in a future with him." Jane moved toward the front of the garden.

"I'd better go, Stephen. Wait for a few minutes before you follow me into the house."

Stephen took her hand and bent over it. "Remember, I am always at your service. You have left me with more questions than answers about your origins, Miss Crockwell, but we Americans have always been a mysterious, independent sort, have we not? Good day."

Mattie followed Jane back to the house through the kitchen, with a wave to Mrs. White on the way. Jane headed off to her duties, and Mattie had just reached the stairs in the foyer with a plan to sprint up the stairs to her room when the front door opened. She turned around expecting to see Stephen, but it was William who entered. He handed his hat and coat to John and raised his eyes to see her. Mattie froze under his gaze, suddenly warm. His face brightened into a loving smile.

"Miss Crockwell, I am so glad to see you are still here."

****

At the sight of Mattie, the constriction, which had gripped William's heart ever since he walked away from her the previous day, eased. He simply could not force himself to remain angry with her any longer, and in the absence of anger, he had only sorrow and happiness left to him—

sorrow at her choice to leave, and happiness that he had the opportunity to meet her and know love.

He had ridden away in the early morning hours with the express intention of spending the next three weeks at his hunting lodge in York, but he got no farther than the first inn along the road before he realized he could not bear to be separated from Mattie.

He had returned posthaste, fearful that she would refuse to speak to him again. But here she was on the staircase before him, lovely in a pale yellow dress with high color in her cheeks. Did she blush to see him?

"William," she said with a catch in her breath. "You're back!" She seemed frozen on the staircase; her hand gripped the banister.

William hoped the emotion clearly apparent in her voice was joy to see him.

"Miss Crockwell, I must speak to you in private," William said urgently. "I hope you can forgive me—"

He swung around at the sound of the front door opening, surprised to see Stephen Carver opening the door unannounced. John jumped forward to close the door behind Stephen, who stopped short at the sight of William. His eyes traveled toward Mattie on the staircase.

"William! You are back!"

Stephen's words echoed Mattie's, and William looked between the two, both of whom stared at him. Something about Stephen set his teeth on edge at the moment, but William could not decipher the origin of his distrust. How did Stephen know he had left? He clenched his jaw and narrowed his eyes as he addressed Stephen.

"I did not hear your knock, Carver," William said with frosty politeness.

"I had just stepped out for a breath of fresh air. My aunt is visiting with Mrs. Sinclair and Miss Sinclair."

William nodded. "I see," he said, though he did not. He had thought Stephen enamored of Louisa, but the way Stephen's eyes strayed toward Mattie at the moment and the look that passed between them gave him concern. William took a deep breath. He had resolved to treasure the time he had left with Mattie, and he was determined to do just that.

"I hope you enjoyed your walk," William said. "I have just arrived myself and did not realize your aunt was visiting. Shall we join them?" He held his hand out to Mattie, who descended the steps with a look of dread on her face. He smiled at her reassuringly. John opened the drawing room door, and they entered the room.

"William!" Sylvie said with enthusiasm. "You have returned!"

William returned his sister's kiss, wondering how many more people would echo those words.

"Yes, my business resolved itself," he murmured inconsequentially. He had left with only a note for his mother stating he was retiring to his hunting lodge for a period, and had made no mention of business, but a pointed look at Sylvie silenced any questions she had.

"Welcome back, William," his mother said quietly. She eyed Mattie and Stephen and himself with a careful expression. "Miss Crockwell, you look well today. Stephen, I hope you found the gardens to your liking. Will you take tea now?"

William exerted great effort to avoid speculating about Mattie and Stephen as they took tea with Mrs. Brookfield, but throughout the visit, he caught several undecipherable looks pass between them. As soon as Mrs. Brookfield and Stephen had left, he slipped the women's company and headed to his library with a vague reference to attending to matters of the estate. He was in no mood to discuss his precipitous return with his mother or Sylvie, but could find no excuse to waylay Mattie without drawing undue attention.

He poured himself a drink and perched on the edge of his desk to stare out the windows onto the grounds, mulling over various ways of gaining access to Mattie for private conversation.

He cursed at the knock on his door. Apparently, his excuses had not been enough to dissuade his family from seeking him out.

"Yes," he said, his voice exasperated. He turned and straightened hastily when Mattie slipped into the room. His first instinct was to stride toward her and take her in his arms, but he fought the urge. Words were the wisest course at the moment, not potentially unwelcome displays of physical affection.

"Miss Crockwell!" He indicated she should take a seat. "May I offer you something to drink?"

Mattie shook her head. She kept her eyes on the general area of his chest, avoiding his eyes, and it pained him. Had he brought her to this? Taken the laughter from her? He sat down across from her.

"I have been thinking of various ways to see you, to talk to you in private, but here you are, having arrived at the most sensible solution."

"I hate the way we parted," Mattie said. She raised her eyes to his, and he saw unshed tears.

"As do I," William said softly. "No more tears, Mattie. I vowed I would not badger you any further in the matter of staying or returning. This is what I wished to convey to you as soon as I arrived but was prevented from doing so by my mother's guests. I left this house in such misery, selfishly so, knowing full well that you suffered too. And yet I could not rise above my own grief to tend to your discomfort. For that, I most abjectly apologize. Please forgive me, Mattie." He rushed on lest he forget the most salient point. "I love you and I wish you to remain, but I understand completely if you feel you cannot. Things must have changed very much over the centuries that come between us, and I cannot in all conscience ask you to give up the life you have known, let alone your country, to remain here with me."

His heart ached to see tears flowing freely down his dear love's face as she gripped her hands tightly, but she needed to hear the words. He himself would have gladly prostrated himself and wept like a child if he could. He rose, kneeled down before her on one knee and pried one of her cold hands loose to bring it to his lips. He pulled a handkerchief from his pocket and handed it to her.

"Do not cry, my love. We still have a fortnight and more to enjoy each other." He held his breath. "If you still feel the same as I do?"

Mattie wiped at her face with his kerchief and nodded. She pushed herself to the edge of her chair and wrapped her arms around William's neck.

"I do! I do! I love you, William, and I don't want to leave you, but—"

William lifted his head and covered her mouth with his own before whispering against her lips.

"You need explain no further, my love. I understand. Let us enjoy the time that remains."

****

Over the next few weeks, they did exactly that. William remained at Mattie's side throughout the numerous dances and balls the family was required to attend, giving rise to comment and speculations regarding his intentions. His mother remonstrated with him on a continuing basis, but he advised her that he cared not a whit for the opinions of others, and that he would not deny himself the pleasure of Miss Crockwell's company while she remained in their time.

He was not always able to seat himself next to her at the various dinners they attended, however, and it was at one of these that he gritted his teeth when she was seated next to Stephen Carver at a dinner given by Mrs. Covington. Stephen and Mattie greeted each other as old friends, and he wondered how their friendship had come to pass. It seemed to be more than just fellow compatriots sharing a few stories. Mattie had given him no cause for jealousy, and yet he felt jealous nonetheless. He watched Louisa across the table from Stephen, eyeing them with an expression of sadness, and he resolved to speak to Mattie as soon as possible. That opportunity presented itself shortly after the men joined the women for an evening of cards.

William managed to maneuver Mattie away from the general

conversation. He wasted few words given that the room was small and their tête-à-tête would soon be interrupted.

"Mattie, I wonder if you are aware of Miss Covington's regard for Mr. Carver."

Mattie turned surprised eyes on him. "I *had* noticed, William. I didn't know you had."

"I have known Louisa all my life, and she is not able to hide much from me. However, the expression of unhappiness on her face at dinner is not one I wish to see again. You and Stephen seemed very cozy, and I imagine she thinks you have a fondness for one another." He swallowed hard on the words.

"Well, good!" Mattie surprised him by saying. "Maybe she'll get off her duff and pay attention to him. At least, that was my plan. I offered to talk to her and ask her how she felt about him, but I haven't seen much of her." Mattie looked in Louisa's direction. "Maybe I'll go ask her now."

"Your plan? I am not certain what 'get off her duff' means, but I can infer, my dear. What do you mean 'your plan'?"

"I talked to Stephen several weeks ago, the day you came back as a matter of fact, and I volunteered to talk to Louisa. He's in love with her, and he wants her to go back to America with him, but he doesn't think she will."

"So, you have become a matchmaker?"

Mattie grinned, something she had been doing often of late. Like him, she seemed to have put away her grief for the moment. His heart thrilled to the brightness of her smile.

"I thought I might. I'm going to tackle this thing between Sylvie and Thomas too."

"Oh, my dear. I wish you well with that. So, you and Stephen are not…" William struggled for words.

"In love?" Mattie offered. "No, I'm in love with *you*."

William's face heated, and he coughed behind his hand. "Miss Crockwell, how brazen of you!" He returned her smile with one of affection. "Do not ever change."

"You say the nicest things, William," Mattie said softly. She looked over her shoulder to where Louisa sat on the sofa and drank tea while others played cards.

"I'm going in," she said as she sailed off.

CHAPTER FIFTEEN

"Louisa, I wondered if I might talk to you," Mattie said as she slipped onto the sofa next to Louisa. Mattie noted that Stephen, playing cards, watched her with an alarmed expression. She wasn't sure if he really wanted her to talk to Louisa or not, but folks in the Georgian era rarely seemed to say what they truly meant, so she decided to move things along.

"Certainly, Miss Crockwell. I hope you are enjoying your stay?" Louisa's smile was not as wide as Mattie had seen it, and Mattie knew she needed to clear the air as soon as possible.

"It's wonderful. I'll be going home to America soon." Mattie hated to say the words, but they seemed like a good opening for a difficult conversation. "What do you think of America? Have you ever been there?"

Louisa looked taken aback for a moment, but she quickly schooled her face into an expression of polite interest.

"No, I have not. Mr. Carver returns soon as well, I think."

"Does he? I didn't know that. Have you ever thought about visiting America?"

Louisa shook her head. "No, not in reality." Louisa's gaze traveled to Stephen, but she quickly looked away when she saw Stephen watching them. Mattie watched the exchange with a sigh.

"What if..." This wasn't as easy as she'd thought.

"Yes, Miss Crockwell?"

Mattie forged on. "What if you fell in love with someone who lived in America? Would you consider moving there?"

Louisa's eyes rounded. She opened her mouth to speak and closed it again. She took a hearty sip of tea. Mattie looked over her shoulder toward William with a pained expression.

"No, I have not contemplated such a thing, Miss Crockwell. No more than I have contemplated marrying a Frenchman or an Italian." Louisa's pink cheeks were indecipherable. Was she mad? Embarrassed? Mattie hoped she wasn't blowing it, for Stephen's sake.

"It's a beautiful country, Louisa. Stunning." Mattie stalled as she pondered other tactics.

"Yes, I am sure it is. I have heard Mr. Carver speak of it."

A full-frontal assault was required. Mattie threw one more look over her shoulder toward William who watched with a small smile of support.

"Ah, yes! Mr. Carver," Mattie said. "Yes. Well, that's what I really wanted to talk to you about."

"I did not realize you and Mr. Carver were so…well acquainted, Miss Crockwell, but it would appear that you are."

"We're not," Mattie said with a tilt of her head. "We're just fellow Americans."

"Yes, of course," Louisa said with a look that suggested she thought otherwise.

Mattie took a deep breath. Here goes!

"Look, Louisa, the thing is…Stephen is in love with you." Mattie let it go and waited for the reaction.

Louisa gasped, and her eyes flew to Stephen, whose attention had been captured by the game once again.

"Miss Crockwell! That is a very bold statement. How can you possibly know such a thing?"

"Well, one look at him says it all, but as it happens, he told me so."

"He told you? I find it odd that he should discuss such a thing with you before addressing himself to me." Louisa stiffened as if she was affronted. These people and their rules, Mattie thought. Argh!

"Well, I asked him," she shrugged. "I've seen him watching you, and I suspected he was in love with you. So, I asked."

Louisa looked at Stephen once again, her cheeks rosy. "And he told you he was?"

"Yes. I think though that he hasn't said anything because he thinks you wouldn't want to go with him to America." Mattie felt she had said way too much, but she wasn't sure that Stephen or Louisa would follow up. It seemed like some of the romances in Jane Austen's Georgian-era books took forever to develop given the era's propensity to *observe the niceties* above all else and to treat strong emotion as a less than desirable trait. But then, Stephen was American. Maybe American societal mores were already different in this era.

Louisa turned back to Mattie and pressed her lips together. Mattie winced. She *had* said too much! Drat!

"*If* I were in love with my husband, I would follow him to his home. That is our custom," Louisa said serenely, as if she spoke of an abstract future subject. Mattie stared at her.

"Really?" Mattie breathed.

Louisa cleared her throat and took another sip of her tea. Her eyes strayed toward Stephen, still engaged by his partner in conversation. "Yes, of course."

"So, are you saying you feel the same way about Stephen?"

Mattie saw Louisa swallow hard, and her chest heaved as she took in a deep breath. She looked at Mattie and blinked.

"Yes, Miss Crockwell. I surprise myself by disclosing to you that I do, in fact, feel the same." Her lips curved softly.

Mattie glanced over her shoulder toward William, resisting an urge to throw him a thumbs-up signal. He must have seen something in her face because he smiled broadly. She grinned back and returned her attention to Louisa.

"Will you tell him?" Mattie nodded toward Stephen.

"I am afraid I cannot. Mr. Carver must initiate such a discussion."

"I'll tell him if you want," Mattie offered. Otherwise, it wasn't going to get done, was it?

Louisa chuckled. "You cannot simply walk up to Mr. Carver and declare my undying love for him, Miss Crockwell. We are not so hasty in these matters."

"No, no, of course not. I won't," Mattie promised. Well, of course she was going to.

Louisa nodded and lowered her eyes to her tea.

Mattie spun her head toward Stephen, willing him to look up so she could communicate nonverbally. Luckily, he did look up at that moment. His eyes traveled to Louisa first, and Mattie almost jumped up and waved to get his attention. She did raise an abrupt hand to her hair, startling Louisa. Stephen met her eyes, and she gave him a slight, almost imperceptible nod. His face broke out into a bright smile, and he looked away to speak to his partner.

"Miss Crockwell, did you just signal Mr. Carver?" Louisa said in a strident hiss.

"Well, yes, I think I did," Mattie said with a beaming smile. Stephen rose from the table. "I think I'll just go talk to William over there."

"Miss Crockwell, you must stay!" Louisa whispered, her eyes flying toward Stephen, who approached.

"No, I'm sorry, I wish I could, but William is calling me." Mattie rose swiftly and moved toward William.

"Well played, my dear," William said quietly as she sprinted to his side. "I stand in awe of your skills." They watched as Stephen took a seat beside Louisa and she poured him a cup of tea.

"Thank you. I've always been a bit of a matchmaker. Did it all the time in high school. Made up for never being able to get a date myself."

Mattie looked up to see William staring at her with a perplexed expression.

"I do not have the faintest idea what you said, my love, but if you are suggesting you had few suitors when you were in the schoolroom, I should certainly hope that was the case."

Mattie shook her head with a smile and turned to watch her handiwork as the couple spoke together.

****

Their engagement was announced a week later, a week in which Mattie reveled in William's company on drives, horseback rides, picnics and walks—always with a chaperone, either Sylvie or Jane, but occasionally with Louisa and Stephen as their courtship progressed. In that week, Mattie had studied Sylvie around Thomas as well, and she concluded that the key to Sylvie and Thomas' happiness was for Sylvie to do as Louisa did—accompany Thomas to America. She wondered, though, how Mrs. Sinclair might take the loss of her only daughter.

She tucked her hand in William's arm as they followed the foursome of Sylvie, Thomas, Louisa and Stephen around the path by the lake after a picnic one day. Sylvie seemed to have relented and walked beside Thomas, but they continued to behave as strangers.

"William, you agree with me that Sylvie and Thomas are in love, don't you?"

"Yes, my dear, I do." William smiled and looked down at Mattie's upturned face.

"What if the solution for them was for Sylvie to go with Thomas on his adventures? What if she, like Louisa, agreed to accompany Thomas to America? How would your mother take that?"

William looked toward the foursome ahead of them and sighed.

"Not very well, I am afraid. She would miss Sylvie terribly. Additionally, there is the issue of grandchildren. Would they grow up English or as Americans?"

"Not to mention she wouldn't get to see them very often," Mattie murmured. "Does it matter whether they grow up English or American? Are we really so different?"

"Not in my opinion, but I believe my mother feels the cultures are very different."

"I hope she's not comparing me to other Americans of your era. I don't know how other Americans in this era act, but it's far different from how we behave in the twenty-first century, no matter what country one lives in."

"I cannot say, dear one. My mother, of course, was also a child during the Rebellion, and there were the more recent rumblings in 1812 regarding Canada. There is always some animosity, some mistrust for the colonies in members of that generation."

Mattie shook her head. "Gosh, sometimes I feel like I'm way out of my league. To hear the American Revolution called the Rebellion. It was all so long ago. The way we learn about the revolution and the War of 1812 as children is that Americans were patriots wanting independence and the red coats, the British, were oppressors." She peered up at William's face to see if she offended him.

"I see that you worry about my sensibilities in this matter, Mattie. Do not. I feel no proprietary claim for America, save for one American, and do not harbor grudges over past conflicts."

"I'm glad."

"I am pleased to hear you say so, dearest."

****

Mattie sought Sylvie out in her bedroom that afternoon before the evening's engagement.

"Sylvie? I wondered if I could talk to you?" Mattie said when Sylvie called to enter.

Sylvie, lovely in a pink wrapper, set her teacup down and rose.

"Mattie! I am so glad you have come. I have been pondering a matter about which I think only you can advise me." She took Mattie's hands and pulled her down to the settee where she'd been sitting.

Mattie surveyed Sylvie's face. Her cheeks were high with color, and her normally guileless blue eyes flickered away. Unusually knitted brows replaced her normally sunny expression, and she chewed on her lower lip.

Mattie gave Sylvie's hands a gentle squeeze. Her planned matchmaking efforts would have to wait for another day. Sylvie was troubled about something.

"What is it, Sylvie?"

Sylvie seemed to take a deep breath.

"Thomas wants to go to America with Stephen and Louisa when they leave." A single tear slipped down Sylvie's face.

Mattie, taken aback that Sylvie had raised the very subject she'd come to talk to her about, struggled for words. This time she'd practiced what she was going to say, as she had not with Louisa, but the words seemed hollow at the grief in Sylvie's face.

Sylvie clutched Mattie's hands tighter.

"I am afraid he will never return this time," she whispered in a strangled voice. "He has asked me to marry him, to go to America with him. I cannot leave my mother. How can I leave everything I have ever known to go to a wild, untamed country?"

Mattie, unsure of Sylvie's reaction, put her arm around the younger girl. Sylvie, at first rigid, relaxed against Mattie's shoulder.

"Forgive me, Mattie, I did not mean to disparage your country, but I am so afraid," Sylvie said on a sob. She broke down then, and cried while Mattie held her. Sylvie was right. Mattie probably did have a better understanding for what Sylvie felt than others. After all, she'd left not only her century, but her country. England *was* different. It didn't matter that they spoke a common language. At times, the language was no more recognizable to her than French might be.

"I understand, Sylvie. I understand," Mattie said soothingly.

Sylvie's sobs slowed. "Yes, I thought you might," she said with a shaky smile. "I love Thomas, you see. I have loved him all my life, ever since I was a child. And I know he has always loved me." She straightened and pulled a handkerchief from a pocket in her wrapper. "But this adventurous spirit of his. I fear I cannot live up to it. I fear I will disappoint him, Mattie."

Mattie waited. Sylvie seemed to have more to say.

"My mother knows how I feel about Thomas, and she has never discouraged me. Yet I feel she would be devastated if I were to leave. She has never expressly stated such, but a daughter knows these things."

She reached for her teacup, and stopped abruptly, turning to Mattie with dismay. "Forgive me, Mattie. I did not offer you tea. Shall I ring for another cup?"

Mattie shook her head. "No, thank you. Go on with what you were saying."

"I think William would encourage me to go with Thomas," she said. "But I lack the adventurous spirit which possesses Thomas. Tell me about America, Mattie. I know the America Thomas travels to must be far different from yours, but tell me what you can."

For the next hour, Mattie told her as much as she could, both in a historical and modern sense. She avoided describing too much about present-day technology, but discussed customs and traditions—at least, those that seemed to have existed for the last century or so. She described the beauty of the United States, with its mountains, oceans, deserts, lakes and rivers.

Sylvie asked questions often, and Mattie struggled to find the appropriate answers. Sylvie chuckled, some of her normally happy disposition returning. "I know you are telling me all that is good in your country, Mattie, and dispensing with anything which might discourage me, and I accept this. My apprehension has lessened now than when we first spoke. And if Louisa is there, I shall already have a friend. I do not know, though, how my mother will fare." Sylvie sighed. "Still, William will be here. He will produce an heir and secure the future of Ashton House, ensuring that my mother continues to have a home."

She gave Mattie a sly look, her cheeks taking on a rosy hue.

"Perhaps this is something you will be part of, Mattie?"

Mattie blinked.

"What?" She knew what Sylvie was asking, but preferred to stall.

"You and William," Sylvie pressed. She covered Mattie's hand with her own. "I thought...there was affection between you. These past few weeks..."

Mattie swallowed hard. "There is, Sylvie. There is."

Sylvie's face brightened.

"Then you will stay? Has William made you an offer?"

Mattie shook her head. "No."

Sylvie's lips drooped.

"No to which? You will not stay? Or William has not made you an offer? I cannot believe the latter is true. William is quite infatuated with you. It is apparent to all. I know he cares not a whit for your origins or connections."

"I can't stay, Sylvie," Mattie squeaked out. "I'm sorry."

"Oh, Mattie!" Sylvie cried. "It is I who must apologize for haranguing you so. No, of course, you must return home if that is your desire. Is there a chance you can return?"

Mattie shook her head again. "I have no idea." She hadn't even thought of that. Could she return? Even now, she wasn't sure she could get back home.

It was Sylvie who now consoled Mattie with a gentle embrace.

"I see this is a difficult subject for you. Forgive me, Mattie. I think it must be time to dress for dinner. I cannot keep you any longer, though I feel I must have many more questions. Thank you for your counsel regarding my own future."

She rose with Mattie and followed her to the door.

"Regardless of what may occur in the future, Mattie, I shall always consider you a good friend and a sister." She planted a kiss on Mattie's cheek.

****

William found it difficult to keep his attention on his dinner companions, so desirous was he of private conversation with Mattie. His mother had all but given up on the proprieties regarding a chaperone for Mattie in William's company, and had resorted to treating Mattie as the distant cousin they had declared her to be.

He had no special information he wished to impart to Mattie, but simply wished to bask under her smile and the light in her eyes. The passage of time had flown over the past few weeks, and less than one week remained until the next full moon. He had promised Mattie he would not entreat her further to remain with him, and he had honored his word, though he could not count the times he had wished he could plead with her yet again.

As if Mattie knew he thought of her, she raised her eyes and favored him with a smile of affection. Hardly appropriate at the dinner table in such a large gathering, but he cared not. They had little time left for artifice.

William returned her smile, hoping she would be available to join him in the library at evening's end, or perhaps a walk in the moonlight. No, he thought, not the moonlight. The time for her departure approached, but had not yet arrived. He dared not risk any premature time-traveling adventures.

A tinkling of a glass at the end of the table caught his attention, and he turned toward Lord Hamilton who stood, his glass of champagne held high as if in toast. Beside him, his mother kept her eyes discreetly lowered, but the unusual fiery red color of her cheeks concerned him. What had Lord Hamilton said to her to bring such strong emotion to her normally controlled countenance?

"If I may." Lord Hamilton's voice boomed over the guests. "An announcement!"

The crowd quieted and turned toward him.

"I have the happy honor to announce that Mrs. Sinclair has consented at long last to become my wife, the future Lady Hamilton!"

William drew in a sharp breath as the sound of surprised exclamations and several titters was heard. His mother raised her eyes and looked directly at him, and then to Sylvie a distance down the table. She returned her gaze to William's face, an unexpected vulnerability showing in her eyes.

William grabbed his glass and jumped up.

"Hear, hear!" he said, silencing the comments. "Many happy felicitations!" The guests rose in unison and raised their glasses. "Hear, hear."

Lord Hamilton took his seat once again, his cheeks almost as bright as those of William's mother. She threw William a look of gratitude, and he met her eyes with a curious tilt of his head and a smile but no more. Truth be told, he found himself stunned by the news, never supposing that his mother would really accept Lord Hamilton or a removal from Ashton House.

As his mother turned her attention back to Lord Hamilton, William tore his eyes from the scene and looked toward Mattie, who watched him with wide eyes. Aware that several guests studied him discreetly to assess his reactions, he dared not show blatant emotion on his face, but he gave her a reassuring nod.

So, he was to be left alone with the estate. It was unclear if Sylvie would go with their mother or with Thomas, as they seemed very intimate that evening, but she would soon leave. Of that, William was certain.

And Mattie would leave as well, sooner than his mother or Sylvie. He studied the length of the dining room—the long table festooned with flower arrangements, glowing white porcelain place settings and stemware, the guests immaculately dressed in starched shirts and dark coats as well as colorful dresses and hair adornments, the portraits of ancestors covering the walls and the six crystal chandeliers which cast a warm glow over the festivities.

There would be no more dinner parties in the house once his mother removed to Lord Hamilton's estate and Sylvie followed Thomas to wherever he might go next. No more balls, no more card parties. He did not regret the notion, but reflected on the concept almost dispassionately.

Still, he would miss the women in his life—his mother, Sylvie and Mattie. He wondered how often he would slip into the kitchen to find comfort in a warm cup of tea with Mrs. White.

A sudden thought occurred to him, and he returned his gaze to Mattie, her attention now captured by the older gentleman sitting beside her. If his mother were in Lord Hamilton's hands, and Sylvie removed with Thomas, what would prevent him from attempting to return to Mattie's time with her? His heart thudded against his chest. Surely, there must be some way he could turn the estate over to a manager, perhaps even put the house up to let. The latter idea galled him, but the gist of the matter intrigued him.

The dinner seemed interminable following Lord Hamilton's announcement. It was several hours later when the family was finally able to speak in private, the guests and Lord Hamilton having gone home.

His mother sat on the sofa, Sylvie beside her. He had asked Mattie to await him in the library, and she had consented.

"You can imagine what a surprise this is, Mother," William said unnecessarily.

"Yes," she replied briefly. William and Sylvie waited, but their mother laced and unlaced her fingers in an uncharacteristically nervous manner.

"But Mother? I thought you had sworn off marriage," Sylvie said.

"Such vulgar language, Sylvie, please." Her mother smoothed an imaginary wrinkle in her skirt.

William surprised himself with his next question. "Do you love him?" A flowery sentiment to be sure, but loving a woman from the future had indelibly changed him.

His mother's cheeks brightened, and she threw a quick glance at her son.

"I surprise myself by saying this, but yes, I do."

"Mother! How delightful!" Sylvie said. She hugged their mother impulsively.

"I am so pleased for you, Mother," William said in a more restrained fashion. "Lord Hamilton is a fine man. I have always thought so."

"As have I, dearest." Their mother almost beamed...almost. "I apologize for not discussing the matter with you children beforehand, but Lord Hamilton—Jonathan—was so beside himself with the news, just decided this evening, that he could not wait to announce it. Perhaps he fears I will change my mind." She smiled playfully.

"When do you intend to hold the wedding, Mother?" Sylvie asked.

"We do not see any reason for delay, and we have discussed marrying as soon as the banns are posted, perhaps in a fortnight."

"So soon," William murmured. In a fortnight, Mattie would be gone. Too soon.

"Yes, will that present any difficulties, William? If I am not mistaken, I hear a bereft note in your voice."

He returned her wide smile. "Not at all, madam. I do not cling to my mother's apron strings."

She laughed, an unusually light-hearted sound.

"Sylvie shall still remain here, will you not? Or do you wish to remove with me to Hamilton Place?"

"As it happens, I have news of my own," Sylvie murmured. "Thomas has asked me to marry him, and I have consented!"

"At long last!" William commented without surprise. Their broad smiles at dinner had left him in no doubt. "It was never a question of if but of when, I think."

"Sylvie! What a surprise!" their mother said. "I must admit I thought you and Thomas would never come to an understanding." She kissed her daughter's cheek. "I fear we shall leave William all alone."

"Actually, Mother, we will honeymoon on the voyage to America...with Stephen and Louisa. Thomas wishes to visit there for an extended period, perhaps even relocate there."

"Sylvie!" her mother remonstrated. "Not America! So far..."

"I worried that you would receive the news poorly, Mother, and I have resisted Thomas's proposal for weeks both because of my own fears of leaving England and because I did not care to leave you. But you are beginning a new life of your own, Mother."

"You are right, of course," their mother said with a droop of her lips. "But grandchildren?"

"If you wish to see my children"—Sylvie blushed—"you must come to visit me in America. I am certain, though, that William will provide you with English grandchildren."

William looked away.

"I am not as certain of that as you, Sylvie," their mother said. She rose and kissed her children on the cheek. "Again, accept my felicitations. It is late, and I have much work to do for the wedding...for two weddings now. I will say good night."

They parted ways, and William hurried to the library, opening the door quietly to find Mattie asleep in one of the large chairs. He cursed himself for having left her so long and hoped she would understand he'd had no recourse, as one did not simply walk away from one's mother on announcement of her engagement.

He sat down in a chair across from Mattie and studied her to his heart's content. He loved the cinnamon color of her hair and the way the curls fell across her cheeks and onto her neck. Pale cheeks underscored her long, dark lashes, and she tucked a small hand under her cheek. The lilac gown she wore reminded him of the soft purple hue of early-morning clouds as the rising sun lightened them.

He returned his gaze to her face to find her watching him with a smile. He went down on one knee in front of her and took her hand in his. Though he had dreamed often of such a gesture, of falling to a knee and begging for the honor of her hand, his promise to himself prevented him from asking her yet again.

"Dearest, you looked so peaceful. I hated to wake you. I did not intend to leave you here alone so long."

She straightened and covered his hand with her own.

"That's all right. So, your mother..." She let the words hang.

"Quite the surprise," William said with a wry smile. "I thought she had dedicated herself to enjoying her freedom as a widow."

"Are you upset? Happy? Thoughts?"

"I am happy for her. She seems to genuinely care for Lord Hamilton. I do not think I realized that, so involved have I been in my own affairs."

Mattie smiled.

"It is my pleasure to inform you that your matchmaking efforts have once again been successful. Sylvie announced her engagement to Thomas this night."

"Really? Wow! That was fast! I'm so happy for her, though I'm not sure I had much to do with it. I went to talk to her this afternoon, but she raised the subject first. I think she'd already decided. She just wanted to know more about the United States. And she was worried about leaving your mother, but that seems to have resolved itself very conveniently, hasn't it?"

William nodded. "Yes, it does. I must admit I will miss her, though."

Though it was not his intent, Mattie's smile faded. Tentatively, she put her hands on either side of his face, and he covered them with his own. He struggled to keep the misery he felt from his eyes—that Mattie too would soon be gone.

"I know, William, I know," she murmured. "But the passage doesn't really take that long, does it?"

Let Mattie think he mourned Sylvie's departure.

"No, dearest, the passage does not take more than seven days."

Mattie's eyes narrowed.

"This isn't about Sylvie, is it? You're talking about me."

William leaned in to kiss her. "I vowed not to press you further to stay, Mattie, and I shall not. But I must admit to experiencing some grief at your pending departure. I cannot deny it. Please believe that I attempt to hide it from you."

Mattie pressed her lips against his, and he wrapped his arms around her, desiring nothing more than to hold her to him forever. He tasted salt, and pulled back. Tears spilled down Mattie's face.

"There, there, my love. Do not cry. I am a beast. I promised you I would not add to your grief, and yet here I am again reducing you to tears."

"It's not your fault, William. It's me. I don't want to go either. I want to stay with you forever."

William stiffened and studied her face. "Are you saying…?"

Mattie shook her head, and his heart dropped to his stomach. "No, I can't stay. But it doesn't mean that I don't want to. I love you. I will always love you. I can't imagine a day when I won't love you. I don't know what strange power brought me to you, to the hero in my book, but I don't regret one minute of it."

William lowered his face to her hands and kissed them.

"I just don't know how I can give up everything I've ever known, all the things that keep us alive, the safety, the security of life in my time. I'm not saying it's perfect or even particularly safe, but it's a lot safer for a woman in my time than it is now."

"I can protect you, my love." Even as he breathed the words, he cursed himself. No pleading. He must let her go.

Mattie smiled at him, love softening her eyes.

"I know you can, William, and I trust you with my life. But there is a limit to what you can protect me from. You can't protect me from illness that is curable in my time. You can't protect me from cancer, from infections, from complications of childbirth. You can't give me the right to vote, to drive a car, to fly to the States, to turn on a tap of hot water."

William rose to his feet, his body feeling suddenly old.

"No, you are correct. I cannot do any of these things for you."

Mattie jumped up and wrapped her arms around his waist, pressing her face against his chest.

"I'm sorry, William, that sounded awful! I'm not trying to hurt you. I'm just trying to explain."

William put his arms around her, resisting the urge to pull her tightly against his body lest she think he meant to bind her to him.

"I understand, Mattie," he whispered against the top of her head. "I understand."

Mattie raised wet eyes to his.

"I worry about you here in the house by yourself. Your mom will be gone and so will Sylvie. I can't bear the thought of you living alone."

William smiled, though he did not feel happy. "Perhaps I shall travel more," he said. "Perhaps I shall visit Sylvie in America."

Mattie smiled. "Maybe you should," she whispered. "I'd like to think of you there when I return. To think that you had been there."

"Shall I visit your Seattle?" William asked.

"Can you? Is there transportation to Seattle in the early 1800s?"

"I do not know. I shall make inquiries," William said. He looked at the clock on the mantle. "It is late, my love. You must get some sleep."

Mattie's arms around him tightened. "I don't want to. Can't we take a walk or something?"

"I thought of that myself earlier, but was concerned the moon might be nearing full." He gave a short, discomfited laugh. "I worried the moon might snatch you from me early."

"Not likely." Mattie chuckled. "Besides, don't we both have to wish on the same thing at the same time? Didn't we decide that might have been the catalyst for the time travel?"

William nodded, and took her hand. "Let us walk." He pushed back the curtains and opened a door from the library leading onto a terrace with the garden beyond. He looked up and paused. His throat tightened. The moon loomed large above them in the sky.

Mattie looked up, her grip tightened on his hand. "It can't be full yet. It hasn't been thirty days. We still have three more days. We'll be okay if we just don't wish. Right?"

William took a deep breath. "Yes, of course, you are right. It has not been thirty days. We are only at the twenty-seventh day. I have been counting."

"I promise not to wish to go home," Mattie said with a weak chuckle.

"And I promise not to wish you will stay, as difficult as that may be for me."

They stepped down from the terrace and moved across the lawn toward one of the gardens. William tucked Mattie's hand in his arm as he tried to ignore the large silver orb overhead. The lights, still on in the house as the servants cleared from the dinner party, illuminated the gardens just enough to be able to see.

They strolled along the rectangular pond, one of William's favorite spots in the garden. The moon, ever omnipresent, reflected in the still waters, its image broken only by the occasional clump of lily pads.

William absentmindedly covered Mattie's hand with his own.

"As long as we are joined like this, the moon cannot separate us, I think."

"Even if the moon has anything to do with it at all," Mattie said in a quiet voice. "I still have no real idea how I got here."

William looked down at her. "I believe with all my heart that you are here because I wished for you, though I did not know it at the time."

Mattie's step faltered. "Oh, William," she breathed.

He paused and pulled her into his arms. "I love you, Matilda Crockwell. I shall never love another as I love you. I would do anything I can to help you return home as I know it to be your heart's desire, but I cannot reverse my love to help send you back." He bent his head to kiss her, folding her to him. "I wish only for your happiness," he whispered against her lips.

Mattie froze. "Don't wish," she whispered. But it was too late.

His arms were empty.

CHAPTER SIXTEEN

Mattie opened her eyes. She lay on the balcony of her apartment in Seattle, her head pressed against the wooden railing. Lights from the surrounding apartments broke the darkness—those and the moon overhead.

She attempted to scramble to her feet, her skirts twisted about her ankles. Her skirts! She still wore Sylvie's lilac dress. It hadn't been a dream. She'd really been there in the Georgian era!

"No, no," she moaned as she managed to right herself. She stared at the moon. Was it full? What had happened? Had she wished? She gripped the railing tightly, her nails digging into the resistant wood.

William! Where was William? She'd been holding on to him. He'd been holding on to her. Did he travel with her? She yanked open the balcony sliding door and yelled his name, uncaring of the neighbors.

"William," she shouted. "William." She tried to remember where the lights were, so long ago, and yet only a month. Switching the living room light on, she scanned the room, scanned the kitchen then ran down the hall to her bedroom. Please, please, let him be sitting in her chair, holding her book and wondering how on earth he got there!

But the bedroom was empty. The adjoining bathroom was empty. William wasn't there.

Mattie spied the book on the small TV tray by her chair. She grabbed it, sank into what had once been her favorite place in the world and pressed the book she had once loved so much to her aching chest while she cried. The power of her sobs frightened her as she gasped for breath. Could one survive such pain, such heart-wrenching grief? How could she find William again?

Wish again! She held onto her book and ran back to the living room to burst onto the balcony. She kissed the cover of the book and held it up as an offering to the moon.

"Please let me get back there! I wasn't ready. We didn't say goodbye. I don't want to say goodbye. He wished for my happiness. Was that what did this? His wish? You weren't even full. How could you let this happen? Is this my happiness? Wasn't I supposed to wish, too? Please send me back. He must be so worried about me. Please, please, please…" Mattie's trembling legs gave out, and she sagged to the balcony floor. Several lights from neighboring apartments had come on, but she didn't care.

"Please don't do this to me," she begged. "Please let me go back. I *wish* to go back."

Nothing happened. She remained where she was, kneeling on the balcony, embracing the book as if it were William himself.

She waited and wished all night, hoping the moon would relent and send her back. Certain no one had ever stared at the moon so long; she thought she must have memorized every crater and valley on it. The sky lightened, dark purple turning into lavender and then a soft mauve. She stayed with the moon until she could see it no longer as the sun rose.

Stiff from sitting in a rigid position in the cool air all night, she rose slowly and entered the apartment. She returned to her bedroom and dropped into her chair, wondering vaguely how long she had been gone. Running her hand along her dress, she told herself that she had indeed been gone though because she didn't remember buying an empire-waist satin gown to traipse about the house in.

She slipped off her black satin slippers—Sylvie's slippers—and pulled her feet up under her. With the book pressed to her chest, she closed her eyes and willed herself to dream. To dream of William.

Her last thought before she slept was that she would try again that night. And every night while the moon was full. And every night that it wasn't full.

****

A month later, Mattie still retreated to her balcony every night to wish on the moon, even when she couldn't see it. She knew it was there. In the intervening weeks, she had tried desperately to bury herself in her book again, to find William within its pages, but she couldn't find the courage to do more than stare at the cover without opening the book. Somewhat numb at the moment, she dreaded any return to the pain she'd experienced when she had first returned.

She'd been let go from her job, having truly been gone for almost a month without giving notice, but she hardly cared. Savings helped her

184

pay long-overdue bills, and she resisted looking for another position until she found out what would happen on the next full moon.

"What happened to you?" Renee, her coworker, had asked over the phone. "When you didn't come to work the next week, I came to your apartment looking for you, I called your landlord, I even called the police. I tried to cover for you at work, but they only believed the dead grandmother story for about two days."

"I wish I could explain, Renee. I really wish I could, but I can't," Mattie said. Of course, she wouldn't have explained. Her time with William, in 1825, had been hers and hers alone. She couldn't share that with anyone. Even in modern times, they still locked people up for being crazy.

"Can I come see you, Mattie? I'm worried about you."

"Not right now, Renee. I'm so sorry. I just need to be alone. I think I had a nervous breakdown, and I need to be alone now. The doctor said it's best for me." Her story didn't feel far off the truth.

"Mattie! Were you in the hospital? Because you can get your job back if you were in the hospital! Are you all right? Oh, Mattie, I'm so sorry."

"No, I'm fine. I'm not coming back to work for a while. Doctor's orders," Mattie murmured.

"Oh! I see." Renee paused as if waiting for Mattie to fill in more details, but Mattie had exhausted her thought processes with the few lies she'd dreamed up. In fact, she couldn't remember the last time she'd actually been honest with anyone, either in this century or the nineteenth century. She wondered what it would feel like to be totally truthful with someone, anyone. Well, perhaps she had been more open with William than with anyone else.

"Okay, well, call me if you need anything, Mattie. And let me know when I can come see you."

"Okay, Renee. Thanks." Mattie hung the phone up and set it on the table beside her chair.

She looked at the book once again, running gentle fingers across the cover, allowing them to pause on William's face. No, Lord Ashton's face, she corrected herself. She looked at her bedside clock. She still had an hour before moonrise. She'd become quite the expert at the different phases of the moon over the past month.

Tentatively, she lifted the book and settled it on her lap. She toyed with the edge of the cover, noting that the pounding of her pulse grew louder in her ears, sometimes erratically, as if skipping a beat. She dragged in a deep breath and opened the book, the pages falling to a well-worn spot in the book.

"The moon shines for us because it has given me my heart's desire."

Rather than cry, she surprised herself by smiling. So hokey. She hadn't been in any danger at all, had she? Not from men who wanted to kidnap her for her fortune or her virtue, not from stagecoach robbers, not from French or American spies.

The name of the author, at the top of every other page, caught her attention once again. *I. C. Moon.* Mattie blinked and stared at it again. She closed the cover and looked at the large print. *I. C. Moon.* Good gravy! Was that a play on the words "I see moon"? Her heart thudded even louder. She remembered, though, that no author biography was included in the book.

With shaking fingers, she riffled through the book until she found the copyright page. The book was out of print, that much she knew because she would have bought it to keep rather than worry about having to return it to the library.

Original work by I. C. Moon first published 1859 by Sinclair Publishers Limited, London, England. Twenty-sixth printing 1950, Sinclair Publishers International, New York, New York.

"Sinclair Publishers," Mattie said aloud. "Sinclair."

William's company? To think otherwise was too much of a coincidence. Had William begun a publishing house? She noted again the New York address and the word *International*. The company appeared to be prosperous.

Who was I. C. Moon? Mattie bit her lower lip, waves of excitement coursing through her body. It could only be one of two people. William or her—the only two who "saw the moon." She tried to imagine William writing a romance in 1859. It hardly seemed likely that he would write a romance novel. Had he survived until 1859? That would make...would *have* made him sixty-four at the time of the first publishing of this book.

The internet! Why hadn't she looked the author up on the internet before? Were there other books by the same author? None were shown in her book. She could look up Sinclair Publishing and see what its history was as well.

She tucked the book under her arm and dashed into the living room to find her laptop. Perched on the dining room table, she turned it on and waited for what seemed like hours for it to warm up. Finally, her browser came up, and she keyed in *I. C. Moon*, which prompted a myriad of sites regarding the moon, some she'd already been researching over the past month. She scrolled through the pages looking for any references to the author. Several links to web pages came up, and she clicked into them.

I. C. Moon, pseudonym for Georgian- and Victorian-era American romance author rumored to be Matilda Sinclair, wife of William Sinclair, member of the landed gentry and owner of Sinclair Publishing. Mrs.

Sinclair published an impressive forty-two romance novels in her lifetime, all published under the umbrella of her husband's company. Her novels, featuring paranormal elements of time travel often involving the moon, continue to be read today but most are out of print. A list of the books followed.

Mattie read the paragraph again and again, trying to comprehend the enormity of what it said. *Matilda Sinclair*! Her heart thudded against her chest. So, she *did* go back—and for all her whining, *had* apparently lived in the nineteenth century. And she had married William. Thank goodness no death date was given in the article. She opted not to read any other websites associated with the pen name, which seemed to be more about her books than details of her personal life on the off chance she would see something she didn't want to. She couldn't imagine anything worse than knowing the date of her death, except for the date of William's death.

As much as she wanted to click on references to Sinclair Publishing, which she noted from the references appeared still to be in existence, she balked at the thought of possibly seeing William's name plastered on the top of the site along with his birth and death dates, such as one might see on a wall of portraits of CEOs.

Though she longed to know William's future—and her own—she couldn't risk looking. It seemed likely that she had lived a long time— long enough to write and publish forty-two novels.

A sudden thought occurred to her, and she keyed in several more names. A broad smile spread across her face as she read the screen. A site on American culture in the 1800s revealed that none other than Mr. Thomas Ringwood had been the publisher at Sinclair Publishing in New York. A portrait of an older, more distinguished Thomas with lamb-chop sideburns and mustache, and Sylvie, the spitting image of her mother albeit in Victorian dress, accompanied the article. Despite her best efforts to screen the article with her eyes half closed in anticipation of seeing dates, Mattie wasn't able to avoid seeing the dates of their deaths on the website, and although she knew a moment of grief, she was comforted to know they'd lived long lives.

One particular biographical site noted that Mrs. Sylvie Ringwood and Mrs. Louisa Carver, New York socialites, were heavily involved in charity events, as were their husbands, prominent publisher Mr. Thomas Ringwood and banker Mr. Stephen Carver.

Mattie touched the screen with her fingers as if she could touch the people she'd come to know.

She finally dragged her eyes from the computer and looked around her apartment, studying the furniture with a critical eye. She was going back. Everything could go. The only things she needed to keep were family photographs, letters, personal documents such as her passport—just in case—and the book. She was definitely taking the book. Perhaps a small donation to the library to cover the cost would be appropriate. And she'd take a few things with her, since it seemed clear from the fact she didn't arrive in either the past or present naked that whatever touched her traveled with her.

Mattie wasted no time setting her plan in motion. From her experience the month before, she now knew that depending on travel on the exact night of the full moon wasn't foolproof. The moon had its own plans. She needed to be ready to go that very night, and if she failed to travel that night, then the next night, and every night after that until she returned to William…as history proved she would.

She made a stop at the bank and withdrew all the money in both her checking and savings, leaving only a small amount to keep the accounts open. She converted the money to a series of cashier's checks. She made her way to a one-stop legal documents store and picked up a power of attorney. Her final stop was to a discount and grocery store where she picked up a few things for the "trip."

She returned home in the late afternoon, anxiety rising as she realized how much really needed to be done if one planned never to return.

As much as Mattie wanted to hear Renee's voice one last time, she opted to send her a letter instead. Renee would have too many questions and was even likely to call the police again if she thought Mattie was off her rocker—especially after she read Mattie's odd letter.

Dear Renee,

So much has happened to me over the past month, I can't even begin to describe it. I haven't really been "ill," and I'm sorry I lied about that. I've been away—far, far away. I wish I could tell you about it, but I can't. You wouldn't believe me if I did.

You asked me to let you know if I needed anything. I need your help now. I have to leave tonight, and if not tonight, then sometime in the next few nights. But I'll be gone before you get this letter.

I've enclosed the key to my apartment. I've left cashier's checks, a power of attorney for you and the keys to my car on the coffee table in my living room. I can't take much with me, so I'm asking you to dispose of my things, sell them, give them away…whatever works best for you. You can keep my car or sell it. The money is for you to do with what you want. You can keep it or donate it. It's yours. I can't use the money where I'm going.

I know these requests sound bizarre, and I don't blame you for panicking. But please don't. I'll be all right.

I met a "man." You know, "the one," but he doesn't live here. He lives far away, and I'm going to join him. He's wealthy, so I don't need any money, the car or my furniture. There is no computer service, no postal service and no telephone service where I'm going so we won't be able to stay in touch with e-mails, letters or phone calls.

Take care, Renee. I'll miss you! And thanks for taking care of everything for me.

Love

Mattie

P.S. Find books by I. C. Moon in the library. I'll say hi to you in them! That way you'll know I'm okay.

Mattie slipped the letter and her apartment key in the envelope and made her way down to the mailbox to drop it in. The postman had already come and gone for the day, so she knew she'd have plenty of time before Renee got the letter.

She returned to her apartment, and packed a large duffle-type bag with the photographs, letters and personal identification. Although she could see the potential for disaster if the identification were found someday, she suspected it would be better she have something on her— even if far-fetched. She packed the things she'd bought for the trip— over-the-counter pain medicines, antibiotic creams, bandages, cold medicine, toothpaste and spare toothbrushes, feminine products, diaper cream, baby aspirin, antacids, a small bottle of her favorite perfume, deodorant, hand soaps, small bottles of shampoo and conditioner, safety pins and anything else she could ransack from her bathroom.

She had a thought and ran to her computer to find some information, which she printed out and stuffed in a side pocket of the bag. She finished off by throwing in some underthings, warm socks for her feet and her small digital camera, then spent the next fifteen minutes sprawled across the overstuffed duffle bag, squeezing each side as she struggled to zip it closed.

At last she managed, and she sat back on her heels to survey the bag. She hadn't packed nearly as much as she thought she might need for a lifetime in the nineteenth century, but she'd done the best she could on short notice.

She looked out the window. Dusk had come and gone, and she didn't have much time. She removed her jeans and t-shirt and slipped into Sylvie's dress, stockings and slippers. She stuck her hair on top of her head as best she could.

Dragging the heavy bag out to the balcony, she looked up to see the moon just above the roofline of the other apartment buildings. It seemed full to her, but the lunar calendar said the moon would not be full until the following night.

Mattie was taking no chances. She wasn't sure if William stared at the moon and wished for her return at the exact same time, but she hoped he was. She sat down on the balcony floor, clutched the bag and stared at the moon, wishing she could return to William.

As she had a month ago, she wished all night, struggling to keep her eyes open, fearful that if she fell asleep, she would miss the "window," or whatever mechanism helped her travel through time before.

And as happened last month, the sky lightened at dawn, dimming the moon's light, and she remained on the now-cold wooden floor of the balcony—alone. She rose to her knees and laid her head against the railing, one hand clutching her bag, the other pushing against the pain in her chest as if she could massage it away.

"Please don't do this, Mister Moon," she whispered. "Don't leave me here, without William. I-I don't think I can do this." She pulled the book from a side pocket in the bag and held it up. "Wait! Look! This is me! I'm *supposed* to be there. Send me! I know you have something to do with it. You control the tides. Surely, you can control time as well."

Mattie waited, held her breath and stared at the outline of the moon dropping toward the horizon. After a few minutes, she dragged air into her lungs, lowered the book and clasped it to her chest.

"Fine, not today then, mister, but I'm not giving up! I'll see you tonight."

She rose awkwardly to her feet and grasped the bag to drag it back inside. She turned to look at the moon one last time and felt her knees buckling as she fell forward.

****

William leaned his elbows on his knees and dropped his face in his hands. Dawn approached, lightening the night sky, and Mattie had not returned. No matter how much he begged and pleaded for her, the moon had denied him his heart's desire.

His body ached from sitting for hours in a fixed position on the bench in the cool night air of the garden. He'd had the gardener move the bench to the exact spot where he had found Mattie only two months prior.

As Mattie had noted, the moon had appeared full for several nights, and he was uncertain which was the one noted to be the "full moon." They had all looked perfectly rounded to him. And so he had waited in the garden all night for the last three evenings as he had the month prior, and would resume his vigil again for several more days until the moon brought her back to him.

William had no idea what Mattie's life was like in the twenty-first century, but he believed with all his heart that she loved him. Whether her love for him was enough to overcome her hesitation to stay with him in the nineteenth century remained to be seen.

He turned to study the house. Ashton House. Was it worth giving up the woman he loved? If he had the chance to do it all over again, would he try to travel with Mattie to her time? To leave the estate without heirs, without management, to become a derelict, abandoned relic in future? His mother and Lord Hamilton might see to it in their lifetime, but when they passed on, who would care for the estate, for the household staff, for the tenants, for the land?

His throat ached as he contemplated a choice that was not available to him. The question of whether he would return with Mattie to her time, or live out his days with her in his time was moot. Mattie was gone, and he had no idea if she would—or could—ever return.

He reached for the garment lying on the bench beside him—the same garment he had brought with him to the garden every night at dusk. He pressed the softness of Mattie's pink robe to his nose and breathed in her scent, a delicate floral fragrance reminiscent of roses.

"What do you mean she just disappeared?" Sylvie had asked the day after Mattie vanished. Tears had flowed down Sylvie's cheeks. William held her, struggling to keep his own devastation in check.

"We were walking in the garden, and she vanished, Sylvie. That is all I know. I can only assume that somehow she was returned to her own time. I hope that is the case." William swallowed hard at the thought of anything worse befalling Mattie.

"Is she returning?"

"I do not think so, dearest. I am sorry." William released his sister and regarded her. At the moment, he wished himself a woman so he too could shed tears to relieve the ache in his chest.

"No, William," Sylvie said with a watery smile. "It is I who am sorry for your loss, which must be great compared to mine. I cannot imagine how you must feel."

William thinned his lips into a semblance of a smile, but said nothing. He could not trust himself to speak of the pain of loss.

"Miss Crockwell is gone?" their mother had asked quietly as she entered the drawing room.

Both Sylvie and William nodded, yet neither spoke.

Their mother sighed. She approached William and kissed his cheek. He returned the kiss and moved away to take up a position leaning on the mantle. He lowered his head to stare into the cold hearth. His mother joined Sylvie on the sofa.

"I am truly sorry, William. Although you are aware I did not wish you to return with her, I almost hoped she would stay."

William raised his head.

"Miss Crockwell did not plan to leave last night in such an unexpected fashion. But as suddenly as she came, she vanished. I know she would have wished to say goodbye. As for her staying, she never had any intention of remaining in the nineteenth century." William forced the words out in an even tone.

"I did not realize that," his mother said. "And yet you gave her your heart, knowing she would leave if given the chance?"

"Mother!" Sylvie said, aghast.

William's eyes flew to his mother's face. They rarely spoke so openly to each other, and never of matters of the heart.

His mother's eyes flickered but she maintained her gaze.

"I do not mean to be vulgar or insensitive, William, but I was concerned what might happen to you if she chose to leave."

"Yes, Mother, I did give her my heart...unconditionally. In the beginning, I will admit, I turned from her in anger when she told me she could not stay in our time, that she could not give up the life and comforts she has known. But I soon realized that it was not her fault, and that given the same circumstances—were I transported to the Middle Ages, I might insist on returning to my own time as well. I decided then to cherish the remaining moments we had together, and I did. Every moment."

Sylvie's cheeks burned a bright red and she looked down at her clasped hands, but said nothing.

His mother sighed again. "I am sorry for your loss, William. What will you do now?"

"I will wait and hope and wish for her return every night while the moon is full, and when the moon is not full, I will simply wait until the next full moon and begin the process all over again."

His mother rose and approached him.

"That seems a very lonely life, William. It is not what I would wish for you. How long will you wait?"

"Until she returns to me," he said quietly.

Now, in the garden, as he stared at the outline of the moon slipping down in the sky, he wished with every breath in his body that Mattie would return to him.

A sound like a thud from behind caught his attention, and he turned.

There, on the ground, lay Mattie, half buried by a large cloth bag, a book clutched in her hand.

He jumped up and ran to her, dropping to his knees to push the heavy bag aside and cradle her in his arms. The book slid from her hands. She wore the same dress she had worn the night she had disappeared a month ago.

"Mattie! Mattie, my love!"

She opened her eyes and looked at him. Her eyes widened, and her face broke into a wide smile.

"William! I'm back. I finally got back!"

"Oh, my love, you have returned to me," William muttered as he kissed her and spoke at the same time. "I thought never to see you again."

"I've tried and tried to get back, William. I prayed and wished and cursed the moon, waiting night after night," she cried as she held onto him.

"I cannot believe that you have returned to me," he murmured, burying his face in her hair. He rocked her back and forth like a child.

"I love you, William. I knew that even before I was taken back the last time." Mattie struggled to straighten to a sitting position, and she regarded him. Loath to release her, William kept hold of her hands.

"And your concerns? Your fears? What you must give up to be with me?"

Mattie smiled, almost serenely, and William studied her face. What had brought on this change of heart?

She patted the bag next to her and picked up the book.

"I've brought some of the comforts of home with me to last as long as they can, and this book tells me that I was always meant to be here. I'm not afraid anymore, William. Everything is going to be all right."

William eyed the book curiously.

"I'll tell you about it later," Mattie said softly. Her eyes widened as she looked over his shoulder. He turned to follow her gaze.

"Look how bright the moon is," she said. "Even as it disappears below the horizon, it seems to be glowing its brightest."

William stared at the moon for a moment. Mattie was correct. It did seem to shimmer more brightly now than at its zenith.

"It shines for us, my love, because it has given me my heart's desire."

"And mine," said Mattie softly. "Quick! Before the moon changes its mind, kiss me, William. Kiss me and don't let go!"

William did as the love of his life requested, and he kissed her thoroughly as the moon beamed down upon them.

EPILOGUE

Mattie looked up to see William poking his head through the nursery door, an inquiring look on his face.

She smiled and nodded. The baby slept soundly, one tiny fist resting against her cheek.

"Is she well?" he asked as he stepped in quietly and approached Mattie's rocking chair.

"She's fine," Mattie said as she raised her face to his kiss. The touch of his lips never failed to send a thrill up her spine.

William sat down in a chair beside her and leaned forward to look at the baby.

"The image of her mother," he murmured with a smile. With the tip of his index finger, he smoothed a red curl on the baby's head.

"How's it going down there?" Mattie asked.

"The drawings you brought have the engineer puzzled, but he feels he can devise a system according to the specifications noted."

"I'm sure he can. Just remember to tell him that the wastewater can't be vented into the surrounding waters. It's going to be some years before they come up with proper wastewater treatment, but I couldn't figure out how to download plans for wastewater treatment facilities."

William grinned. "Rest easy, my dear. We shall have your *indoor plumbing* in place before long."

"I hope so." Mattie returned his grin. "I'm managing everything else pretty well, but that's the one thing I really don't think I can do without."

William yawned behind his hand. "Forgive me."

"You look tired, William," Mattie said softly. "I think I would sleep through the baby's crying if you didn't bring her to me every night."

"I surprise myself that I am attuned to her crying. I did not realize it was possible to raise an infant without the services of a wet nurse and nanny."

"I know that's a big change for you, and I appreciate your consideration." Mattie leaned over to kiss his cheek. "Thank goodness Jane has agreed to take over as governess when it's time."

William took her spare hand and brought it to his lips.

"I did not fall in love with you, dearest, because you do things as we have always done. I fell in love with you because you are singular, you see things in your own way and you do things in a different way. It is not consideration, Mattie. It is love. As you returned to me for love, I dedicate my life to easing your transition to my time because I love you."

He rose and bent to kiss her lips once again.

"I must return to the engineer." He crossed the room to the door, and paused, turning back.

"It is a full moon tonight, my love. Shall we make our wish as usual?"

Mattie smiled. "I wish to live a long and happy life with you."

"Yes, that is the one," William said. "This time though, I must include 'I wish to live a long and happy life with you and our child.'"

"I'll see you tonight," Mattie murmured as she blew him a kiss. "Under the full moon."

"Under the full moon," William echoed.

ABOUT THE AUTHOR

I began my first fiction-writing attempt when I was fourteen. I shut myself up in my bedroom one summer and obsessively worked on a time-travel/pirate novel set in the beloved Caribbean of my youth. Unfortunately, I wasn't able to hammer it out on a manual typewriter (oh yeah, I'm that old) before it was time to go back to school. The draft of that novel has long since disappeared, but the story still simmers within, and I will finish it one day soon.

I was born in Aruba to American parents and lived in Venezuela until my family returned to the United States when I was twelve. I couldn't fight the global travel bug, and I joined the US Air Force at eighteen to "see the world." After twenty-one wonderful and fulfilling years traveling the world and the birth of one beautiful daughter, I pursued my dream of finally getting a college education. With a license in mental health therapy, I worked with veterans and continue to work on behalf of veterans. I continue to travel, my first love, and almost all of my books involve travel.

I write time-travel romances, light paranormal/fantasy romances (lovelorn ghosty stuff), contemporary romances, and romantic suspense. Visit my website at http://www.bessmcbride.com

Made in the USA
San Bernardino, CA
20 February 2015